REND ME, THE WAYWARD KNIGHT

BOOK TWO IN THE HEARTWOOD TRILOGY

Z.M. CELESTAIRE

DREAMING IN COLOR

Contents

Content Warning

THIS BOOK CONTAINS DEPICTIONS of self-harm, suicidal ideation, depictions of panic attacks, implied substance abuse, domestic violence, and instances of magical violence. Reader discretion is advised.

Chapter One
The Storm

Micah Stillwater peered through To a Tea's paneled windows with his hands cupped around his eyes, but the view awarded him little more than a flurry of snowflakes the size of cotton balls. It was the beginning of December, which heralded the largest snowstorm in years. Lights from a passing snow plow flashed yellow against the cars parked on the curb, which were rapidly disappearing under the accumulating snow. He grimaced and straightened, clicking off the neon OPEN sign.

"Nobody's gonna get very far in this storm." He turned from the window with a pit of worry in his stomach. He looked eastward, toward the river, and made a mental note to go out to Lilydale to check on the Folk tomorrow.

He'd managed to get the other two baristas home after closing was finished, but not Diana. She sat on the countertop by the register, sipping a bright orange Thai tea and scrolling on her phone. She had loosely braided brown hair and wore tights under a pair of black denim shorts—very poorly chosen for the season, Micah thought. Not that he was a bastion of being appropriately dressed, as his boyfriend liked to point out. At least Diana wore Docs with wool socks.

"Why aren't you trying to get home?" she asked, glancing at him with cool gray eyes rimmed with eyeliner. That was what Diana had been like for the year she was at To a Tea: cool, snarky, and put together. Much like Micah, she was older than most of the high school baristas and didn't need to be given the same basic and redundant direction as the younger kids. She was kind to every customer, and didn't bring any drama to work. As far as Micah knew, she was working on a Master's degree at one of the nearby universities. Maybe Saint Kate's.

"'Cause I couldn't convince you to go home," he replied with a laugh. He slid onto the counter next to her and folded his hands, surveying his shop with a frown. With all the chairs and stools up, it looked ominous, like a cursed forest. The art showcase for the month was grim, too. Dead trees and dark skies filled the paintings on the walls. Andrew warned him the exhibit was going to look depressing, especially during the holidays. But the artist who asked for the showcase had seemed like she needed it. "I gotta go down with the ship. Can't leave till the crew does."

"I mean, you could. I've closed alone. I know the alarm code."

Ignoring the comment, Micah said, "Listen, I gotta make

a call. But I want you to try to get a car home for yourself, okay? I'll pay. They hike the prices during storms like this, but they'll show up anyway."

Diana made a noncommittal noise and quirked a corner of her lip. He bonked their elbows together. Then he jumped to his feet and disappeared around the corner into the back hall of the shop. He let himself into the windowless manager's office and closed the door. The space was still a disaster relative to how he kept his brownstone on Saint Claire, but it was better than when he first took over the store. He had organized all the mandatory notices on the walls into neat rows, and gotten a greenhouse lamp to keep some plants alive on his filing cabinet. Spinning on the squeaky chair by his desktop monitor, Micah used his office landline and dialed Andrew Vidasche's cell number from memory.

Andrew picked up on the first ring. "Hey, are you okay?" His voice vibrated Micah's bones. It was a particular twist of gravelly and airy, like the sound of two flint stones scraping together.

"Yeah," replied Micah. "I'm still at the shop. One of my baristas is stuck here."

"Your dad had the weather channel on all afternoon. This blizzard is insane." Andrew's Scouse accent came out when he pressed his *A* into a lilt. "Do you want me to come and get you?"

Micah twirled the phone cord on his finger. "I wanna say

no? I gotta take care of Diana. Then I'll make it home. It shouldn't be more than a couple hours."

"How are you going to 'make it home'?" Andrew pressed.

"I'll fold some shadows…"

Andrew paused. Micah could feel the argument coming before he even heard it. "That hasn't been working consistently, Micah. You almost dumped yourself in the river last month."

"Andrew." Wounded pride sharpened an edge into his voice.

Heedless, Andrew said, "I can make it up there in probably thirty minutes. The Saturn has made it through many blizzards."

"Andrew."

Andrew gave a growl of frustration, "Why won't you let me come get you?"

"'Cause it's not a huge deal! Just be a bit patient, okay? We're perfectly safe here for the moment, and I need to take care of her first."

"You really don't."

Sighing, Micah said, "I'll text you in a few minutes, okay? I was trying to call to check in. Not to get badgered." He dropped the phone noisily back into its cradle. Sliding his black beanie off his head, he slapped it onto his desk and then leaned back in his chair, glaring at the stained ceiling tiles.

Things were tense with Andrew right now. They passed

their second anniversary over the summer, and Andrew had formally moved into the brownstone. He had changed then. Pulled away. Micah didn't know why, and no matter how he asked the question, Andrew had nothing to share on the matter. He wondered if it was because they were together too much. Micah was new to cohabiting, and had to learn boundaries, and learn to hear the things Andrew left unsaid—which was a lot, it turned out. Regardless, he couldn't get Andrew back. Micah felt Andrew's emotional absence like a fog which swallowed them both up. Micah realized within that formless gray space that he had no idea who he actually was.

Enormous power stirred in Micah when he confronted his mother in the Redwoods, but when he came home to Minnesota...it all went back to sleep. Micah made sure he visited Ingrid in Lilydale once or twice a month, but his visits were short and uneasy. All the Folk stared at him, and his shoulders tingled during his whole stay.

What was worse was how Lilydale shook loose all these memories from the Redwoods, making it almost torture to be there. It was for his father's sake, but it was also for his own. The twenty years Micah spent growing up in the Redwoods had been sharp edges, backstabbing, loveless trysts, and sickening overindulgence. Lilydale might be softer, but the basic routine there struck him as very much the same in essence.

It didn't help that he seemed to be a disappointment

to the Folk in Lilydale. Everyone seemed to expect him to be a remarkable force of nature now, but he had few Fae abilities he'd identified and none he could do at will. At least his relationship with Ingrid was better now. That was enough for him, and so was having a normal job, and a…relatively normal family.

Julian Stillwater went to weekly bingo, and water aerobics, and made dinners for many of their neighbors throughout the week. Otherwise, he kept to himself, focusing on maintaining the brownstone on Saint Claire, and keeping Cinnamon company after Fadil passed away last winter. Julian actually seemed more stable since being rescued from the Redwoods. Not perfect, still prone to nightmares and dissociative spells. But not as jumpy, not always yearning for Fae-spelled foods. Andrew and Sam, safe humans who knew about Lilydale, helped Julian stay grounded.

"Micah?" *Tap. Tap.*

He jumped, pulled from his…brooding. Wheeling the chair over to the door, he spun the knob and cracked it open.

Diana peeked inside. "The earliest a car's gonna get here is an hour."

Returning to position with his head back and eyes on the ceiling, Micah took a fortifying breath. "Okay. That's nothing." He sat up. "Want to do inventory?"

She snorted. "You gonna pay me for it?"

Micah shrugged. "Seems fair."

Near the front windows, silhouetted by snow billowing off the awning outside, Micah sat on a stool at the counter with glass jars of tea leaves in front of him. He held a thick ream of paper and a highlighter. They worked quietly for a while, checking tea quantities against the manifest and preparing for reordering, or letting stock run out on items that weren't selling.

Diana picked up a jar and side-eyed him.

He blinked. "What's that look for?"

"Who'd you need to call? Was it that tall red-haired guy who comes in?"

Micah blinked again. "Uh. Yeah. My boyfriend."

Smiling with dimples in both cheeks, Diana put her chin in her hand and said, "Well how about that. It just takes a blizzard for Micah to self-disclose for once." She paused. "Isn't he a lot older than you?"

Eight years younger, actually. That was another issue that sat in the back of his thoughts at all times. In the two years since they'd gotten together, Micah hadn't aged at all. Every month or so he would inspect his reflection against photos from his first summer with Andrew. But not so much as a single wrinkle had appeared. Toward Diana, he tried to make his grimace more coy than dreadful. "Looks that way."

"Anna and Faith would be devastated if they knew you're gay," she added, referring to two of the baristas who were the most attentive to...literally everything Micah did.

"Yeah, I'm not," Micah said automatically. Apparently he still hadn't lived through enough social movements for people to stop making assumptions about his sexuality based on his partner.

Diana cringed, and then resumed shifting through the tea jars while Micah highlighted. She finally said, "Sorry. I was presumptuous."

He glanced up from the papers with a faint smile. "It's all good," he said gently. "I'm used to it."

Diana's cheeks colored. "I didn't ever think you were gay, for the record. On the other hand, I've never seen you flirt with...anything."

Smirking, he said, "I do save most of my flattery for cats."

"Oh god."

"Yeah. I'm a cat guy."

Diana swallowed and then said in a hurry, "You're just a pretty respectable guy, I mean."

Looking down at the paper and highlighting a quantity line, Micah shrugged. "I'm in charge, so I try not to mess around."

"You're only human."

Micah bit down hard on the inside of his cheek to keep himself from snorting. He was glad he was looking at the paper to mask the way his eyes bugged. When he contained himself, he looked back up and said, "Would you prefer if I was flirting with everyone?"

Diana blushed again. "No! That's not what I meant."

He grinned.

"I just meant it's hard to tell if you're even into anyone." She hugged her arms across her chest and stared at the jars on the table, picking one up and giving it a turn before setting it back down and pushing her hair behind her ear. "I don't mean—"

"Hey." Micah patted her elbow. "I'm giving you a hard time." Her shoulders relaxed and she pressed her hand to her cheek with a timid smile. Shifting uneasily, Micah explained, "I've been with Andrew for two years. I haven't really thought about anyone else since then. He saved my life." Micah's mind served him an image of Andrew in the backseat of his Saturn, soaked by rain and bloodied by a sword swung by Micah's own mother.

Diana traced the shape of a jar lid with a finger. "Lucky."

"I am. Very." He scrutinized Diana. "Is...everything okay, for you? Are you avoiding going home? I've noticed you're usually at a table reading long after your shifts."

She grimaced. "It's usually homework, but...yeah, that too, I guess. Home...isn't great." Diana shrugged. Micah waited for her to continue. "Bought a house with my boyfriend. After that he showed his true colors."

Micah leaned across the counter toward her. With an earnest shine in his orchid eyes, he said solemnly, "If you're ever unsafe there, I've got plenty of space at my place. Okay?"

Turning away quickly, Diana dabbed at the corner of her eyes. "Why are you so nice?" she muttered.

Micah glared at the tea on the counter. "Seems like your bar is set pretty low." He shook his head. "Look, this is stupid. I can do inventory Friday morning." Shuffling the papers together, Micah got up and started putting back the jars of tea. Diana looked confused but didn't argue, letting him slip around her with their shoulders brushing as he passed. "It's a blizzard," he said. "We don't need to be productive when crazy shit happens."

Diana's gaze roved the tea shop. She chewed on her lower lip for a moment. Then she grabbed a paper cup for hot drinks off a stack near her and flipped it in her hands. "Wanna play the cup game?"

"The what?"

She scoffed, "You don't know the cup game?" Diana squeezed around him and pulled down two chairs at a small table next to the windows.

Micah thought ruefully about growing up in faerieland. A lot of human childhood experiences were not had. He plopped into the chair across from her, the cold air seeping through the window chilling his shoulder. Outside, the street was eerily deserted at a time when it was usually crowded with diners. Micah wasn't actually sure how he was going to get home. He was about to pull his phone from his pocket, but then Diana started drumming on her cup and flipping it over her hand. Micah paused, quizzical and amused.

"Are you interested in magic, Micah?" asked Diana. "The crystals you wear, the gauges, the colorful hair..." She glanced up when Micah took a short breath. "I am too, that's why I ask. And I believe in small magic. Like rhythm, and carefully chosen words, and intention."

Micah's shoulders relaxed. "Yeah. Of course."

She hummed while she flipped and tapped, smiling faintly. Then she slowed down to teach him, and commended him when he caught on quickly. When he meant to pass it to her, he fumbled and the cup went flying. They both laughed and lunged at it.

He caught it first before it hit the floor, but barely, and Diana's hand closed around his. She then swooped in with confidence, lashes fluttering shut as she pressed her lips to his and kissed him. Tasting cardamom, Micah froze, his heart climbing up into his throat as everything fell into chaotic confusion inside him.

Clasping her shoulder, he snapped back into his body to push Diana away.

A clod of snow thumped loudly against the window next to them. He jumped and pulled away, the confused shock from the kiss replaced by a blast of dread. Over the snowball plastered to the glass, the window showed a familiar fox-like face framed by auburn hair under a furry hunter's cap.

Micah swore, kicked back his chair fast enough that it

toppled, and tore through the front door. It was heavy and hard to push open against the piling snow. He squeezed through the crack, giving Andrew plenty of time to trudge down the street back the way he came. "No, no, no, Andrew, wait, wait, stop. You're too fucking fast! Slow d—*oof!*"

Andrew spun around as Micah face-planted into the snow in a short-sleeved shirt and jeans. Micah shot up like he was spring-loaded, spitting out a clod of snow. Andrew didn't think twice as he hauled Micah back to his feet and brushed him off, slinging his scarf off his shoulders and pitching it at Micah.

Face burning despite the weather, Andrew continued the trek through the calf-deep snow back to his Saturn idling on the road. Tears jumped into his eyes, but they melted into the snowflakes on his lashes. Things had been...rough, a bit, since the summer. But this was worse than Andrew anticipated, and confirmed all his worst fears.

Micah called from behind him, "Andrew, please don't think—I–I would never—"

"We need to get home," Andrew declared, not turning around. He climbed onto a waist-high snowbank that had iced over during a previous storm, and down past it into the empty street. His winter boots were plenty sturdy for this, laced tight and insulated by wool socks underneath.

As Andrew yanked open the driver's side door, Micah clambered over the snowbank after him. Winter stripped Micah of his easy way of moving. It was startling for Andrew to adjust to during the first winter and still strange now during the third. Hitherto all gracefully connected to the natural greenery of the world, during the winter Micah regularly slipped on patches of ice, tripped on chunks of frozen snow, and wore the wrong shoes out and soaked his feet to the bone. It was annoying. Winter was still natural, and who was Micah to decide what nature he connected with and which he rejected?

Trying to keep the sneer from his tone, Andrew asked flatly, "You're just going to leave your jacket? We could get stranded."

"Why did you come?" Micah asked instead of answering. On any other day, Micah would be warmed by Andrew's insistence to help. But if Andrew hadn't shown up...Diana shouldn't have kissed him, and Micah shouldn't have let it fluster him, but he could have dealt with it immediately. Shut her down. Hell, he could have fired her.

The streetlights glinted on the vial of Micah's blood Andrew wore as a pendant from a cord around his neck. He hadn't taken it off in two years, not since Micah got Chamomile's help to protect Andrew from any Fae abilities Micah didn't know he was using. Now it rested on the top button of his coat, as if he'd used it like a homing device to find Micah in the storm.

All that work, only to find someone kissing him.

"I told you that you didn't need to come." Micah stammered, "Not because I've been doing a-anything behind your back…I didn't want…I just, you didn't tell me."

Andrew's eyes turned dark and angry. "Didn't I? Check your phone," he snapped, still hovering over the door of the Saturn. Snow crowned his head and turned his cheeks ruddy, his eyes glassy and reflecting the street lights a dozen times over. On the verge of angry tears, in his black double-breasted pea coat, Andrew looked tragically handsome. "Your dad practically put my jacket on for me. He's been losing it all day."

Micah's heart sank. "Oh. God." He dug out his phone and flicked briefly through the number of texts from Julian and several from Andrew. At the bottom, a text from a number he didn't have saved said *I'm so sorry.*

Pulling his sleeve over his palm and wiping his face, Andrew said, "You need to get home."

"Can't I ex—"

"No!"

Micah swallowed. He blinked back tears because he had nothing to cry for. It was *his* lips that tasted like someone else. "I'm sorry."

Andrew watched the piling snow on the roof of the Saturn, gathered his wounded feelings in a pile, and stuffed them down. He said blankly, "Are you getting home with me, or are you finding your own way?"

"C…can I?" He indicated the passenger door.

"It's why I came." Andrew slid into the car and slammed his door hard enough that the car creaked on its suspension. He glared at the steering wheel while Micah got situated in the passenger seat, wrapped in Andrew's Leinster tartan scarf, combing back his green hair with his fingers. His hair never darkened after the Redwoods, staying lighter than the turquoise it was when Andrew met him. Now it was a leafy, sage green, wet with snow, cut in the same way as before with the sides buzzed short and the hair on the crown of his head effortlessly tousled to the left.

Andrew looked back at the road, which was already choked by fresh snow even though he'd been behind a plow on his way out. The Saturn groaned, the wheels spun and smelled like rubber, but they made slow forward progress.

Micah glanced at his phone when it buzzed on his lap.

"Already getting texts from your new girlfriend, eh?" Andrew's voice was brittle.

Micah flipped his phone over and buried his face in his hands. "I don't know what to say."

On a bridge over a railroad track not far from the brownstone, the Saturn's wheels slipped and lost traction. Andrew cursed and switched into third gear, but nothing changed. He reversed, twisting in his seat, trying to avoid the treads he'd made in the road, and then he revved and slammed on the gas. The back tires of the Saturn fish-tailed and sent them toward the curb. Micah clenched his jaw and gripped the handle over the door. Then the car stopped again, a stinky exhaust cloud forcing its way inside through the closed windows. Andrew switched into park. Snow blossomed in the beams of the headlights like static on a television.

Tears ran freely down Andrew's cheeks. He sniffed messily, grabbing a fast-food napkin and wiping his face. "I've been afraid of this since we got together."

"What?" Micah's hand fell against his chest, the disbelief and horror palpable.

"You're...too good for me. Everyone loves you...and you had Chami...or even that...that buff faerie in the Redwoods..." Andrew's voice broke and he folded his arms on the steering wheel and hid his face. "I'm boring. I'm so dreadfully human. I—I don't even know the geography of my own home country, did you know? Told you Liverpool was in the east when it's northwest. Should have been your first clue. I'm weak and sad and you're so—"

"Andrew, please," Micah said desperately. "That's not at all what this was. I did not predict, intend, nor ask for that to happen. And yet, it happened, and that's my fault," Micah said, touching Andrew's shoulder. "I was just telling her—"

Andrew flinched away from his touch. "Please don't."

Micah's heart dropped. Tears stung his eyes, but once again he steeled himself and swallowed them back, swallowing and swallowing until the feeling subsided. He hugged himself tightly with a savage shiver.

"I need you in the driver's seat," Andrew said abruptly, straightening, wiping his face dry with his sleeve. He switched the car into neutral. "I'm going to get out and push. When I knock on the boot, slam on the gas. Keep the wheels pointed toward the road. Okay?"

"I can help push." Micah unbuckled, ready to jump out.

Sharply, Andrew told him, "No. You're wearing a T-shirt." His voice was dense with....mockery, Micah realized with a lurch. Andrew got out of the car and slammed the door on him. His head spinning and stomach knotted with shame, Micah shimmied into the driver's seat and switched gears as Andrew went around the back of the car.

When Andrew got back to the bumper, a wave of nausea hit him and he leaned over the trunk, biting down on a cry. His face burned from the coarse wool of his jacket sleeve, from the cold, from the urge to weep more. Andrew pounded a fist on the trunk, gritted his teeth, and shoved his shoulder into the rear of the car. The wheels screamed, spun, and then gained traction. Andrew leaned and shoved, and then the Saturn started to move. With the sudden shift, his boots slipped out from under him. He crashed onto his hip and smacked his head on the bumper.

After the car window buzzed open, Micah called, "Are you okay?" The Saturn was still crunching forward, but was slowing down.

"*Don't* stop!" Andrew scrambled to his feet and tripped around to the passenger door as the Saturn made it to the crest of the hill. He yanked open the door and fell inside.

"Keep flooring it," he instructed, shutting himself inside the Saturn, brushing off his sleeve and his pants. Wet clods of snow flew off him and landed with a *plop* on the window console.

Micah's jaw was clenched, his knuckles turning white around the wheel. Andrew rubbed his forehead where the flesh was tender, wincing, trying to ignore Micah's look of concern.

They conquered the worst part of the drive, and made it down the street to Saint Claire. Parking in front of the brownstone was messy, and the Saturn would need to be adjusted when the snow stopped. This was an expected inconvenience during a blizzard, when abandoned cars in ditches or on back roads became a norm, and being towed was a relief more than a threat. But they made it, mostly into a parking spot, and Micah was mercifully silent.

As soon as Micah cut the engine, Andrew threw open the passenger door. Climbing between the snowbank and the curb, he trudged back towards West Seventh in the direction of his shop, Magic's Computer Repair.

Micah stood in the deep snow, goosebumps rising on his bare arms, watching Andrew flee across the street. He called desperately, "Seriously, Andrew? Can't you stay and fight with me?"

Andrew stopped and turned back. Fat snowflakes settled on his shoulders. His chin quivered slightly, though he tried to suppress it. With eyes that were a dark void, he shrugged. "Can't I let you go?"

"To what?" cried Micah. "There's nothing else I want!"

Tears beaded on Andrew's lashes. "I don't believe you." He stuffed his hands in his pockets, turned away, and faded into the chaos of the storm.

CHAPTER TWO
THE PANIC

MICAH ENTERED HIS BROWNSTONE alone, glancing at Andrew's extra shoes by the door, smelling his almond scent in the air, and trying to tamp down the sour taste of dread. He trudged up the stairs, his socks soaking wet and leaving footprints on the wood. The living room was empty and the kitchen was dark, so he went up the next flight to his father Julian's level. He peeked in his dad's bedroom and found him folding laundry.

"Hey, Dad. I made it home."

Julian looked up with a pair of pajama pants in his hands. He was midway through his sixties, his thick black hair finally going gray around his temples, wire glasses perched on his nose. He had light brown skin and vivid amber eyes. Micah wished he'd gotten Julian's eyes and not just his Pakistani complexion. It would have been better than the obnoxious, magical purple irises Micah inherited from the Redwood Queen.

"Oh, what a relief." He scrutinized Micah. "You look

miserable. Where's Andrew?"

Micah stared at the light on in the ceiling to push back his tears.

"What happened? Come here, kiddo." Julian gestured to his bed, so Micah slunk over and sank down onto the mattress as he covered his face with his hands.

"I think I just broke Andrew's heart."

"Oh, now." Julian put his arm around Micah's shoulders. "What'd you do?"

"Someone kissed me at work." With a sniff, Micah sat up and wiped his hand across his nose. "Andrew saw her do it."

Julian sighed. "What happened? With the girl."

Micah shrugged, shaking his head. "I don't know, Dad. I was just trying to be nice."

"You have that effect on people." Julian smiled. "It's your nature. And the cute face I passed on to you." Julian pinched Micah's cheek. "Doesn't Andrew know how much kissing you did in your teens in the Redwoods?" His voice caught only slightly when he said the last word.

"All the more reason to not mess around now." Micah's voice was tight and defensive. The person he was before Andrew hardly seemed real. Being single and moving from tryst to tryst, even once they were in Minnesota, he couldn't even imagine it anymore. All the lying and, most likely, all the charming he'd done to make sure he could gorge himself on pleasure and then vanish.

"I didn't mean you ought to." Julian patted his hand.

"I just don't think Andrew seems like he'd throw away your relationship so easily." He stood up from the bed and resumed folding laundry.

Micah ran his fingertip over the diamond of his *Ingwaz* tattoo on his left index finger. "He doesn't seem like himself right now."

Midway through folding a shirt against his chest, Julian paused. He nodded slowly. "I agree. He's seemed different ever since this summer. I wonder if he hates living with us." Julian grinned. "We do argue a lot."

"I've asked him a hundred times." Micah scraped his hair back from his forehead. "I *have* given him plenty of times to admit that we annoy him. He says that's not it."

"Not *yet*." Julian snorted. "He ain't seen nothing yet. I haven't even had an episode since he moved in."

Micah stared at him for a moment, wondering about that himself. These days, Julian's bad days were becoming more and more spaced out. But he had never even told Julian that the Redwood Queen actually stole him away. As far as Micah knew, Julian was none the wiser.

Finally Micah shook his head. "Andrew won't give me any explanation. Just says he's fine. When we all know he's not."

A strange expression flickered over Julian's features before burrowing out of sight. He finished folding the shirt and put it in his drawers before leaning against the dresser. He spoke to the pendant light hanging from the ceiling in the corner, not to Micah. "Have you considered there's a chance it might not have anything to do with you?"

Micah blinked. "I mean...I suppose. But I wish he would tell me either way."

"I know." He looked down, opening and closing his mouth as if testing some words without speaking them. His shoulders began to hunch before he caught himself, biting his lip. Padding up to the bed, he sat beside Micah, wringing his hands. He said with a faint tremor in his voice and ghosts in his eyes, "Take it from me, Micah. There are some truths that would paralyze us if we speak them aloud."

Up to his hips in scalding bath water, Andrew sat hugging his knees to his chest, trembling. He stared unseeing at the silver faucet and his warped reflection stretched long and thin, like a specter. He'd been in his tub for thirty minutes, and he had only moved to refresh the hot water when it cooled.

"Andrew?" Sam rapped his knuckles on the door. "Hey. Are you okay?"

Jumping, splashing water over the edge of the tub, Andrew glanced at the door and tried to speak, but his lips felt stuck together. In response Sam turned the bathroom door handle and cracked open the door.

"Andrew? Do you want to talk?" Peering through the crack, Sam blinked a hazel eye at him behind tortoiseshell glasses. Sam was twenty-six, and Andrew's sole coworker at Magic's Computer Repair and Programming. Unsettled by the blank look on Andrew's face, the way it didn't even seem like Andrew recognized him, Sam nudged the door open further and said, "What's up? Are you okay?"

For as many weeks as Andrew had been hiding, he knew by the look on Sam's face that it was over. He was caught. Sam's worry shot fire through Andrew's numbness and unleashed his despair. His slender features crumbled; tears jumped into his eyes. He crushed his face into his knees as a sob he'd been holding in since August ripped its way out of his chest, despairing and hopeless. Once it broke out, he couldn't stop the weeping.

"Oh. Oh, no. Andy." Sam shuffled into the bathroom, the toilet lid clinking as he sat down beside the tub. He'd sort of known Andrew hadn't been doing well, but this was terrible to see. Worse by far than when Ingrid had been stalking him. That had been a frantic sort of desperation. This was beyond that. Andrew was like a lost little boat, unmoored, in the shallow water of the tub and hidden behind his hair with his fingers dimpling his biceps and his knuckles blanched.

"I d-don't know if...I can do this anymore." His voice turned into a desolate whimper as the words squeezed out of him.

A cold jolt of fear ricocheted through Sam. "Do...do what? Andrew, are you suicidal?"

Andrew lifted his head, snot and tears shining. "I—I have to break up with Micah." Saying it aloud crushed Andrew's chest so all his breath whooshed out.

"You *what*? What happened?"

Andrew couldn't answer. The sketch of his rib cage expanded and pressed against his skin every time he gasped for air, highlighting the sharp pink scar above his hip from the Redwoods.

Panicking, Sam dug his phone out from his sweats and sent a quickfire text to Micah. Andrew might be in a disagreement with him, but Micah was the only person who would know what to do.

Down the street, Micah leapt to his feet from his living room couch, ejecting his orange tomcat Cinnamon from his lap. He had his phone in his hand with a single-worded text from Sam: *Help.*

"Micah," cautioned his father, halfway to taking a drink from a mug of tea that matched Micah's, "give Andrew space."

"Oh, you know...I'm going...uh...somewhere else."

"Yeah right. You don't have other friends."

Shooting his dad a nasty look, Micah dropped his phone in the pocket of his joggers. Then he took the stairs down to their entryway two at a time, pulled on his dad's Columbia jacket, and tugged on his heaviest boots. He tightened the hood of the jacket, picked up a pair of fleece-lined leather gloves, and then he exploded into the fray. In proper footwear, it was easier to run than when he left work. But the snow was too deep, and Sam's text was too terrifying. He had to risk it. Micah reached for the empty air, grasped a ribboned shadow a street lamp cast through a branch, and pulled himself inside.

Andrew was right: folding shadows like this worked maybe every third time. Micah had tried it regularly in the last two years, but the safest time to do it was instances like now, when he was buzzing with anxiety. Otherwise, the shadows spit him back out, like failing to catch a wave on a surfboard.

Though he didn't break stride, the weight of the snow stopped affecting him; the shadows bent him around and through it. He jumped out again when he reached the curb beside the red awning of the two-story building that was Andrew's shop on the ground floor and the apartment above it. When his boots hit the snow on the sidewalk, Micah lost his balance and pinwheeled his arms desperately to stay upright. He gritted his teeth, realizing Andrew was right to scorn him in the winter. The snow and ice turned him into a toddler barely able to keep his feet under him. Embarrassed and frustrated—even though nobody was there to watch him—he thrust his hands into his jacket pockets and shuffled around the side of the building.

Micah had the third and final set of keys to Andrew's building, so he let himself through the large steel door around the back near the parking lot where Sam's Honda sat gathering snow. He hurried up the squeaky stairs. At the top, he shook off the snow that had already collected on his shoulders and hood, stomped it off his boots, and then opened the front door.

The television was on but silent in the living room in front of him, with Sam's large gaming laptop open on an IKEA coffee table as if he'd abandoned it suddenly. And that was when Micah heard Andrew crying.

The sound dug into his ears like sharp fingernails, filling him with a terror that made his hands go numb. He dropped his coat on a cushioned stool near the front door, kicked off his boots, and hurried past the kitchen to the bathroom door, where Andrew's sounds were getting louder. He entered without knocking, the door whacking into Sam's knee.

Sam waved off Micah's apology as he leapt off the toilet seat, shimmied out of the way, and squeezed Micah's arm. "I'm in over my head," Sam whispered, "but holler if you need me."

Naked and hugging his knees, Andrew whipped his

head up when the door opened. Micah was a mirage seen through tunnel vision and a sheen of tears. He had changed into a knit sweater Andrew had bought him, stuck his hair under a brown beanie, and looked down at Andrew with lips parted and eyes wide and dark, usually violet but now almost burgundy.

"No," cried Andrew. "Please, I don't...I can't..." His heart hurt, clawing inside his chest like a wild animal; clutching his head, he shied away and wedged himself into the corner of the tub. He felt rather than heard Micah kneel beside the tub; warmth radiated off his skin.

Breathlessly, Micah asked, "Is this all about me?"

"No!"

"Can I help you calm down?"

"Yes," he wept.

Micah tugged Andrew's arms down from his head and then pressed one hand to his back between his shoulder blades and the other against his sternum. Like Andrew did to him in Lake Sylvia, before they went into the Redwoods. Under Micah's palm, Andrew's heart was a staccato frenzy.

"Come on, Andrew. You need to breathe. Slower. In, out."

"I can't." Andrew shook off Micah's hands so he could curl up into the fetal position. "It's too much."

"Okay, then we're getting you in bed." Micah grasped Andrew's biceps. "Come on."

"No," wept Andrew, though some small, trapped part

of his brain deeply buried beneath the panic desperately wanted to be warm and dry and held. His body was vibrating, dizzy with anxiety, his ribs aching with the labor of his shallow breaths. "I can't." Andrew grabbed the wire-wrapped blood ward and yanked. The wire around the vial bent and came free of the cord. He tossed it at Micah and said, "T-t-tell me to do it."

Clapping it against his chest, Micah opened and closed his mouth. "Andrew, I don't want to do that for the first time—"

"I w...won't listen t-to you otherwise."

"I don't know how to do that on pur—"

Despairing, Andrew clutched his temples and started to weep again.

Micah curled the vial into his palm, calculating. Then he slipped it into his pocket. "Okay," he said, relenting. "All right. Fine. Look—look at me." He tried to tip back Andrew's chin which was pressed into his chest. Andrew didn't respond, fighting against Micah's grasp, nearly unrecognizable beneath his shroud of despair. "Babe. C'mon." Micah stroked his high, bony cheeks, coaxing, coaxing, coaxing his face up and his body to relax. "Andrew. Darling. C'mon, babe. You're okay. Be calm."

Drawn to the sweet music of his voice, Andrew pushed through the panic to meet Micah's gaze. Tears flicked off Micah's lashes as his irises turned like coffee filling with cream, burgundy to lilac, as if the light in the room had shifted. Micah's soft hands caressed his cheeks and made him shiver, enveloping his wild and wayward heart in something cozy and silky like an infant being swaddled. Abruptly, his body followed suit: his pulse cut itself in half, from frantic to languid, exterminating the fire crawling over his skin with a cool rolling mist. Stunned, he coughed and rubbed his throat, blinking rapidly.

Micah released him at once. "D-did I hurt you?"

Clutching his chest, Andrew shook his head, reaching for Micah with his other hand till he closed on his fuzzy sweater sleeve. Micah wordlessly helped him up from the tub and held onto his waist as Andrew unfolded. His knees were wobbly as he stepped onto linoleum, still trembling, teeth chattering. His heel slipped and his weight shifted, trying to take him down to the ground, but Micah wrapped a warm, soft arm around him and held him up.

Anxiously thinking about how much Andrew probably didn't want him here, Micah began, "I can let Sam take over—"

Silent, gulping in air, Andrew shook his head and stumbled alongside Micah past the living room. His wet feet squeaked on the kitchen tiles and left footprints when they trod onto the carpet in the second bedroom in the corner of the flat. Sam was close enough to see Andrew's answer, and blinked in understanding as he pushed his glasses up and watched them pass.

Micah flicked on the light switch in the barren bedroom. Andrew's bed was made neatly in the far corner, his dresser on the wall across from it, red curtains closed over the small window.

The room was unadorned, and filled Andrew with a new kind of sorrow as he pulled back the covers and climbed into bed. This would be his life without Micah. Plain, cold, and hopeless. Tears still squeezed out of the corners of his eyes, residual, like the last grumble of thunder on the tail of a storm. He could think again, and the tunnel vision retreated. The sudden tranquility almost made him giddy.

Micah put a handful of tissues in Andrew's palm. Gratefully, Andrew cleaned up his messy face and then dropped them into the small waste basket Micah held out.

"I didn't know you had a history of panic attacks." Micah kept his voice to a gentle whisper. "That looked terrible for you."

Andrew didn't answer. Rolling onto his side facing the wall, he flipped the dusty covers up over his head and stared at the pinpricks of light coming through his sheets. It had been at least five years since he'd last fallen apart like this. In the middle of Ingrid's haunting, when he thought he would never have relief. But even then...even then he didn't feel this empty.

"Andrew, I know...I know...what I did. But I hope you understand that I can't leave you until I know you're going to be safe." Micah turned the blood vial over in his fingers, wanting to sit on the bed but not moving.

Andrew snorted. "Who cares."

Micah shot back, "Me, obviously. I don't have feelings for anyone else. I love you, Andrew."

"I don't care that some girl kissed you," murmured Andrew. "I mean. I do. But…"

"I can't hear you."

Sighing heavily, Andrew raised his voice. "Get in bed then."

Micah sagged with relief. He climbed onto the space near the pillow, his weight rolling Andrew's body back toward him so they leaned together. Andrew didn't move away. His usually cool skin was hot and feverish, making Micah's heart lurch. The only other time Andrew had felt so warm was outside The Squire on the night they met. Was Andrew so warm now because he'd just been hyperventilating, or because Micah had used Fae magic to calm him down?

"I said I don't care that some girl kissed you," Andrew whispered under the sheets. "I saw her do it. I know you didn't initiate it. I…I just think…I'm h…"

Gently, Micah scrunched up the sheets to see Andrew's face. He cringed back from the light, and Micah jumped up and ran to switch them off.

When he came back, Andrew was on his back staring blankly at the dark ceiling. Then Sam knocked lightly on the door, stepping in with an awkward wave.

"Hi." Before they could answer, Sam went on, "I'm sorry if I was wrong to call Micah over, Andy. It...it was the first thing I could think of. I've just never seen you like that. But I figured, it's Micah, and anyway, he helps Julian when he—"

"You weren't wrong," Andrew said to the ceiling.

"Can I do anything? Do you want some water? T–to drink?"

Andrew managed a tremulous smile. "Sure. Sorry. For the scare."

Sam picked his lip and then smiled. "Nah, I get it. Mental health." He patted the door frame. "Micah? Anything?"

Mustering a smile for him, Micah shook his head.

Sam disappeared. The refrigerator clunked open and shut around the corner. When he ran back in with a glass of water and a metal straw, Andrew struggled upright and took it with a faint smile. Sam said to him, "Let me know how else I can help. I'm probably gonna be up for a bit." On Andrew's dresser, Sam clicked on a table lamp, casting gentle light across the room. It glinted on a moonstone ring kept on a tray beside it. He turned back, serious. "Hey, Andy. I just want you to know that I love you. And I hope you feel better. That's all, bye." Awkwardly, Sam scuttled out of the room, his bedroom door thumping closed on the other side of the living room.

Micah reached down to the bare cord around Andrew's neck so he could loop the vial back onto it.

Andrew shook his head, straw in his mouth, and pushed Micah back. He said with his teeth around the straw, "I don't need it back on." Lowering the cup, Andrew said more clearly, "I think I want to keep your calm chemistry flowing. Especially b-because I want to know what happened, back at your shop."

Micah slumped against the headboard. "Yeah. Okay."

Andrew reached around Micah and set the cup on the windowsill. He paused, wanting to press his lips to the curve of Micah's neck above his sweater. The sudden wave of desire was staggering. Andrew wondered if it was from the absence of the blood ward, but he knew better. He hadn't cooled to Micah since the moment they met, not even now, when Andrew was facing the end.

The heat of Andrew's deep, slow breath rippled across Micah's throat. Goosebumps prickled his skin as he strained to resist the urge to stop Andrew's lips with his own.

Tearing himself away, Andrew leaned back, tucked his knees up, and pulled the covers to his chin. Then he turned and watched Micah, waiting.

Micah pulled off his hat, dropping it over the edge of the bed. "What do you want to know? I...I want to tell you helpful things, and I don't want to hide anything, but I don't even understand how it happened."

"You're desirable." A humorless, nearly hysterical laugh tumbled from Andrew's lips. "People stare at you and long for you wherever we go. Men, women, everyone. It's constant. I become a public enemy when people realize I'm 'with' you."

Micah made a face. Truthfully, he never really noticed people checking him out, especially not since meeting Andrew. "Well, regardless. The woman was Diana. She's, I don't know, twenty-eight? Thirty? She's in grad school for...I don't know. Something."

"I'm oddly comforted by how little you know about her." said Andrew.

"She has been completely beyond my notice," Micah told him emphatically, "with the exception of her excellent customer service and sub-par tea-making. That was my first time ever being alone with her. She certainly wasted no time." Micah raised his eyebrows. "And if I didn't take that damn tea shop so seriously and came home when you told me to, I could've avoided the whole thing."

"Until the next time," said Andrew.

Micah's expression hardened. "I don't follow."

"Until the next time. Or the next person who falls for you. Or the next time you wish you could kiss someone pretty, but you're stuck with me, as I wither and get creaky and fat."

"Andrew, what?" Micah was incredulous. "What are you talking about? This isn't at all how I think. I thought you'd know that by now." It was true that Andrew had never thought extraordinarily well of himself over the course of their relationship, but he'd never admitted explicitly he believed he wasn't good enough for Micah.

Andrew glanced at him, and then away. He quickly wetted his lips with his tongue and then blurted, "You should forget we met. I'm holding you back."

Hot rage shot through Micah with such intensity that he snapped, "Shut the fuck up."

Andrew sat back as if struck. His expression grew blank and guarded and he curled a lip. "Excuse me?"

"You are a choice I choose every single day," Micah said, hoping both of them could pretend like his voice hadn't broken.

"I don't bel—"

"Stop *saying* that. You can't say you don't believe me. If you don't believe me then that means you don't trust me, and I hate that." Micah's teeth bared around his words, contorted by his disbelief and heartbreak. He inhaled and held his breath, blinking rapidly, smoothing his features. *Stay neutral. Don't lash out.*

Andrew just stared at him, blank and distant, bony shoulders hunched.

More quietly, but still with an edge of frustration in his voice, Micah asked, "What is going on with you? We got through a whole calendar year together last year and I never heard a whisper of doubt about my feelings. Now, you make fun of me every time I say something nice to you. You sleep less than I do. You've gotten *skinnier,* if that's possible. You yell at me and even Sam and sometimes my dad over the smallest things, and then you clam up and won't talk for an hour."

Andrew's eyes glistened with sudden tears. A vein rose on his forehead. He started to cry again, silent, pressing his lips together. Finally, he swallowed, the apple of his throat bobbing, and he whispered in a voice that broke, "I'm so depressed."

"What?" Micah's eyes widened. Then his shoulders slumped. "Oh." He reached out and brushed Andrew's hair over his shoulders. "Oh, Andrew. I'm so sorry. I didn't...I should have put it together."

Wiping his cheeks, Andrew took a few unsteady breaths. "It wasn't your responsibility. I've dealt with this my whole life and I...I should have known. But I thought I'd be rid of it, to be honest, when I found you. So I stopped going to therapy, and...this summer...this episode hit me harder than any of the others." He stifled a hiccupping cry. "I was buried by it before I even realized. And the thoughts now, they're so much worse now that I'm not alone."

"How come?"

Andrew curled up, shrinking himself, forehead on his knee, hugging his chest. "I don't understand why the fuck you chose me, back at the bar where we met. I don't understand why you choose me now. It doesn't make any sense. And...and I'm mad at you for it."

"You're mad at me because I love you," clarified Micah,

trying and failing to hide his indignation.

"If you'd never met me, I could've just killed myself and been done with all of this." Andrew choked on the possibility, on the longing for such final relief.

Watching Micah's expressions shift through the veil of his hair, Andrew realized he could physically feel the emotions passing. Incredulity, to heartbreak, to frustration, to sadness and back again, back and forth with dizzying speed. It was like the seasons kept changing, how the smell of the air outside shifts, Micah's anger like scalding sunshine hot enough to blister, while his sorrow was the cold snap in autumn. Micah pressed his lips together, brows furrowing a line into his otherwise unblemished tawny skin.

Andrew went on, "Being around you and...and Julian, and even Ingrid...it's reminded me how...how incredibly, painfully abandoned I have been by anything resembling family."

Micah looked away and began lamely, "My dad adores you...and...and there's Sam..."

"Stop. Micah, it's not your problem to fix." Andrew waved his hand. "I'm not looking for you to cheer me up. Nothing about how I think right now is your problem to fix. *I'm* the broken one. *I'm* the hopeless one. Don't make me your problem."

"You're not my 'problem.'" Micah put the word in air quotes, scornful. "And I should remind you that this whole breakdown was triggered because I kissed someone. Why exactly am I getting away with that? How did this spiral so much?"

Tearful again, Andrew insisted, "You should be able to kiss someone. You should be able to shine your blinding light everywhere. I'm only snuffing it out."

Another flash of frustration. Andrew felt it like heartburn in his chest. Was this the effect of not wearing the vial of Micah's blood? Was Micah always this emotional to everyone around him—so much that you could taste his feelings?

Micah gritted his teeth. "Stop telling me how you're making me feel."

Andrew looked away, silent.

"Listen," continued Micah, gentler, "I messed up tonight. With Diana. And I'll take responsibility for that in any way you want me to. But if you don't consider us over, then I'm not letting you convince me to leave you. Got it?"

Andrew pushed his hair behind his ear, running his hand down the side of his neck. He wiped his cheeks dry and then stared at the threadbare rug next to his bed. "All right," he murmured.

"Now," Micah said, his voice a lullaby with only the sweetest notes, "how can I help lessen the depression? What do you need?"

Andrew shrugged. "I'm back on my therapist's schedule in two weeks. I...I can't do much else but wait it out. Try not to get suicidal. Er, *more* suicidal."

"That doesn't feel like enough."

Andrew sighed. "There's something I've been thinking about since this summer, actually." He glanced across the small room at the moonstone ring on his dresser.

Micah followed his gaze and went to pick up the ring. He held it out to Andrew, who slid it onto his finger.

Watching the light glint against ghostly blue flecks, Andrew thought in silence for a moment. "You got to save your dad when the Redwoods lured him in. Just like you two, my mum and I were on our own. And just like your dad, the Fae-spelled foods caught my mum, too. Only I ditched her. Just...got angry and bounced." He sighed, soft and remorseful. "I don't know if she died, or had a heart attack, or ran away," Andrew went on. "And ever since Ingrid found your dad in her scrying glass, I've been hoping I'd just stop caring what became of her. But being in Lilydale has had the opposite effect. So I think I need to ask for Ingrid's help, and see where my mother is. She already said she would, remember? That first autumn we were together."

"Okay. Yeah." Micah nodded. "I'm surprised you waited this long."

Andrew stared at the ring, spinning it on his finger, tears pooling in his lower lashes. "I really haven't wanted to care. I wish I could just grow the memory of my mother into a tree."

Micah paused. He understood the reference, but the implication that Micah never thought of the Redwood Queen anymore was misguided. She'd still been his mother. Even if she'd never so much as hugged him, the biological cords could never truly be severed. It was just that Micah mostly felt terror at the thought of her, and relief to have her gone. The absence of Andrew's mother clearly came as no relief for Andrew.

His foxlike expression torn, Andrew opened his mouth and then closed it.

"And?" Micah urged softly.

Andrew blinked. The tear he dislodged fell almost in slow motion, a tiny drop of tragic starlight reflecting the lamplight a hundred times over. "And if my mum is still alive...I want to go to her." He paused. "Alone."

Micah's shoulders dropped. He rolled his head down and grabbed a handful of his hair. Cynicism and sarcasm burbled behind his sternum and begged to come out with a sharp rebuke or sarcasm. "Sure," he managed instead.

Andrew stole a quick glance at Micah out of the corner of his eye. He had learned over the last two years what it looked like when Micah was gnawing on the inside of his cheek, a habit Andrew was convinced lived on even though Micah hadn't self-harmed anymore since that night in the mountains. It was his indicator that Micah's attempt at nonchalance was a lie, and that Andrew had just hewn the bond between them with an ax. He explained, "Maybe it's the thing I have to reconcile between me and myself."

"I brought you with me to *my* mother," Micah muttered.

Andrew smiled halfheartedly, nudging their elbows together. "She and I were fast friends, eh?"

Micah grumbled wordlessly.

"Will you come with me to Lilydale tomorrow to see Ingrid?"

Micah eyed his smile with the smallest flicker of resentment. It was easy for Andrew to smile as he was pushing Micah away to carry on without him. It was easy for Andrew to leave him behind. He swallowed painfully, and by the way Andrew still looked soft and at ease, he must not have picked up on Micah's frustration. Good. Determined to keep it to himself, he fixed his bangs and pushed down the negative feelings. Maybe he could deal with them later. At least, that's what he always told himself. He wetted his lips and then answered, "Yeah. I wanted to see how they held up in the storm anyway."

"I'm sure Ingrid took good care of them." Andrew's head spun, and he had an ache behind his eye socket. He slid down his pillow and onto his back, hair spreading out around his head like a mane of fire. The smell of sage and turmeric swelled over him from Micah's clothes, bringing with it a clear vision of the brownstone, which always smelled like that. Andrew gazed at Micah's chiseled chin and plush lips just as Micah pushed his sweater sleeves up to his elbows. Andrew hungrily followed the reveal of his tawny forearms, forgetting everything else about this godforsaken blizzard at the sight of those rippling muscles beneath a fine layer of moss-green hair.

Micah glanced down at him, swallowing. For how the night had gone, this was an intimate arrangement, with Andrew laying in bed naked and still damp from the bath. He was radiating heat from the exertion of his panic attack as if he was a woodburning stove. The half-lidded stare from Andrew's coffee-colored eyes was reminiscent of that night at The Squire. They talked about that night now and again, but Andrew was dismissive of it, treating it like a silly meet-cute rather than Micah demonstrating a reckless amount of power he couldn't control.

Micah dug his fingers into his thighs, looking away as Andrew burrowed deeper in the blankets. "You should get some sleep."

Andrew responded with an ambiguous purr, which drew Micah's eyes back to his face and that irresistible quirk of his lips.

Micah started to get off the bed. "I can go h—"

But Andrew reached up, grasped the collar of his sweater, and pulled Micah down on top of him. He pressed their lips together, sweeping away any residue of cardamom and tamarind. Andrew's cool hand reached under Micah's sweater and held him by the small of his back, his touch tingling like a breeze after a rainstorm. Then he lifted the sweater up and over Micah's head, pulling him free of it.

Hair mussed, Micah leaned on his elbows for a moment,

searching Andrew's face, looking for eclipsed pupils and scalding skin. He swallowed, collecting himself, intent on pulling back any escaped Fae influence.

Andrew hummed in irritation over Micah's delay. His high cheekbones were bright with color, and his lips were slightly parted. His hands roamed across Micah's bare chest. "Micah," he pleaded raggedly.

Micah bit his lip, and Andrew's eyes devoured the sight of it. Micah asked, "Wh...what if you can't...consent right now?"

"I can and I do," growled Andrew, and untied Micah's pants.

Chapter Three
The Scrying

Micah leaned over the island in Andrew and Sam's small kitchen, clutching a half-finished cup of coffee in a maroon and gold mug. He sat near the yellow-leaved bromeliad he'd given Andrew at the co-op two years ago. It was barely alive.

When he came out of the bathroom, Andrew was wringing his hair dry with a small towel, wearing only the same pair of jeans he had on the night before.

It was unusual that Micah didn't join Andrew in the shower. It was a cue to Andrew that things were still quite wrong, and it set his teeth on edge. Andrew looked down at Micah as he came around the island, perching on the seat next to him. Micah stared seriously into his mug, hair pushed back off his forehead, knee bouncing restlessly against the stool.

"What's the matter?" Andrew asked.

Micah didn't look up. He took so long to reply that Andrew wasn't convinced he was going to. Finally Micah acknowledged him with a fleeting glance. "I feel weird about last night."

"Yeah, can't be great having to help your grown-ass boyfriend through a total mental breakdown." Andrew's voice was high and breathy with derision.

"Not that." Micah picked a black cat hair off the rim of his mug.

Andrew waited. When Micah remained silent, he stood up and clicked on his red electric kettle to boil some water. He scooped some fragrant tea leaves into an aluminum mesh tea ball, about to drop it into a mug he grabbed from his cabinet. But the mug had the little bubble tea and leaf logo for To a Tea on the side. He set it back on the shelf and picked up a red-glazed mug from a thrift store instead.

Micah shifted uneasily. "I meant when you wanted to have sex."

Andrew leaned against the counter, staring at Micah's hunched shoulders while a sharp waft of peppermint touched the tip of his tongue when he took a breath. It wasn't from his rooibos tea.

Uneasy with Andrew's silence, Micah turned around on the stool to face him. Andrew watched him with that infuriatingly blank expression again as if just waiting for Micah to elaborate.

Micah ground the inside of his cheek between his teeth, hard enough to feel a pinch and taste a quick burst of copper on his tongue. Hoping to break Andrew's silence, he added, "I mean that I wasn't confident that I wasn't still charming you, and...I don't think you know how disturbing I still find it that I charmed you into kissing me that first time in the bar. I know we worked out well and everything, but—"

Andrew blinked slowly with catlike indifference.

"Any thoughts on the matter?" Micah said impatiently.

Cool and formal, Andrew said, "I was in my right mind last night when we had sex." He picked up the boiling kettle and filled his cup with steaming water. He spread his hand across the porcelain mug; it was hot enough that he reflexively began to drop it, but he steeled himself and held tight. "And it seems like if you're concerned you still can't control those abilities, there's a fairly obvious solution."

Micah recoiled. Andrew's tone stung like he'd sliced Micah with his iron blade. And the implication that Micah wasn't doing what he had to do in order to master his Fae abilities was just as insulting.

Lifting and dropping the tea ball with his thumb and forefinger, Andrew avoided Micah's wounded gaze. His thighs clenched together as he endured his burning palm.

Finally, Micah said, "Yeah. You should put back on the blood ward I made you."

"No." Andrew's voice was flat. "That's not the answer."

"How I deal with being Fae is not up to you, Andrew," Micah told him sharply.

Andrew's eyes flashed. "You're *not* dealing with being

Fae."

They were locked in a silent stare-down for several beats. Then Sam came out of his room, humming Taylor Swift as he pulled on a sweatshirt.

When his head popped out of the hood, he stopped in the doorway to the kitchen, eyes growing wide. "Uh...am I interrupting?"

Micah ended the stare-down first. Of course. He gave Sam a weak smile. "Nah." He turned his back on Andrew and lifted his mug to his lips. He was embarrassed by how much the coffee rippled in his shaking hands.

"I'm being an asshole." Andrew's voice trembled, ambiguously talking to either Micah or Sam.

"What else is new?" Sam gave a hollow laugh. He poured himself some coffee from the pot and then picked up a fuchsia beanie from the counter next to Micah.

Scuffing his toe against the laminate in the kitchen, Andrew glanced up at Sam. "Hey, I need to go up to Lilydale this morning to talk to Ingrid. But I was going to come back down and work afterwards, if that's okay."

"Okay," said Sam, neutral as he ever was when they talked about Lilydale around him. He sipped his coffee and then pushed up his glasses. "You going up there for something in particular? You guys usually just go up on the weekends."

Andrew paused. "I'm finally going to ask Ingrid to use her scrying glass to look for my mum."

Sam looked away, rubbing the stubble on his chin. "Surprised you didn't do that this summer after you started talking about her."

Micah straightened, looking at Andrew. Andrew was welcome to talk to Sam about whatever he liked, but hearing that he'd talked about his mother with Sam and not Micah...the sting was there, whether Micah wanted to care or not.

As if sensing his stare, Andrew looked down, picking at a cuticle. "Uh. Yeah. You know how it goes. I'd rather pretend I don't care. But my trauma has forced my hand, I guess."

Sam sucked his teeth. "So this is a very big deal. Take the rest of the day off then, goddamn it. What did you always tell me when I missed a day for school or called in sick?" He stepped into a pair of checkered flats by the door, kicking his left foot back to fix the heel.

"I don't know," Andrew lied.

Sam rolled his eyes. Then, with a halfway decent British accent, he said with a flourish, "The shop won't burn down, and the viruses won't win. Take a fucking break."

Andrew scowled. "You would need to take the day from my pay."

Sam snorted. "I would not."

"That's how running a business works." Andrew leaned down, fixing Sam with a stern look. "If I'm not working, then you make the money I would make."

"You know I'm doing programming projects on my own," Sam insisted. "And those I get to do in my pajamas on the couch."

"Moving up in the world." Micah directed a little two-finger salute at Sam.

"Thank you. Thank you." Sam gave a theatrical bow. He opened the front door and gave them a nervous smile. "Take the day off, Andy. If you show up to work, I'm locking you out."

All Andrew could manage was a tight smile as Sam left and shut the door softly behind him. A gust of frigid air rolled across the floor. Micah lifted his bare feet to the chair rung.

Goosebumps on his skin, Andrew lowered himself onto the other stool. Micah stared at his coffee.

"That day this summer?" Andrew nodded toward where Sam had just been. "When I was moving into the brownstone. I found this..." He spun the moonstone ring. "...Box of old stuff, and I... " He swallowed.

"You what?" pushed Micah, stomach clenching, blood pounding in his ears as his heartbeat doubled.

Andrew wetted his lips. "I've been thinking about suicide every single day since."

Micah remained motionless, tears pooling along his lower lashes. "I..." He swallowed thickly. *I wish you would have told me,* he wanted to say. But that was the wrong thing to say. Everything was the wrong thing. Micah had fallen for all the fake smiles, the warm embraces, the peaceful nights. It was hardly Andrew's fault that Micah had been so oblivious.

"Andrew, that must have felt terrible for you."

"If I don't...take care of this little brain meltdown of mine," whispered Andrew, "then there will be worse than a bathtub panic attack happening."

Hot prickles of terror crawled along Micah's shoulders as he put his forehead on his palm. "You shut me out," Micah murmured. "You made sure I had no way of knowing. Or did I miss it all?"

"I don't know." Andrew shrugged, twisting a damp strand of his hair around his finger. "I was trying to fool myself, too. There was nothing to admit to if I was convinced I was fine."

They sat with the space between them full of tension, where the only certainty was that everything was wrong.

"I'm sorry," said Andrew quietly. "For what I said about you. I got defensive. I got thrown off when you said you felt weird about sex. I really appreciated, needed, and enjoyed it. So I had no idea."

Micah couldn't bite his tongue fast enough. "I had no idea you thought I was doing a shit job as a faerie." He sighed coarsely and pressed his fingers to his eyes. "Sorry. I'm sorry. You're not wrong. It's just, uh...I guess you're not as honest as I thought."

Andrew hesitated. "It doesn't serve us for me to tell you

what to do."

"How do you know?" Micah snapped "You haven't given us the chance. You've been visiting Lilydale with me for two years, Andrew, watching me around the Folk and thinking about how dumb I looked with them."

"Not at all," said Andrew quickly. "I just—I know you've spent a long time wanting to avoid magic, and maybe that's not the best strategy...Julian has seemed okay, and I mean, you could make it useful for yourself..."

"All right." Micah's tone suggesting that it very much was not.

Desperate to finish the thought, Andrew hurried on, "All the Folk—like Syabira, and Lina, and Chami obviously—they just seem so ready to help you, and if you—"

"*All right*," Micah interrupted, shooting Andrew a glare out of the corner of his eyes.

Andrew fell silent. Releasing his hand from his mug, he curled and uncurled his scalded fingers.

Micah caught Andrew's wrist and inspected the angry red skin of his palm, clicking his tongue. "Took one out of my book."

Andrew laid his hand on the counter, palm up, dropping his head between his shoulders. "I'm at rock bottom, Micah."

"Yeah." Micah sighed softly. "I'm getting that."

Pinching the bridge of his nose, Andrew forced out the words. "I think...even...even if I...uh...don't go to find my mum...I might just spend a few nights here by myself." After all, if he was alone...maybe he could just end it.

Micah held his breath while he ordered his body to keep his emotions to himself. He held his breath until he thought he could easily pass out. Then he unclenched his jaw and managed flatly, "Whatever you need."

As they unloaded from Micah's car at the parking lot for Pickerel Lake, Andrew clipped his snowshoes on and asked again, "Are you sure you don't have something to say?"

"No. I'm just tired. Your bed sucks," answered Micah. If Andrew didn't know any better, he might have believed him.

Already snapped into his snowshoes, Micah locked his car and tromped off the flat paved lot and onto the frozen lake. He spotted the slight movement of Ingrid and Chamomile peeling off from their perch on a dead tree and started to wave, relieved—oh so relieved—for company besides Andrew.

Chamomile tore over the snow like a child possessed in a bright pink jacket and fluffy boots. Close behind her was Micah's tall half-sister, hips swinging as she approached in a sweater dress and knit tights.

"Ingrid," Micah called, accusatory. "The windchill is like,

twenty below! Wear a jacket."

"I like this weather," remarked Ingrid.

"See? This weather's great." Andrew cast a sidelong look at Micah.

Though he was nothing like Ingrid, her half-brother was still more gifted with Fae talents than Ingrid could have anticipated, especially as she remembered him on the day he was born. Smaller and more fragile than Fae babies—the few Ingrid had seen—he had been held first by Ingrid after the human midwife cleaned him of the gore of childbirth. The Redwood Queen had frowned at the sight of him, sniffed, and gone to sleep. He'd cried for hours, but Ingrid didn't put him down until at last he'd settled.

Now, Micah looked unsettled once more, with shoulders hunched and his jaw clenched. He shivered under his winter layers, nightshade eyes splashed with a tinge of burgundy. Ingrid wanted to pinch his cheek or pull on his ear to see if she could pull back the shroud of sadness over him.

Andrew cleared his throat. His red hair stuck out from under his scarf like spikes of dead leaves. He pulled his hands out of his pockets, both gloves curled into fists. "Gifts."

Chamomile nearly ripped his arm off, screeching ferociously, "I *love* Andrew gifts!" She dropped a pocket watch down from a tarnished gold chain, her blue eyes round as saucers. Andrew winced, rubbing his shoulder before holding a gleaming bronze blade out for Ingrid. She took it and admired the gilded ivory handle with her eyebrows raised and a quirk of her scarlet lips. Andrew bent his knee in a slight bow, his eyelids crinkling slightly, but in a way that didn't bring any light to his hollow umber stare. Something was wrong with him, too. Not just Micah.

"Winters have been easier since Ingrid arrived," said Chamomile, "but easiest yet this year. And easier now today than yesterday."

"Linguistically oblique, but that's good. I think," Andrew said drily.

Chamomile sneered at him. Then she went on to both of them, "The Lady of the Bluffs was quite in her element during last night's storm. Wait till you see what she erected."

Before either of them agreed, Ingrid and Chamomile took their arms and slipped with them into the shadows made by the claws of the naked trees. Andrew had learned to close his eyes, as it helped lessen the nausea and the disconcerting impression that he was moving inside, rather than through, his surroundings. He and Micah instinctively clung to each other despite their circumstances, because they'd found it impossible to keep their footing any other way when in the shadows.

They emerged at the northern perimeter of Lilydale. It was different now, though. No longer was the faerie compound simply fenced in by a low cobblestone wall. It was like a terrarium now, only the glass sides were...ice.

Mirror-bright, cloaking the compound from view with the reflection of the bluffs around them. Twenty feet tall, easily, with only a chink here and there where the Folk could pass through. A fortress, now, rather than a derelict brickyard.

Chamomile gestured toward an archway in the ice, eyes alight with excitement. "Feel." She stuck her arm inside. Micah followed suit, thrusting his arm out. Chamomile jumped and snatched his glove off. It was in the single digits—he should have felt the bite of the cold immediately.

But he didn't.

Bewildered, Micah stepped inside. He unzipped his jacket and unwound his scarf. "What the actual magic."

"I know!" squeaked Chamomile.

Andrew ducked inside after Ingrid, craning his neck back. You could still see the sky, but it didn't seem the same. Like a porthole into summertime. Wild but not. He gazed at the wall, reaching out and touching the slick ice that seemed almost to breathe like an ancient beast. "Ingrid, this is amazing. You've truly elevated what is already an impressive little patch of magic."

"More literally than you know." Ingrid's sly expression suggested she wasn't going to elaborate.

Lilydale spread over the bluffs with its eastward edge against a twelve-foot limestone cliff. It was the size of a modest provincial estate, maybe fifty yards in any direction. There was a grove of mismatched trees that grew tall and strong in the northeastern corner of the compound, where the majority of some two dozen Folk took up roost in hammocks or baskets. The center of the compound was an old brick kiln that now served as a modest throne with a seat Ingrid made herself with her uniquely magical artistry. Behind it was an evergreen garden plot growing fruits, vegetables, and flowers tenfold more splendid than the hothouses of the Arboretum.

In addition to the sweets Folk liked to bake for their own pleasure, the produce from the garden had an intoxicating effect on humans. It wasn't intentionally overwhelming to humans. Creatures made of magic like the Folk just naturally changed what they touched.

Since Andrew and Micah had gotten together, humans still showed up daily trying to get a taste of the magical food. Whether or not they got it depended on who they ran into outside Lilydale. Some Folk couldn't be bothered to refuse, while some couldn't be bothered to acknowledge them, and let the person get bored or frustrated and wander out. In the last two years, at least, the Folk had gotten less inclined to allow humans into their revelries. This winter, the human intruders had all but ceased, as if word had spread that Lilydale was closed.

The winter in Lilydale was less dead than beyond the walls, but less green than in the summer. The garden plot was spelled to withstand the brutal winter temperatures, to remain ever-green. But now, insulated by the ice walls, everything felt mild within the compound. The air was cool and still, not suffocatingly cold. There was still quite a bit of snow on the frozen ground, but it had melted off the limestone steps which ran in aisles near the north and south ends of Lilydale. Snow dripped from the trees. Several Folk behind the kiln throne were having a snowball fight.

"Dude, it's like, Hollywood-winter in here," exclaimed Micah.

"I know!" Chamomile bounced with delight.

Ingrid preened under the positive attention, tucking her hair behind her ear. "What brings you two out here?"

"Well, I wanted to check if you were okay," Micah said. "Clearly, undue worry."

"Indeed." Ingrid patted his back. "I always have things under control."

With his eyes steadfast on the wall, Micah's expression split with a humorless smile. "That must be nice."

She blinked at him.

Chamomile kicked off her winter boots straight up into a tree over their heads. Someone in the branches gave a yell. Unheeding, she wiggled her toes. "You know, before Ingrid got here, we used to hibernate with the garter snakes all winter," said Chamomile. "Now we get to celebrate Yule, and craft with spruce and pinecones. And also, now, I get to be *barefoot.*"

Ingrid turned her uncanny scarlet gaze on Andrew.

"Why else are you here?"

Andrew swallowed. He glanced at Micah, but as if on cue, Micah unclipped his snowshoes. He scooped up a handful of snow and then took off toward the Folk having the snowball fight. Chamomile hollered and tore after him.

Andrew rolled his eyes heavenward. "Cool."

"You're troubled," observed Ingrid. She turned and motioned toward her shelter, which stood alone on the highest eastern point of the compound, made of intact brick with a cast bronze door. A large winterberry bush grew outside her door, bursting with bright red fruits. Andrew unclipped from his snowshoes and picked his way after her, stepping in her footprints in hopes it would make him less likely to slip. At her door she glared at his winter boots until he bent and pulled them off, wiggling his numb toes. Only when he was in his stockings did she move and let him inside. The brick floor was warm and toasty, and when he crossed under her lintel, the candles circling the room whooshed into life. She pulled aside a crushed velvet curtain and allowed the clear winter daylight into the room.

Ingrid invited him to sit around her low round table on a pile of cushions. The candles filled her room with heat, so much so that he had to unzip from his jacket and slide off his snow pants. He set them aside on the bricks and unwound his scarf while she bent toward a heavy shelf next to the table. It held her Seeing glass, masked under a silk cloth, a stack of cups and mugs, and several lidded tins. She picked up one of the tins and popped back the lid, scooping leaves into an aluminum tea ball.

"What happened to you?" Ingrid asked. "You smell like cortisol."

Andrew blinked. "Um, how exactly do you know the name of the human stress hormone?"

She peered at him, waiting, not supplying an explanation.

Andrew peered back at her, waiting.

Scowling, she yielded. "I like science. It makes sense."

"Nerd." Andrew smirked and settled back on his cushions. It was ridiculous how much he enjoyed Ingrid, especially after they first met when he slashed her with an iron switchblade and he barely escaped with his life. For five years she'd haunted and stalked him. Truthfully, it had taken most of his first year dating Micah for him to fully believe Ingrid wasn't waiting for him to just let his guard down before she pounced. She gave him gifts, mostly antique books, but also a handsome seax much nicer than the one he'd bought off eBay. Her last gift before he'd told her he'd forgiven her had been a gilded iron dagger with a mahogany handle. She'd had to wrap it in a full bolt of silk and burlap to handle it. Even though he now came to Lilydale as a friend, he still wore the dagger in a holster on his ankle, even today. Most days, he also had his seax strapped to his back.

He watched as she struck a long-stemmed match, and

then held it aloft underneath the kettle. The flame continued burning long past its natural lifespan, until the water in the kettle started to bubble and boil. Then she filled a red chinoiserie pot with the steaming water and dropped the tea ball inside.

"Ahem." She raised an eyebrow.

"Oh. Uh." If he'd learned anything about Ingrid in the past two years, it was that he could skip the niceties of conversation which humans expected. "I'm very depressed." He paused and shrugged, dismissive, when Ingrid gave him a silent look of alarm. "Last night I had a very bad panic attack. You know, tunnel vision. Think you're going to die. Hyperventilating. Micah had to pull me out of it." Andrew tapped the hollow of his throat where Micah's blood ward usually rested.

"By biting you?"

He coughed. "That was later."

She picked up a larger rectangular tin that said it was from Grain Belt Beer in Minneapolis. Her long, slender fingers were tipped in black nail polish, as they usually were, but she wore no rings today. She pulled out a slice of thick, grain-studded bread and set it on a small clay plate, and then pushed it toward him.

"Grain-heavy bread boosts serotonin," she explained when she noticed him staring at her. "I didn't make it. I bought it at a market."

Andrew nodded slightly. Sometimes, with Ingrid especially, Andrew forgot to be cautious about Fae-spelled foods anymore. So far, he left Lilydale in the same state he entered it. So far, he hadn't lost track of any time among the faeries. And at least with Ingrid—unlike Micah—if those words had come out of her mouth, then she couldn't be lying about it.

Ingrid cut herself a slice of bread. "How did Micah do, handling his power of influence without your ward on?"

He dropped his gaze, picking at the sleeve of his fleece. "I honestly expected to lose track of the whole night. I think I kind of hoped to. But as soon as he lowered my heart rate and got me back in my head, he stopped influencing me. He made it seem easy."

She nodded. "Good. He needs to be less afraid of that ability. Properly managing your ability to charm is quite feasible. I could encourage you to laugh, but I could stop you before you passed out."

Grimacing at the bleak example, Andrew tore a corner of the bread and popped it into his mouth. It was sweetened faintly with honey. "I think I'm having an identity crisis," he told her.

"Oddly, I can relate."

The remnants of his grimace turned into a smile.

Ingrid's eyes were lit with a dozen candle flames, turning her scarlet irises soft and rosy. "So I suppose you've been thinking of your mother." She brushed an invisible piece of dust from the silk over her Seeing orb, recalling when he asked about her on a summer night two years ago.

Rolling back his shoulders, pushing a stray lock of hair behind his ear, Andrew explained, "I just...when you walk away from someone, or someone walks away from you, or both...you know how you can't just help but think about them every day, wondering if they're thinking about you?"

Ingrid nodded, returning her gaze to stare at the candles, a faint frown on her slender lips.

"Or she's just dead. But that would...let me rest, too."

"It does," she agreed. "At least, it has worked that way for me." She picked up the teapot, filled two matching teacups, and pushed one of them toward Andrew.

The sting of lemon balm wafted forth, and Andrew picked it up and inhaled deeply. Lemon balm was his favorite. He was pretty sure Ingrid had caught onto that.

"What was her name?" she asked. She delicately lifted the orb down onto the center of the table.

"Liath," he told her softly, staring at the golden contents of his cup.

"Liath?" Ingrid repeated. Her tone drew Andrew's gaze; one slender dark eyebrow was raised over her forehead. "Is she a Druid?" The other brow went up. "You're named Andrew because you're actually Celtic?"

Andrew stared blankly at her for a moment. "Ah, yeah, I guess." He shrugged. "Nan and Pa, the Ryans, were from Leinster. But my dad's from Liverpool, and never let mum go back."

"I love Leinster." Ingrid's sigh was dreamy.

They let the common ground spread between them without speaking for a moment before they both began to laugh.

"What are the odds," laughed Andrew.

"I believe in fate," said Ingrid suddenly. "Don't you?" She didn't wait for an answer, pulling the silk cloth from her Seeing orb and folding it carefully into a square. As her reflection stretched around the crystal and danced with the candlelight, she glanced back up and asked, "Do you happen to have an item that belonged to her? When it's someone I know, I need less to Seek them, but when it's not—"

"Actually—" Andrew twisted the moonstone ring free from his finger. "I suspected I'd need this."

Ingrid reached across and plucked it from his palm. She turned the ring over in her fingers and nodded appreciatively. "Of course you did." She brushed the table clean and laid the glinting ring on the square of silk. Then she adjusted her long legs, sat on her knees, and released a long, measured breath.

Resting his hands on his knees, Andrew remained very still as Ingrid whispered like a trickling creek, her breath clouding the surface of the orb. In the seat of his belly, Ingrid's magic stirred. It made all the small hairs on Andrew's skin stand on end. He knew historically if an object meant to be Seen didn't exist, then the orb would stay dark. So when a cool white light flickered in its core, Andrew's stomach flipped. It could still be bones in a grave, he supposed.

But in the center of the crystal, a modest cabin flickered into view, situated at the foot of a cresting hill heavy with shrubs and conifers. Beyond the hill, a long dark shoreline stretched, with a barge slowly creeping across the water.

Andrew sucked in a breath. "Superior?"

Ingrid let the image go dark, panting slightly, scrunching her nose as she relaxed her shoulders. "Well, she's out there alive. But I didn't recognize where. You did?"

"Yeah. Haven't you been up to Duluth?" Mum had only brought him up there once, when he was sixteen, having organized a deal with a hospital orderly to get a large number of pain pills. She'd set Andrew up at a grubby coffee shop and tried to pretend like he didn't know what she was doing.

At least they'd gone to the lake while they were there. In the northern end of Minnesota, all the small cities were built along the shores of Lake Superior. It was the largest freshwater body of water in the world, deep and frigid year-round. The shores were rocky and littered with driftwood, and enormous barges drifted slowly across the waters carrying mass quantities of iron and limestone ore eastward.

"Is that in the Iron Range?" asked Ingrid.

"Yeah."

"Then no. You won't find Folk living comfortably up there."

Andrew made a quizzical face, and then the words settled in. "Oh," he breathed, realization dawning as he nodded. "I suppose the ground is filled with iron. Doesn't feel good up there, eh?"

"I tried to stay, once." Her gaze went distant and haunted. "Imagine a migraine so bad you feel like you're constantly going to vomit, but vomiting would be a relief, so you don't. But it never goes away, not until you leave."

He cringed. "Understood."

She shook herself in her wolf-like way and blinked at him. "Micah should be fine enough up there, though, being half-human."

Taking back the moonstone ring, Andrew looked down guiltily. "I'm not bringing him with me."

Ingrid gave Andrew a strange look. "Are you ending your relationship with him?"

Slowly shaking his head, Andrew said quietly, "No, not entirely. I just...need some time with myself."

"How do you 'not entirely' end a relationship?" There was a sharp edge of protectiveness in her voice, but she remained still and calm as she lifted her tea cup and sipped from it, her long dark lashes veiling her gaze.

"I want...Micah to be sure that I'm who he wants to be with."

"Has he given you reason to believe you're not?" she

asked quickly.

"N-no, he hasn't given me reason to doubt him."

"So he is sure about the relationship, but you are not." Ingrid set down her cup. "But you're making it seem like his problem. Am I understanding this?"

"Ingrid—"

She unfolded herself from the floor and glared down at him with finality. The smallest flicker of fear tickled his stomach as she fixed him with her scarlet eyes that had haunted his nightmares for years.

"Go on this trip by yourself." Ingrid shrugged one narrow shoulder. "I don't care. But don't pretend your reasons are something they're not. Come along, then. Now you've annoyed me."

Andrew sighed heavily and stood up, not shocked by the dismissal due to the number of times Ingrid had used that very specific sentence on him or Micah in the last two years. As he stuck his arms through the sleeves of his jacket then struggled into his snow pants, Ingrid went to her large pillowed bed on the floor in the corner and rummaged through a wooden trunk at its head.

"But here." She held out a twisting golden neck band. "This is something I brought home from Leinster. I'd like your mother to have it."

"That's so sweet of you." Andrew accepted it in his outstretched hand, strangely reverent.

Ingrid waved a hand dismissively. "It's pragmatic. It

should be with a native, not me."

He smiled. "Decolonizing. I like it."

"You're a British man. You are the worst of all the colonists."

He snorted. "Rude."

"Quite."

"Thanks for doing this for me, Ingrid. I owe you more than a letter opener next time."

"Might I request an antique hand mirror?" She rubbed her chin thoughtfully, looking down at her crystal. "I want to see how easily the scrying practice translates. Oh. And some Oreos."

"Yes, your ladyship," laughed Andrew.

The top floor of Micah's brownstone was an open level with a master bathroom in the northwest corner and a row of windows on the eastern wall. Last year, Micah and Andrew had gotten a leather couch and coffee table to fit into the corner under the windows. They'd put a short bookshelf next to the couch that had slowly filled with a collection of Andrew's books.

There was an outlet beside the shelf where Andrew was currently charging his best laptop. He had tortoiseshell glasses perched on his nose, his hair tossed back in a bun, and a canned energy drink next to him. On the other end of the couch he had several sketches on printer paper of the cabin from Ingrid's glass. He should have taken a picture on his phone, but it was easy to forget about technology when surrounded by the magic in Lilydale. It was just as likely Ingrid would have sliced off one of his fingers if he'd tried.

Micah was at his computer desk, distractedly playing Stardew Valley. His shoulder blades tingled with the wrongness of not helping Andrew pore over a map of the North Shore. But he hadn't been asked, and he wasn't in a position to bother Andrew. He kept catching his knee bouncing, and was close to going to bother Julian instead of sitting in uncomfortable silence.

His heart kept forgetting his relationship was in such flux. With Andrew just on the couch across the room, any time he cleared his throat he drew Micah's eye. And then any time Micah saw his narrow face pinched with concentration, he wanted to go over and kiss him till he caused a distraction. And then any time he had the impulse before remembering that Andrew was leaving by himself soon, it was like someone was crushing his windpipes.

"Andrew," he blurted.

Andrew looked up at once, but it took a moment for his eyes to clear and focus. He raised his brows, and then picked up his can to take a drink.

Micah's resolve faltered. He turned back to his computer

without saying anything.

"What's up?" Andrew pressed.

"Never mind."

Andrew frowned at Micah's back. Under his desk, Micah's leg was bouncing rapidly enough to make the wheels of his chair squeak. "Micah."

"You're busy." Micah didn't turn around, tapping his keyboard.

"Micah. Please, talk to me."

Micah's leg went still. He minimized his game so he was just staring at his desktop. The wallpaper was a picture of the two of them together. After a moment, Micah opened an empty browser tab and stared at that instead. "I was wondering if you could maybe go back to your place."

Andrew searched for something to say. But there wasn't anything—it made sense why Micah was uncomfortable with him here. Opting for silence, he closed his laptop and stacked the sketches of the cabin on top of them.

Micah turned his chair around at the sound of Andrew packing up. He picked at a hangnail. "I just feel confused. And I know you're busy trying to get ready to go. And I don't want to distract you with my nonsense."

"I get it. It's fine." Andrew spoke stiffly.

Micah's expression fell. He stared at his hands. "We're on a break, right?"

Andrew hesitated. They hadn't exactly put it in those terms yet. It felt...final. Stalling, Andrew leaned around the bookshelf to unplug his laptop. But he knocked his energy drink with his elbow; it tipped over and clattered across the wood panels. Fizzy liquid splashed over the floor.

Swearing, Andrew set aside his things and jumped to his feet, crossing the room quickly to Micah's bathroom. He pulled his red towel off the wall and hurried back to his spill. Micah was already on his knees with a handful of paper towels, mopping up the mess in silence.

Andrew knelt beside him and lamely held the towel on his lap. "Sorry."

Micah didn't say anything. He crumpled up the papers. Then he shifted his nightshade gaze to Andrew, expression guarded, raising his eyebrows with an unspoken prompt.

"Oh." Andrew had hoped he'd gotten out of answering. "I guess—I don't like calling it that. A 'break.' That's not—I mean, my point is for you not to be stuck with me. I want you off the hook."

Micah's eyes grew colder and darker, almost ultraviolet.

Andrew was spouting the same bullshit that he had the night before, which meant he hadn't bothered to listen. Micah decided not to repeat himself.

Andrew insisted, "There's so many other people who would die to go on a date with you. Diana, for example."

As the rift between them widened, Micah simply stared at Andrew, unspeaking.

Andrew shifted uneasily. "I think you should see other people when I'm gone." If he had to keep repeating himself, he would. If he could only get Micah to agree...

Flatly, Micah said, "I'm going to ask you again." His voice betrayed the slightest tremble. "Are we on a break?"

Andrew grimaced.

Standing up from the floor, Micah pitched the wet paper towels across the room into an aluminum basket by his desk. It tipped off balance, spinning noisily before falling over and rolling in a circle. The paper towels tumbled back out.

Micah raked both hands through his hair as he paced in a tight line by his windows. Andrew stood slowly, picking up his laptop and papers, still not saying anything. Still not finding the courage to admit to himself and to Micah that he wanted a break. He hugged his things to his chest, searching the recesses of his brain for some other solution, some conviction that he could do all this and keep things as they were, without breaking Micah's heart. But his heart was a cold, barely beating stone behind his sternum, and Micah deserved better.

Micah curled his hands into fists. He stopped pacing and said in a strangled whisper, "For fuck's sake, Andrew. Just say it."

Sighing softly, Andrew looked at his feet. "I want us to take a break while I'm on this trip."

Micah tasted salt on the back of his tongue as he stubbornly swallowed his tears. He glared out the window, eyes burning.

Andrew couldn't look at him. "I don't know how to be a good partner right now. I've been trying to live in the moment while I'm with you, but I'm failing. My mum is haunting my thoughts. I'm exhausted. I-I don't know what will happen when I find my mum, but whatever it is, I swear I'll come back with more of myself to give you."

They were both silent for several uncomfortable minutes. Andrew couldn't so much as move. None of the previous night's emotions rolled off Micah, who was motionless and staring out the window. Absolutely nothing came off him. Somehow, that was much, much worse.

"Um, if you'd like, I can call you when I'm heading out."

Micah shook his head almost imperceptibly. "Whatever you need," he finally said in the voice he used with strangers.

Andrew nodded even though Micah wouldn't see. His throat tight and his eyes stinging, Andrew crossed to Micah's wardrobe and picked up the duffel bag he'd packed with all his warmest clothes. He stood by the door out of Micah's room, hoping—vainly—that Micah would turn back around. But he didn't, so to his back, Andrew promised, "I'll call you."

Several hours later, Julian climbed the stairs to Micah's

room, Cinnamon trailing after him. He knocked on the door to the top landing, and when there was no response, he let himself in.

The room was dim in the twilight, and unusually silent. Julian made his way over to Micah's bed, where a lumpy, dormant shape rose among the pile of blankets. Julian bent and clicked on the lamp on the milk carton table. When the yellow light spilled over Micah's catatonic, nearly buried form, he hardly blinked. He was hugging a squishy pillow shaped like a cartoon bubble tea.

"Micah," said Julian, sitting by his knees and patting his hip. "I brought you a burger. You've been holed up in here all day, so I assume you haven't eaten anything."

"I'm not hungry." Micah's voice was barely a whisper.

Julian frowned. It was a bit unnerving seeing Micah out of sorts, he admitted privately. His son was a bastion of good spirits and relentless optimism. With Micah's mood falling, it was easy to feel like warm days and sunshine would be gone forever.

"Where's Andrew?" Julian asked.

"Getting ready to leave."

Cinnamon jumped up by Micah's face, found a gap in the blankets, and dove under them to nestle against his stomach. Micah appreciated the heat and the vibration against his body, stirring slightly to finally look at his father.

Julian had a crumpled paper fast food bag in one hand, and a large soda cup in the other. His thick black eyebrows raised hopefully when Micah looked at him. With a sigh, Micah pushed himself up to take the bag, digging inside for the wrapped burger. Cinnamon stuck his damp pink nose out from under the sheets, sniffing so aggressively his nostrils whistled.

Julian crossed his leg and asked, "Where's he going? He snuck out of here before I could ask him." It seemed far from a mutual choice that Andrew was leaving alone, thought Julian as he surveyed Micah's drooping shoulders and downturned lips, forlorn as a scolded puppy.

"I guess his mom is alive. She's up on the North Shore," Micah answered. He took a hearty bite of the loaded burger. It immediately made his stomach roll. Struggling to swallow, Micah set it aside on his nightstand despite Julian's accusatory glare.

Julian climbed up to sit against the pillows next to Micah, grunting with the effort of doing so. "Andrew didn't know whether or not his mom was alive?"

"Yeah. They haven't been in contact since he graduated high school. She got into Fae-spelled foods from Lilydale, and he ditched her."

Julian grimaced. "I'm glad you didn't ditch me."

Micah smiled faintly, leaning on Julian's shoulder.

"How come you aren't going up with him? Isn't that exactly the kind of adventure that you two like?" Julian pulled Micah's laptop onto the bed and clicked into the profile he'd made for himself on it.

As Micah watched Julian queue up their favorite K-drama, he said in a voice that quavered, "I think he's ditching me."

Chapter Four
The Departure

Early the following morning, Andrew's old beige Saturn chugged along the heights of Highway 61. The radio stopped picking up any stations, and the silence was setting Andrew's teeth on edge. Out the passenger window, Lake Superior was a smear of darkness dotted here and there with patches of ice. The sun flashed off them occasionally, turning them into blinding shards of glass.

When he'd gotten back to Magic's, locating the cabin where his mum was had taken another six hours on his desktop, zoomed in on the maps. Dozens of times, he started to assume that even if the cabin was there, he'd never find it. Or maybe it *was* there, and it was spelled to be invisible on the map. It would complicate his search, but even if he didn't find it before he left, he was going out there and looking for it anyway. Fortunately, he was rewarded for his obsessive determination. He'd found the little cabin on the map, the photo taken during a heavy snow and barely visible. It was significantly north of Duluth, so far he would practically be in Canada, somewhere west of a town called Tofte. He downloaded the region's map on his phone and extensively marked up with stops including a snowmobile rental, several vacancy motels along the highway, ranger stops along Superior Hiking Trail in case he got lost, and numbers for emergency rescue services. He had flares, an emergency radio, several changes of clothes, protein-dense foods, and a 24-pack of water bottles. His trunk was packed with a box full of instant heat packets, a package of new wool socks, hunter's gear including heavy denim overalls (to his dismay—not his favorite kind of aesthetic for men), an orange winter jumpsuit, face masks, and all his weapons including a new set of hunting knives. He knew *how* to survive outside, he just preferred being indoors.

Andrew had also repaired the wire to hold Micah's blood on a pendant, and it served as a comfort around his neck. He'd said he didn't need it anymore, but this was different. Now, it was more like a lover's token. A lover Andrew had spurned, but still.

"Yeah, you blew it there," he muttered to himself. "Best thing that ever happened to you. You self-sabotaging sono-fabitch." He glared out at the lake. Why couldn't Micah have just come with him? What godforsaken trauma re-sponse was Andrew stuck inside that he had rejected the most caring and compassionate man he'd ever met? And Micah *loved* him. Supposedly.

That was the whole problem. People never...chose him

first. Micah kept saying he did, but even Andrew's own mother and father hadn't. Not really, not for long anyway. Andrew's father turned on him when he discovered Andrew to be gay, and his mother repeatedly chose drugs over Andrew's wellbeing when he was a teenager. After that, Andrew didn't give anyone else the opportunity to reject him. Until Micah.

And now...Micah's lips on someone else, right in front of him. Andrew blinked, trying to shake off the image, trying to remind himself that Micah hadn't welcomed that kiss. But maybe he'd still liked it. It was easy within the dark stormcloud of Andrew's mind to imagine Micah kissing a carefree woman and wondering if Andrew was worth the trouble.

Cinder blocks seemed to drop onto Andrew's chest, his head spinning like a balloon slipping out of a child's fingers and into the sky. Andrew groaned, thumping against the headrest, harder and harder while it clattered around in his head that *He left Micah* and *that was probably it*. Who would wait around after being told to walk away?

"Fuck," Andrew growled, gritting his teeth.

Stepping on the acceleration, he flexed his fingers and then picked his hands up off the wheel. The Saturn drifted to the right and lurched toward the guard rail between him and the water. Andrew's chest seized and adrenaline blazed down his spine. His body instinctively clenched and his palms slapped down again on the wheel. Back in control, he tapped his brakes, fixed the wheel, and burst into tears. Alone, he didn't bother to stifle himself. His eyes and nostrils streamed, relentless and yet detached from his thoughts as his throat burned with his despairing screams.

He imagined the Saturn smashed to plastic pieces on the basalt below. Imagining him crumpled in the cockpit of the car, bloody, and finally dead. It was what he deserved, honestly, for leaving Micah like he had, at home in the dark with a vague promise of making sure he texted when he could.

The ride into the wilderness made Andrew feel like he never knew anything else besides biting cold, bleached white, powder-blue, and a roaring wind tunnel. The snowmobile he'd rented was deafeningly loud, and it took all his attention to drive one for the first time. The rental shop had let him pay to leave his Saturn in their parking lot, happy enough that he'd paid them extra to rent the snowmobile for a week.

Propped in the clip over the speedometer was his phone, an arrow moving with vague accuracy along the downloaded map of the space west of Temperance River and north of Heartbreak Creek. Very maudlin names, thought Andrew, like the white people had named them after they survived their first long winter.

Snow crackled under the ski blades as Andrew mounted a mild incline. The dead forest parted slightly, the trees thinning. Superior rose defiantly over the horizon to the east, such a dark blue as to look almost black, vast as a sea.

A copse of pine rose between him and the water, wistfulness tugging at Andrew's chest when the lake was obscured. He'd have to make sure he went down to the shore before he went home, even if it was wickedly cold. As he gazed off to his right at the trees, his shoulder blades began to tingle—not with the cold, for he'd already gone numb. He scanned the trees more closely, slowing the snowmobile to a quieter crawl.

The boughs of a hemlock stirred, nudged aside by something nearly as formless as a cloud.

Curious and a little bit unnerved, he killed the engine and let the muffled silence envelope him. Flipping up the visor on his helmet, Andrew pulled up his knee and reversed in his seat, hands on his thighs, gazing silently, patient.

Every time his breath puffed out, he was convinced it was more movement in the trees, but it was just the space he was taking up himself. Maybe he'd imagined it in the first place. But he was in no hurry, and if there was something watching him, then he was going to wait until it showed itself.

"It's all right," he called gently, his voice carrying on the slipstream of the frozen air.

Fox? Coyote? Maybe a frightened deer? He wasn't sure how much more the wildlife diversified this far north. He'd probably be able to spot a moose—

A flash of golden eyes.

Andrew sucked in his breath and held it. He didn't blink, didn't sniffle, even though his nose ran.

Under the deep green boughs of the hemlock—no, the color did *not* remind him of Micah, of course not—the keen golden coins of the creature's eyes bobbed lower, showing Andrew a quivering black nose and the edge of a pointed ear with tawny fur. The sound of the animal's large paw sinking into the top layer of the snow drifted across the still air like a snowflake.

Golden coins blinked, slowly, deliberately, and then the animal vanished into the gray wash of shadows under the trees.

Finally breathing—gasping, honestly—Andrew touched his fingers to his forehead as he swallowed a giggle of delight. The flash of its thick tail as it vanished all but confirmed that Andrew had just met the eyes of a wolf.

He faced the hemlock for a few more minutes, memoriz-ing the shape of the branches and the deep saturated tones of gemstone green and umber. With a satisfied shake of his head, he turned around on the snowmobile and flipped the visor on his helmet back down, gripping the handlebars and giving them the complicated twist and flick to start the engine. When he turned his eyes back toward the path forward, the snowy hillscape was altered and the bones of a building reared out of the burial mound of winter.

It was the cabin. It sat atop the crest of the hill where there had been nothing moments before. Two stories high with a stone chimney, it was made of whitewashed lumber, the shingles on the roof faded and loose. Smoke drifted above it, making Andrew yearn for the warmth from the inevitable fire crackling in the fireplace inside. The sketch of a snowy staircase led up to it from where Andrew's snowmobile had stopped. A cairn of hand-placed rocks stood some feet tall beyond a wraparound porch bearing dried reeds and bound antlers. Except for the one closest to the front door, the windows on the first floor were closed behind red shutters.

Speaking over his shoulder in the direction of the presumably nearby wolf, he said, "I mean, I really shouldn't be surprised Mum's cabin appeared out of thin air. Is this your doing?"

If this was how his trip started—locking eyes with a wolf, who made his mother's cabin appear—then maybe this was what he needed after all. He dismounted the snowmobile, patting the breast pocket of his snow suit to feel for the torque Ingrid had given him.

The cabin door swung outward on silent hinges. A woman held the door open with her knee, emerging into the tundra with a rifle aimed at Andrew's head.

Though his heart did an uneasy little somersault, he obligingly put his hands up.

"This is private property," called the woman, with a rolling Irish brogue, faded around the edges like a thirty year old newspaper. She had auburn hair streaked white and chopped above her shoulders, wearing an oversized flannel jacket, a thick knitted scarf, worn denim, and heavy winter boots. Her face had changed very little: still as narrow as Andrew's, slender and down turned lips, with heavy dark circles under her brown eyes. Immediately, instinctively, Andrew wanted to throw himself into her arms and cry while she stroked his hair and told him it would all be okay. Damn the pain, damn the heartache, damn the wounds they cut into each other's hearts. Mum was still mum. Rifle pointed at his head or not.

When he remained motionless, she said loudly, "You've gotten lost and you should go back the way you came."

Tingling, Andrew slowly lifted off the heavy helmet, and then pulled off his mask. He brushed back his loose hair from his face, crooked the helmet under his arm, and called up, "Can we talk first, Mum?"

CHAPTER FIVE
THE TEA SHOP

STARING AT THE TAILLIGHTS of the Saturn as they left the parking lot of Magic's, Micah shook his head with faint disbelief. "You bastard," he whispered bitterly.

Sam looked uncomfortably up at Micah. "Uh...you wanna come up to the apartment? I can make coffee. We can bitch about Andrew."

Micah grimaced.

As he hooked his elbow through Micah's, Sam added, "Affectionately."

Upstairs, Arwen chirped at them when they came in, standing delicately on the counter and purring when she saw Micah.

"Hi, little queen." Micah scratched her under the chin.

Sam went around into the kitchen and started brewing a strong pot of coffee while Micah sat on the couch and beckoned Arwen. The cat thumped prettily down off the counter and trotted, chirping, up to Micah, immediately turning circles on his knees. It was easier for him to understand a cat's sentiment than to explain how the communication really worked. A smell, maybe. Like the inside of a cat's mouth when it yawned—a bit fishy. Clear words didn't happen as often, at least not with Arwen. When they did, they sort of just appeared in his head, like a jingle you haven't heard in a month. At the moment, Arwen was evidently confused as to why Micah was here but Andrew wasn't.

"He's going on a trip," Micah told her. Arwen looked up and met Micah's eyes, blinking slowly, her tail quivering as she turned her head toward Sam and sat delicately on her haunches. "Well, that's good," he murmured.

When he looked up, Sam was staring at him.

Cheeks flaming, Micah said, "Arwen is pretty chill with Andrew being gone as long as you're here."

"Aw. My baby." Sam slithered around the counter and into the living room before flopping gracelessly onto the couch like a teenage boy. Reaching out, he gave Arwen a scratch between her ears. As he picked up the remote and thumbed through some channels, he glanced at Micah and asked more carefully, "So, you seem like this might be, uh...some kind of break for you guys."

Micah brushed the pad of his finger over Arwen's quivering black whiskers. "Apparently."

"All because some girl at work kissed you?" Sam asked. His bushy brows went up and disappeared under his brownish-purple bangs.

Arwen head-butted Micah's fingers before curling up on his lap and closing her eyes with a satisfied purr.

"Is this the beginning of the end or something?" Micah asked, grimacing so that his chin wouldn't tremble. "Is he just delaying the inevitable?"

Sam dropped his cheek onto his fist. "That I can't tell you. He kept to himself last night. But if I've learned one thing about Andrew in seven years, it's that he gives you the information he knows for sure. So if he says he wants a break for this trip, then that's all he knows."

"So you mean he's gonna go and...contemplate us?" Micah touched the space behind Arwen's ear where her dark fur was the silkiest. He grinned acerbically. "Oof, I'm screwed then. He's gonna be the one thinking he's better off without me."

Sam gave Micah an odd look. "You know, for a faerie prince, you have pretty low self-esteem."

Micah slumped lower on the cushions, burying his face in Arwen's furry chest. She started grooming his hair. "I'm only half-faerie."

"That's like saying 'I'm not rich, my parents are.'" Sam stood up when the coffee maker started gurgling and filled two mugs, dishing Micah a spoonful of sugar and himself a healthy dollop of cinnamon roll coffee creamer.

Micah scratched his neck. "Huh. I guess I hear it." He glanced at the younger boy and then asked, "Are you comfortable telling me any more about what happened with

Andrew's box of stuff? He—he told me yesterday he, um... struggled after that."

Sam's stirring paused. "I guess I don't know exactly. He wouldn't tell me either. It looked like a box of high school stuff. He had a tassel from a graduation cap in there but it was red and white, not maroon and gold, so it wasn't from college. That moonstone ring he still had on his dresser."

"That was his mom's I guess."

Sam nodded, thinking. "And like, a scarf and stuff. But I only saw in the box because I came in while he was crying. Like, deep, tragic sobs from the pit of your stomach. But you know how he is. Likes to pretend like he doesn't cry."

"Biggest hypocrite ever," muttered Micah.

"Oh, I know." Sam laughed. "Anyway, I don't know. He just mumbled stuff about trauma and then put the box back in the second bedroom closet." Sam came around the kitchen counter and held out the coffee with just the sugar. Micah took the coffee with a grunted thanks. Then he blinked, lifting up the mug. Its smooth green ceramic was stamped with the words PLANT DADDY. He turned the message toward Sam with an eyebrow raised.

With a snort, Sam explained, "I got that for Andrew after he brought home that plant you gave him. I know now that you're the plant daddy, not him."

"Ah." Micah shrugged. "I am, aren't I?"

They sipped quietly for a few minutes while Arwen kneaded the blanket folded next to Micah.

"The thing is—" Sam gazed thoughtfully into his coffee. "—Neither of us can do anything if that's what Andrew decides when he comes back. But what I can do is make sure he doesn't ghost you. One time someone ghosted me when they said we were taking a break, and it fucked me up. So I'll do everything in my power to make sure he doesn't do you like that. Okay?"

Micah nudged Sam's arm. "You're a real slick kinda guy, Sam."

"I'm also the kinda guy who will keep you company when you're sad over a boy," Sam assured him brightly. He clinked his mug against Micah's. "Say the word, and I'm there."

Several hours later, Micah shuffled into his kitchen to get a bottle of water and a granola bar. He still wore Andrew's cardigan over his black work tee and joggers, tucking the long sleeves over his hands as he bent over the fridge.

From behind him, Julian said matter-of-factly, "You're sulking."

He turned to where Julian and Sam sat across from

each other at the kitchen table, working with thin, raw phyllo dough and big pats of butter for baklava. Cinnamon twined between Julian's ankles under the table, hoping to lick some butter. On the far end of the table was the yellow-leaved bromeliad, rescued from Andrew's and beginning rehabilitation with Micah and Julian.

"I'm a grown man," Micah argued. "I don't 'sulk.'"

"I think it's cute," said Sam.

"I think it's codependent." Julian sniffed.

Affronted, Micah gasped. "Dad! I am not."

"It's not codependent to miss your boyfriend," laughed Sam.

"It was me for a long time." Julian knowingly glanced at Sam. "Then it was Chami while they dated. Then when she ended things with him, it was me again." He peered at Micah over the rim of his glasses. "You have to have that one person you put all your energy into and try to rescue."

Micah narrowed his eyes. Frustration billowed like a noxious cloud in his stomach. One shameful little piece of Micah's heart agreed with him, but the other protested especially loudly hearing this come from Julian. "Sharp observation there, Dad. Bit unnecessary, if you ask me. Don't you have a role in all this?"

Sam shifted uncomfortably, focusing on the phyllo.

Julian hesitated, noticing Sam's discomfort. His shoulders slumped. He cared about Sam like his own child, and the pink in Sam's cheeks made him afraid to say more.

"Hm?" Micah pressed, arms crossed. A chilled finger of dread trailed down his spine the moment he realized that, if he really wanted to, he could probably *make* his father tell him what he wanted to know. Slow his heartbeat a bit, increase his euphoria, make him malleable. Make him *want* to spill his heart out. God knows Julian didn't do that enough. It would be for his own good.

"I suppose that's the problem," said Julian eventually, rousing Micah from his strange and dangerous musings. "Everybody you try to rescue just lets you do it. Must be your Fae charm."

Sam stifled a little gasp of disbelief. "Jules, jeeze."

Micah froze, more shocked than anything to hear Julian be the one to point out Micah's nature. Micah had nothing to be offended by—he'd been thinking about the same thing a mere heartbeat ago.

Grinding his teeth, Micah studied his father's weary expression for a long moment and allowed it to remind him that Julian was the biggest victim of Fae charm out of anyone. He spoke from a place of bitterness, of a life stolen away from him. He always did. And this was always why Julian could get away with saying anything to Micah, no matter how rude. He didn't even know half of what happened to him in the Redwoods, presumably, or even that the Redwood Queen had stolen him back two years prior, just to lure Micah home. This was why Micah had wished for a life free of Fae abilities, a simple human life at a bubble tea shop. He thought that would be what would save Julian. He'd always thought Julian agreed. To be honest, they'd never really talked about it. They'd just talked *around* it.

Relenting, an apologetic crease appeared on Julian's brow.

Micah let out a sigh through his nose. "I mean, you're probably right. It always seems to come back to my Fae side, huh?"

Julian looked away, nodding slightly. "Sorry."

"Did you know—" began Micah suddenly, despite Sam's presence. Or maybe because of it. And Sam would be there after Micah left, forcing Julian to remain regulated. Finally, Micah wasn't alone to tend to his father's fragile psyche. Finally, he could admit how much it damaged him. "—That was my mother's whole goal for me?"

Julian flinched. The Redwood Queen. His lover, tormenter, captor. "I don't want to—"

"I didn't want to, either," interrupted Micah. "I didn't want to be her docile little dormouse, but if I mouthed off, she'd have you beaten till your ears bled. Found that out when I was eleven. After that, it was all 'Yes, mother' and 'As you wish, mother.' If I flexed any sort of agency or—god forbid—Fae power, then you'd pay for it. It worked quite well, so sorry if it bothers you that I've kept doing that." Despite how Julian shrank in his seat, despite how Sam hid his face under the veil of his bangs, Micah added brightly, "I'd be happy to quit, if you'd like."

The present moment in his kitchen fell apart into a dark crevice of Micah's past he'd buried beneath the mundane life he had in Saint Paul. A necklace of daisies on Micah's fleshy, prepubescent chest smelled sweet as the petals crushed into his skin when he threw himself against his little stump throne on the dais outside the massive redwood tree palace. He was bawling because a sinewy and stone-eyed faerie had watched him grow a daisy between his fingers and then plucked it out and crushed it, sneering at him, calling him runt. But when he sought comfort from the Redwood Queen, she'd brought Julian out of his gilded cage instead and held him by the throat until Micah stopped crying.

As if in that moment again, Micah's emotions slid away from him and into that little cavern in his chest where the anger and the hurt burrowed out of sight. In his kitchen where he stood before Sam and Julian, he blinked several times, looking down where Cinnamon rubbed against his pants with a throaty purr. Micah bent and picked up the large, fluffy feline to cradle him in his arms, rubbing his face in the cat's belly. The faint smell of cat litter and fish and the concerned swell of feeling wafting out of the cat's scent glands, working to ground Micah as it usually did. Fadil might have been a rascally best friend, but Cinnamon was the ultimate nurturer.

"I'm sorry." Micah spoke mostly to Cinnamon. "I'm not going to quit caring about you, Dad. Andrew just told me yesterday he thinks I'm not dealing with being Fae—"

"All due respect to one of my favorite people," blurted Julian, "but what the fuck does he know? He wasn't there in the Redwoods with us."

Sam and Micah exchanged a quick glance. Julian was, of course, talking about twenty-two years ago, but...Andrew *had* been in the Redwoods.

"I know. But he's not entirely wrong." Micah took a deep breath. "Sorry, boys. Not a good morning for me. I'll do better, I promise."

"You're allowed to feel shitty," Sam insisted, coming out of his uncomfortable attempt to be invisible.

Micah snorted. "Not in this house, kid." He went around the table and hugged Sam and then ruffled his hair.

"Aw, come on!" Sam swatted at him like a petulant teenager.

"I'm almost twenty years your senior, in case you forgot." Micah allowed his voice to be a bit deeper, not its usual placating tenor.

"I do forget, frequently. You and I look the same age now." Sam crossed his arms.

"Yes," drawled Julian, "isn't his youth infuriating?"

Giving them both a sardonic grin, Micah left them with a flap of his hand. He struggled into his Docs and bundled up in a sweatshirt and his canvas jacket, pulling on a beanie several times before he got it to sit right over his staticky, slippery green hair. He tried to visualize leaving the film of unease and frustration and isolation behind him as he stepped out of the brownstone, but it was ultimately a lost cause and he knew it.

During the winter, Micah took a ten-minute bus ride down West Seventh and around the corner down Randolph to get to the tea shop. He enjoyed watching the kind of subtle interactions strangers made within the cold confines of the bus. But today he noticed that a person with pink hair kept stealing glances at him over their book, and a man with dreads batted his eyes at him.

This was exactly what Andrew said happened.

Self-conscious, Micah sank against the prickly bus seat and kept his eyes on his phone for the remainder of his ride.

When he hopped off the city bus and stepped into To a Tea, the reality of his work life was assaultive. He jumped in with bulky teenage Colton to prepare tea for the day in the back room, wishing immediately for the winter cold as they sweated over pots of boiling water and brewed gallons of tea. His favorite part about Colton, at the moment, was that the boy basically never spoke. That, and how when Colton was making the tea, he used a pink headband to keep his blond bangs from sticking to his pockmarked face. Micah thought that was endearing.

Diana came in a few minutes later. She was in a black space-dyed sweatshirt and ripped black jeans, and her hair was messily shoved under a beanie. She stumbled when she saw Micah, as if not expecting to see him. Working. At the shop he ran.

Neutrally, he instructed, "Hey. Prep the tapioca pearls, please." He hoped if he treated her like an ordinary employee, she would stop looking so ready to cry. He could have asked about her expression—before this week, he probably would have. But he resented the role she played, even if just as a trigger, in how far away Andrew currently was.

As Micah was squatting to pour a gallon of black tea through a filter to strain, he heard her hit the bag of dehydrated pearls too hard. Diana squeaked, swore, and then spluttered a stream of apologies.

"Party foul," Colton intoned, stirring tea with a paddle.

Micah glanced over his shoulder to confirm she had cracked all the pearls in the bag into shards of dust. He dropped his head between his shoulders and let a sigh out through his nostrils. When he finished pouring the tea, he looked at Diana again. Her cheeks were red and blotchy, and she wiped her nose on her shoulder as she much more carefully cut open and jostled another bag.

Once the shop was open, Micah spent a bit more time behind the bar helping the pair of them with the first dozen customers. It was his most efficient way of checking how the baristas performed without making them anxious.

Except for Diana. She was still trembling and avoiding eye contact with him. Anna, the third barista for the day shift, arrived half an hour after opening. Micah took off his apron to get out of her way. When he passed behind

Diana, she fumbled with a shaker of tea and spilled it on the counter.

Gritting his teeth, Micah paused, swallowed, and then told her quietly, "Take it easy. I'm not going to kill you."

Beside her, Anna's mascara-rimmed eyes darted between them. He could see her calculating what the subtext between them meant.

Diana bent her head and sopped up the tea with a rag, nodding once. Then she turned quickly and faced him, searching his expression, although he was sure whatever she saw would not comfort her at the moment.

She asked in a squeaky whisper, "But are y-you and your boyfriend okay?"

Irritation slashed through Micah's veiled attempt to remain calm. He raised an eyebrow and bit back quietly, "Would you like it if we weren't?"

Diana flinched. Muttering something, she resumed working, picking up a cup for the next tea order and fumbling it, sending it bouncing away across the counter. A customer laughed awkwardly and handed it back to her.

Anna shot Micah a pleading look as she stirred a green slushie with a long spoon.

"Diana," called Micah, leaning on the counter, arms folded, nails digging into his palms. "You seem distracted. Do you need to go home?"

Colton snorted, and Micah glared at him.

Diana was red enough to burst. "Nah, I'll do better. I

promise. Sorry everyone."

"Cool," said Micah as Diana glanced uncomfortably at him. He gestured to her outfit with a finger. "But next time...Anna, Colton, what's our dress code?"

They both recited, "No ripped denim in the shop."

Micah smiled sweetly, strode past the counter, and took the corner toward his office so sharply he almost hit the wall. He closed the door to his office and slumped into the desk chair. Tangles of his hair in his fingers, Micah doubled over with his elbows on his knees and squeezed his eyes shut. He groaned, quietly at first, but the anger and frustration lit as if on dry kindling till he was practically yelling through clenched teeth.

Something rustled. Grounded immediately by the unexpected noise, Micah's head shot up. He blinked in the dim light of his plant lamp, which hung over his row of potted plants. Micah stood up and peered inside the pot nearest him. The aglaonema in it had been happy and deep green when he'd been in his office to drop off his jacket not even an hour ago. Now, its leaves were yellow and drooping, curling brown on the ends. Micah stared at the plant in silence, his heart hammering.

One of the leaves broke off with a soft *snik*, drifting down onto the soil.

"Aw, shit," Micah groaned.

Micah left To a Tea with the afternoon closers set up, pushing through the shop door with his phone in hand and staring at his conversation with Andrew.

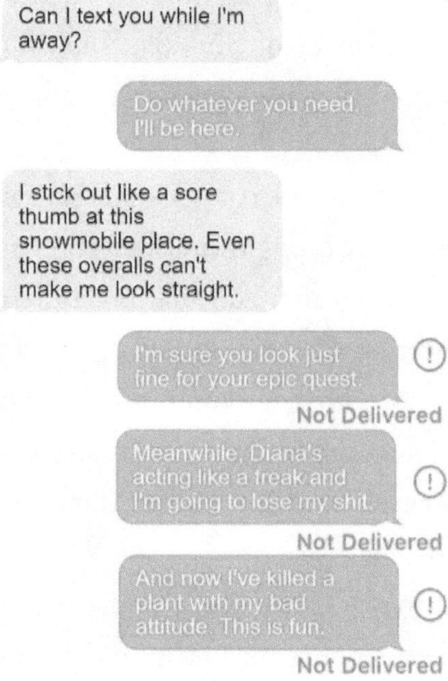

When those texts to Andrew finally went through, it was going to look so ridiculous and—and codependent. Maybe Julian was right. It hadn't even been twelve hours since Andrew drove away, and Micah was going crazy from the silence. But if Andrew wasn't getting any service now, it didn't seem likely he would have it at all while he was on his trip. Maybe Andrew had designed it that way.

The shop door jingled behind him and, against his better judgment, Micah looked over his shoulder.

Diana shuffled hurriedly up to him, hands in her pockets, cheeks deeply reddened. "Micah, please. Please. Give me a minute. I want to talk. Let me smooth things over."

Micah snorted, glaring at the salt on the sidewalk. "*I* want to never see you again, but alas. I'm your boss. Unless you'd like to quit." He gave her a nasty smile, excited by the prospect.

A truck door opened next to Diana, and someone spilled onto the sidewalk, running into Diana and coming straight at him with a raised fist. Adrenaline shutting off all but animal instinct, Micah twisted out of the way. When the short man threw another punch at him, Micah growled and caught him by the forearm, whipping him around and pinning his arm behind his back. Diana gasped, and the man howled in surprise.

"You trying to assault me?" demanded Micah, pulling the man's shoulders against his chest, and gripping the nape of his neck, dimpling his skin. Micah considered with a thrill of excitement what he could do to this person. Charm him into striking himself or make his heart stop beating. As if privy to Micah's thoughts—as if realizing Micah was precisely the *wrong* person to fuck with—the man's pupils contracted with terror, and he smelled like sharp sweat and spoiled meat.

Jaw dropping, Diana looked at Micah for a stunned moment before she turned her eyes on the stranger and exclaimed, "Tom! What are you thinking? That's my boss!"

The bespectacled man struggled in Micah's grip, which shook him loose from his instincts. Micah immediately let him go, dizzy, chest heaving.

"Let me guess," he intoned, glaring at Diana. "This is your dumbass boyfriend?"

The man spun to face him, yellow teeth bared. "Who you calling dumbass? Fag!"

Micah's brows shot up. "Fag? That's a first for me."

Sneering and giving Micah a once-over with pale blue eyes, he remarked, "That's surprising."

It wasn't that he was offended—this man's opinion was dirt under his fingernails—but Micah wanted to punish him for the comment, to make him afraid again. He liked the smell of his fear, and that drove him several steps forward like he was a darkening storm cloud. It worked. Diana's small boyfriend cowered back like a chihuahua realizing it had picked a fight with a lynx.

Diana socked the man in the shoulder hard enough that he staggered, wincing and elbowing her. Even she could overpower him. That meant it wasn't worth it. Conquering a feeble man was no victory.

Micah closed his eyes and sighed, the fire in his belly extinguish, sensation returning to his skin. Or else, proper sensation. When he craved Tom's fear, he felt *everything*.

Hunger. Fury. The cold winter air like glass grinding into his pores. If that was how it always meant to be Fae, maybe he should allow that anger out of the cavern in his chest more often.

Micah sniffed and said so calmly it was like the tempest of his fury had never existed, "So. Tom, is it? Here's the thing. All my baristas are watching right there." He waved at them through To a Tea's wide windows. Colton waved awkwardly back. "So they all saw you try to assault me. If we see you near my shop again, we're going to call the police. Does that make sense?"

Indignant, Tom snarled, "Stay away from my girlfriend, and I won't have to kick your ass."

Micah fixed Diana with a withering glare. "I'm trying to." He turned on his heel and briskly left them outside the shop, listening anxiously for the sound of pursuit. But he only heard Diana chewing out her barbarian boyfriend while he grunted his justification and called Micah a fag again.

When he was far enough away, he wiped his eyes on his sleeve and bit his cheek till he tasted copper. That part of his cheek was swollen and hard under his teeth. He probably needed a better coping strategy.

He pulled out his phone to send Andrew another angry text, but he heard Sam's voice insisting that morning that Andrew had only needed space, not an ending. And the last thing Micah wanted to do was cause an ending because he couldn't control his temper.

It was very clear to him with Tom that he was teetering on the edge of some abysmal fury. A small part of him—likely the responsible son in him which had dutifully looked after Julian for twenty years—told him that being this angry was *bad.* But the part of him lingering in the parking lot watching Andrew drive away, heart breaking into pieces repeatedly...*that* Micah found his fury *thrilling*.

He tried to take a calming breath as he pocketed his phone again.

In through his nose.

Mulberries. He smelled mulberries.

He blinked, scanning his surroundings. He was near a bustling antique shop storefront. It had a small, fancy alleyway near him with a picket fence and bulb lights crossing overhead. The lights glinted on a pair of crimson eyes.

Micah yelped and slipped on an ice patch. Emerging gracefully from the alley, Ingrid fell into step with him and grabbed his pocket to steady him.

"Ingrid! *What* are you doing here?"

Silent, Ingrid glared over her shoulder as she dragged Micah onward down the street.

"Hello! Ingrid! What the hell are you doing here?" Micah stumbled along with her.

"You should have broken his elbow." Ingrid's eyes were narrowed slits.

It took him a moment to realize she was talking about

Diana's boyfriend. "Oh, yeah. That would have been nice."

She glanced at him, then away, and then her gaze snapped back as if processing what he said. Her eyebrows shot up. "You—wanted to break his elbow?"

"Yeah, anyway." Micah planted his feet, trying to stop. "How long have you been spying on me?"

Unbothered by his resistance, Ingrid skated him along over the slick sidewalk like he was a petulant toddler who didn't want to leave a toy store. Honestly, it wasn't the first time that Ingrid had made him feel like that.

"I've been watching you for most of the day," she said plainly.

"Oh my god. What?" Micah's incredulity—and that wild anger—slowly melted away. He managed to get his footing. "Adorable, or creepy? Hard to say."

"I've watched you a great deal since we came to Minnesota."

"What?" Micah squawked.

She shrugged. "You refused to see me, but I never said I wouldn't see you."

Micah linked his arm through hers, nudging their shoulders together. It gave him a bit of a shock—she was Andrew's height. He brushed off the reminder. "Familial love at its finest," he observed with a laugh. "Well, since you're going to tail me anyway, I'd very much like a drink."

"Okay. Come back with me."

Tugging her closer to him, he rubbed his chin thoughtfully. "No...you're going to come with me for a change."

Ingrid grimaced, but didn't argue. She must have been worried about him. It was usually harder to get her to agree to step into a human establishment. She'd needed the blueprints to his brownstone before she agreed to come in. When they started meeting at Amore Coffee, she had spent a month casing it before stepping inside. Now she didn't even know what he was planning, but agreed anyway.

It was rare that Micah saw his sister against such an urban backdrop. Over the last two years, it had almost always been in Lilydale or at the least in Cherokee Park, which was wooded and quiet but easier to navigate than the bluffs. The city streets, meanwhile, made her look feral. Her movements were at once too graceful and too predatory for a human. And her eyes were impossibly bright.

Andrew and Micah had figured out over the last two years that, in public, Micah unconsciously toned his irises down to dim gray. It attracted a bit less attention that way, allowing Micah to relax more when he was out places with Andrew. But Ingrid couldn't be bothered, and it made her look albino, particularly with her alabaster skin.

They left To a Tea behind, making their way northeast back towards West Seventh. The walk home wasn't quite two miles, and the day had warmed up a bit as puffy white clouds settled over them.

"Oh." Micah dropped his gaze, embarrassed knowing he had to tell his sister. "So I was really mad in my office earlier, and I, uh…I think I killed a plant with my feelings."

Ingrid raised an eyebrow. "All right. What does that mean?"

"I don't know." He glared at his Docs. "That I'm a disaster?"

"While true," observed Ingrid, "try harder."

"Strong emotions have driven most of my power eruptions so far. So this negative emotion projected onto a plant."

"Anything more specific?"

"I mean, I wanted to die a little bit."

Ingrid's steps faltered. "Micah—"

Her evident concern made him smile slightly. He patted her hand. "I'm not going to do anything to myself." But he probably wouldn't prevent it. "It was just a passing thought. This stuff happens. There's a lot of stress. And Andrew *may* have been my only positive coping skill."

"That's very alarming, Micah." Her expression pinched like she'd bitten into a berry that was much too tart.

Micah waved his hand dismissively. "It's fine. I'm fine."

"Ah," lamented Ingrid, "to be capable of lying."

He sighed and glared at the heavens before for once turning his attention to considering how his power actually functioned. "But that connection—thinking of death caused dying—would make sense. At least categorically. And if anything, if motivates me to make sure I'm not feeding the suicidal thoughts or negative emotions. I can have them, but giving in to them is different."

Relaxing, Ingrid nodded. "Good. What else might it suggest?"

"That me and plants get along."

Twining a curl around her finger, she frowned. "Crudely put."

"I'm nothing if not crude."

Ingrid rolled her eyes.

"Did I ever tell you I grew a daisy one time in the Redwoods?" Micah asked. "Like, on command, I mean."

She grimaced, silent. Like she didn't want to say anything, since she would have needed to admit she already knew.

"Ah, did you hear about it? Fun. Remember when I said a couple years ago I was forced to believe I couldn't be powerful?"

"Yes." Her voice was a wispy scrap of sound, barely audible.

"Who doesn't love having their growth stunted by their abusive mom?"

"You could try talking about this without the sarcasm." Ingrid still sounded soft and gentle, which made Micah feel considerably worse.

"You used to not be able to catch it." Bitterly, Micah laughed.

"It's Andrew's fault," said Ingrid. "He is always sarcastic." She glanced down at him with an apology creasing her slender lips. "Similarly, regarding the person who tried to hit you...with Andrew away, you need to take better care of yourself."

"Okay," began Micah, defensive, "I'm not walking around every day with people trying to punch me. Also, Andrew is—was—is...I don't know...was my boyfriend, not my bodyguard."

"He can be both." She shrugged. "What did that small, ugly man think you've done?"

He looked back over his shoulder toward To a Tea, half expecting to see Diana on the sidewalk trailing after them like a heartbroken puppy.

"Hello." Ingrid snapped her fingers in front of his face.

Micah swatted her hand away. "During the blizzard, I stayed at work with that woman. Diana. And she kissed me."

Ingrid's eyes widened and she released a long, "Ahhh."

Micah glared at her. "What does that mean?"

Ingrid fell silent as an older couple approached them, arm in arm, smiling cheerily at them. She observed them with a predatory glint in her eye, assessing their threat, assessing their utility. When Micah smiled and half-waved at them, and they passed behind them, Ingrid shuffled her collar and fixed her headband, sliding back into her interpersonal role. Not huntress. Just sister.

She'd always switched around like that. Maybe that meant he could, too.

"Andrew indicated something like this occurred."

"Lovely." Micah kicked a chunk of ice and watched it spin away down the street. "So, do you agree that it seems weird that his reaction was to bounce away to the North Shore?"

"No."

Micah sighed in exasperation.

"You must not understand what it feels like for him with how he left things with his mother."

"What are you talking about? I left my mother, too!"

"You did. But you still have Julian. The two of you have fused into a complete family unit."

"But—"

"And you had twenty years with the Queen. I had a dozen times more than that. I had...too much time and disappointments and wounds with her. It's how Andrew spoke about his mother, too."

Begrudgingly, Micah mumbled, "I guess I could see the difference."

Ingrid fixed her headband again, tilting her chin to cast a contemplative glance to the heavens. "It creates a void. Everything else can be right, but the void remains until something—either reconciliation, or closure—fills it. And no other bond fits the space."

"But why now? Just because he got mad at me?"

"Is it really so sudden? Or were you not paying atten-tion?" asked Ingrid.

Micah hesitated, annoyed. "I guess. He did change over

the summer. That was when he moved the rest of his stuff over to my place."

"Starting new chapters often force reflection on those that are completed. Or unfinished."

Micah squirmed with discomfort. She was right—they both knew it. But it felt unfair that with her tumultuous beginning with Andrew, somehow she understood his existential crisis better than Micah as his boyfriend.

Ingrid lowered her head and blinked at him. She let out a breath that plumed into a small elegant cloud.

He gave her an impish smile. "I bet you think you're real smart, Red."

"Don't be petty," she retorted.

Micah pinched the back of her arm through her pea coat, and she curled her lip at him and snatched her arm away.

Chapter Six

The Mother

Liath Ryan was more awkward than Andrew by far.

Mercifully, she had hot water and fresh tea to offer Andrew when he got inside her cabin. He was sitting next to the front window where, over the frost on the glass, the view from the hill crest was high enough to expose Superior over the toothy trees of Temperance National Forest. The couch she'd put him on was from the eighties, its patterned lime green upholstery faded to puce and sagging in the middle. He sat sideways with one knee up so he could look out the window, but he was still surveying the room.

A deerskin rug sprawled over the bulk of the living room floor. Animal bones and dried flowers decorated the driftwood mantle of the fireplace. Flames crackled and spat within it.

Next to the fireplace was an altar on a black cloth draped over a small plinth. The centerpiece was a stone disc bearing the tree of life, with bundles of herbs, an antler, a rabbit's foot, and unpolished agates circling around it.

Andrew recognized the magical setup immediately. The stone and the antler had both been part of Liath's altar for as long as Andrew could remember, even if she had to keep them in a backpack when they got kicked out of an apartment or an ex's house.

Liath moved silently across the kitchen, which had a modest sink, a wood-burning stove, and a countertop partially obscured by full glass canning jars. A large alchemy setup with a bottle the size of Andrew's head and a narrow long mouth filled the other end of the counter, with a small bunsen burner under the bottle. Bundles of herbs hung to dry from strings tied around an exposed pipe over the western-facing kitchen window.

But once she sat down and picked up her own cup, Andrew thought she seemed very much at a loss for words. He used her speechless delay to recover from the cold, and to let it settle in that he'd really left Micah behind, driven up to the North Shore, and was sitting on a couch next to his mother.

Sixteen years ago, a freshly eighteen-year-old Andrew Vidasche walked in his high school graduation with no family clapping for him in the bleachers. His manager from Good Buy came, and a few of his co-workers, and Andrew kept telling himself that was good enough. Afterward, when everyone was returning gowns in the cafeteria, his favorite science teacher, Mr. Stewart, caught him in a bone-crunching hug.

"Didn't you have anyone come to cheer you on?" the bespectacled older man asked him.

Andrew waved a dismissive hand. "Nah, I'm all right. Onward, you know?"

The man fixed him with blue eyes and a serious furrow in his brow. "Is home safe?"

Andrew paused. He didn't *have* a home; he'd had a floor next to the couch his mum had been sleeping on. She had a boyfriend at the moment who was...at least kind enough not to chase Andrew out. On average, Andrew only had to sleep there once or twice a week. But he was sick of abusing the charity of his few friends and their parents to avoid staying with his mum, so he'd gotten a work-study job as a writing tutor that allowed him to move on campus early. "I'll be in the dorms soon."

"Here." Mr. Stewart handed him a torn corner of paper with an email address on it. "Tell me if you need anything before move-in at the U, okay?" Mr. Stewart smiled. "You're bound for great things, Mr. V."

"Sure." Andrew managed a limp smile.

He left school on a city bus that brought him to the shady apartments where his belongings were. Without a key to the apartment, Andrew waited for someone to come out through the locked outside door before he slipped inside, ignoring their halfhearted protest.

Andrew's heart was pounding as he let himself into the unlocked apartment unit. It was dim and stank of sweat and mildew inside.

On a stained red couch, Liath slumped with her forearms on her knees, hollow-eyed and frowning, her auburn hair dull and stringy where it exploded from a bun on top of her head.

Andrew went behind her to the folded blankets on the floor where he'd slept the night before. It brought flashes of Liath pacing haphazardly in the darkness, whispering about glaciers and piccolos. Crouching, he stuffed his three rumpled T-shirts, a pair of jeans, and his wool cardigan into his backpack, empty and light without any school books.

Liath picked up her head and looked back at him when he straightened, her eyes unfocused, unlike herself. The comedown from the enchanted foods wasn't over yet.

"So happy you made it," remarked Andrew, bitterness clinging to his words like handprints on a grimy mirror.

"To what?" Liath croaked.

"Are you fucking serious?" Despite himself, Andrew teared up. "I'm all you've got, and you don't deserve me."

Lips parting as she looked down at the graduation cap clutched in his hand, Liath rasped, "Ah, shit!" She jumped off the couch, raising her hands. Then, her legs wobbled and she swayed on her feet before collapsing back on the couch, gagging and covering her mouth with her wrist. As Andrew stalked back toward the door, she called after him, "Andrew—"

"You disastrous, self-absorbed druggie bitch," Andrew cried, yanking his backpack onto his shoulders. "Nobody will give a single fuck when you keel over and die. Good fucking riddance."

Liath stared at him, stunned or—she was too dazed, not yet returned to reality. It was one of the two states she was usually in. Drug-addled, or bawling.

He was done. This was the final tolling of the funeral bell. His relationship with her was dead.

"Andrew," she gasped, tears welling in her eyes as her latent processing caught up with her and she realized what he was doing. "No, please. Don't go."

"You sound like my father," snarled Andrew. "Same shit, isn't it? Don't give a shit about me till I'm walking away."

"I'm sorry." She was weeping now, hands trembling so violently it was like she was having a seizure.

"Too fucking late." He stepped into the hall and slammed the door behind him.

On the North Shore, a much more withered Liath stared at her cup, frowning until she got up the nerve to speak. She took a trembling breath, starting to look up but pausing as if she couldn't quite bear it. "I suppose you're quite mad at me."

"I'm not." Andrew waited to see if she would look back up at him. She didn't. He added, "I haven't bothered being angry at you in ten years." He hadn't been angry, true. But he'd hardly moved on from her. That was clear enough, since he'd spiraled enough about her to venture into the bluffs seven years ago, and he'd spiraled enough about her since this summer until she took over his brain and crowded out his ability to focus on anything else, even a relationship he thought made him quite happy.

He drummed his fingers on the back of the couch and looked out the window. "But you have taken up more of my thoughts than I'd like. I'm realizing it's got to be..." He trailed off. It was because of being around Lilydale so often, where he felt a complete absence of temptation to taste Fae-spelled foods. It was so easy for him *not* to want so much as a bite, for him to feel terrified of the thought of losing control. Part of that was because he'd seen their effects on Liath and on Julian, but part of it was because it just seemed so...stupid. He wanted to run from his feelings as often as anyone else, maybe more, but into oblivion?

"It's got to be what?" Liath prompted.

To touch the subject of Fae-spelled foods so immediately seemed like it would be to jump headfirst into Mount Doom before he'd received the One Ring. Pointless, and catastrophic.

Andrew shook his head slightly. "Never mind. It seemed I just had no choice but to hunt you down. Again."

"Again?" Liath straightened. "How often have you tried to look for me? I was around for quite a bit after you..." She trailed off. Couldn't say it.

"Never mind," Andrew repeated, slightly more forcefully.

Liath gazed at him for a long moment, her jaw working while she ground her teeth. She'd always done it when she needed a cigarette. But there was no cigarette smoke clinging to the room, just the sweet burning wood from the fireplace.

"You quit smoking," he ventured.

Liath nodded. "Aye." The single syllable made his eyes sting. Hearing it from her lips reminded him why he couldn't bear hearing anyone with a brogue since he left her. It was *her* thing. She added, "I'm completely sober. Caffeine, alcohol, over the counter medications, everything."

He paused. "Good for you."

"Twelve years." She looked down. "Should have been sooner. Should have tried to quit for you. Lord knows you asked."

Andrew rubbed his cheeks hard enough to make his skin burn. "Wasting no time, eh?"

"I've dreamt of having the opportunity to speak to you again for sixteen years, Andrew." Liath's piercing gaze was the color of iron ore. "I'm overwhelmed, and yes, I suppose a bit eager." She twisted a ring on her middle finger that had a chunk of banded agate in it.

"Mum..." Andrew sighed the word. "I've thought about what I'd say to you for years, too, but I'm just not ready to talk about your addiction yet. I don't know that I ever rehearsed a conversation with you where you were sober."

"Out of curiosity," she said carefully, her tone restrained and her eyebrows raised, "what did you rehearse for this? When you found me."

"I don't know." Tears welled his eyes. "I left an amazing man in the Cities because I just can't fucking get over everything you did. I need you out of my head. You need to fix me."

Liath's chest rose and made Andrew realize how thin she was now. She had always been puffy from pills in his teens. But now she looked wispy. Frail, almost. The shape of her sternum rose visibly through her shirt. Her shoulders, even under her bulky flannel, were too sharp at the slopes.

He added, "And I've done the therapy, and the bridge burning, and wrote the letters I never sent. But here we are. Obsessed with the woman who was so ready to do anything for me unless it meant getting sober."

She flinched. "Why?" She asked the question a little too loudly. "Why, if you wanted so badly to forget me, have you kept looking for me? If I'm nothing but a fuck-up to you?"

Andrew pointed with a finger swinging like a sword, sharp, with his brow creasing with his frustration. "No, no. That is not what I think." He slumped back, eyes slipping closed. "Maybe when I was eighteen I did. Maybe even during college. But when I got done, loneliness set in, and I realized how terrifying it is doing life by yourself. And that I didn't make it easier for you on your own by picking fights and calling you names. Which is what led me to look for you the first time."

Liath lifted her teacup, holding it near her lips at an angle that allowed Andrew to see the amber liquid rippling in her shaking hands. "What did you do?"

"Went to Lilydale," he told her with a humorless laugh. "Like an idiot."

Her tea sloshed, splashing her knee. "Why?"

"I thought maybe you'd be hiding out there or something." He shrugged. It sounded stupid *now*.

"What gave you the idea?" she demanded, sucking down a drink of tea and letting her breath out through her nostrils as if she would smoke like a dragon.

"Well, I found Kate," Andrew continued. "We live near each other and she works at a bar—"

"A bar!"

"—A few miles from my flat. And before you ask, no, she didn't tell me to go, but she did spill enough information to give me the idea." He tapped the rim of his cup, shaking his head slightly. "Honestly, at that time, I'd shifted so much away from how angry I'd been and hoped I could come up there and save you. That you'd just be waiting there for me to hear me say that I wanted you to be better and we could..." He gave a humorless laugh. "Have a do-over."

Liath sniffed, swiping her flannel sleeve over her nose. "When was that?"

"Seven years ago."

"I was already up here. And I never stepped foot in Lilydale, anyway. You know, as soon as you left, I started trying to get off the Fae-spelled foods. But that's partly why I ended up here. Rehab doesn't help that craving. I had to find a sponsor who understood that. This is her cabin."

"That's the part I don't understand," Andrew said forcefully. He clamped his mouth shut. Ten minutes in. He'd been on this couch for ten minutes. He didn't have a plan for once he got here, but he knew this wasn't it.

"Go on." Liath dropped her gaze. "No reason to avoid talking about it."

"I'm around Lilydale all the time." He ignored her jaw dropping. "I could have had Fae-spelled foods *in the Redwoods*. And I'm not interested in it, and I'm not curious about it, and I don't want to engage with magic in that way, by stealing and then letting it control me. So why the fuck, after years and years of teaching me to honor our place in nature, did you chuck all that in the bin and lose your fucking mind to foods that weren't even for you?"

"Wait, what do you mean?" Liath straightened, eyes growing round, leaning forward on the couch. "The Redwoods? Lilydale? What are you doing in those places, Andrew?"

"My boyfriend is the son of the Redwood Queen," he said with a stab of impatience. "It was the Ruby Daughter who used a scrying glass to help me find you. I am very tied up with the Folk, and it has been fairly mundane all things considered. And very substance-free."

Liath fell silent, her eyes still bulging as she blinked hard and ground her teeth again.

"And so I think that's why I've spiraled, because I just want to ask why you had to do it. Why you crossed that line and started to misuse foods from Lilydale." Andrew softened his voice. The question. That was the question which began to form twelve years ago after he finished at the University of Minnesota. That was the question that had slowly driven him mad since he was sixteen.

"I don't know," whispered Liath. "Desperation? You were already so bitter at that point. You had already given up on me. So I didn't have anything to lose."

He wanted to argue, but that was how he ended up in the bluffs where he ran into Ingrid. Desperate recklessness. Clearly that was a trait inherited from his mother.

"I'm so sorry I don't have a better answer," she went on. The skin around her moist eyes turned pink and puffy, dotted with welling tears she blinked rapidly to fight down. "The migraines were so bad and I kept failing and failing to find a way to get by the more jobs I lost because of attendance. It made you so independent so fast, and then you didn't need me anymore."

"That's ridiculous," Andrew retorted.

She nodded, silent, eyes downcast. A tear dripped off her chin and splashed into her tea.

"I've never stopped needing you." The words barely

formed in the air like a single snowflake drifting from the heavens. It reverberated against a choked sob from Liath's throat as she hid her face in her collar to collect herself.

"But there just wasn't space for me," he continued. "What you were doing with Fae-spelled foods was so deeply dangerous, especially when you still had a child you were responsible for. I know I had jobs and everything after I turned sixteen, but technically speaking, you were endangering me. Frequently."

Sobered by his blunt accusation, Liath nodded again, drying her cheeks, giving her ring a spin. "I know. I'll never forgive myself, so I don't expect you to forgive me. But I'm sorry in a way I couldn't have been when I was using. So, so sorry."

He nodded, silent.

"And yet you say you're now involved with the Folk." She lifted her gaze. "How the devil did that happen?"

Andrew laughed, a bit sheepish, a bit lighter, like eighteen years of anger and frustration was a seroma that finally drained during this conversation. "The Ruby Daughter spent five years stalking me after I made her bleed on accident, but that's not really what got me involved."

"The—she what!"

"I think she was working through some of her own mommy issues," Andrew observed, rubbing his thumb on the torque in his sweatshirt pocket.

"As in, the Redwood Queen." Lines creased her brow,

hardening her expression.

"Oh, you know her?"

"Everyone knows her." That's what Chamomile had said, too. "She was infamous. Your nan told me stories of her cruelty toward humans."

"Aye, which is why Micah was very comfortable turning her into a tree." Andrew nodded.

Liath's face grew blank. She blinked hard again. "Beg pardon?"

"Micah's not much for killing," he explained. "So he grew the Redwood Queen into a redwood."

"The Redwood Queen is dead?" Her eyes went round.

"In a manner of speaking."

"And it was her half-human son...your boyfriend—?"

"That's gonna depend." The expression on Micah's face when Andrew was pulling out of Magic's parking lot wasn't going to leave his memory very quickly. Andrew had to come up with a strong argument for himself if he wanted to convince Micah that a break really was just a break.

"Andrew," breathed Liath. "You're more than *involved* with the Folk. You're dating the son of the Redwood Queen, and you're in Lilydale 'all the time?' There's being involved, and then there's practically living like one of them."

He nodded. Over the last two years, being in Lilydale felt as commonplace as strolling through Cherokee Park or going to a brewery. He knew Micah felt more uncomfortable, as there was much more attention on him there than on

Andrew, but that also meant Andrew could simply...relish the crisp enchanted air in the compound, and the music, and the view of the river basin. "I suppose so. Ingrid—the Ruby Daughter—and I have surprisingly quite a bit in common, temperamentally and psychologically. She sent a gift." He pulled out the torque and held it out.

Motionless, Liath stared at it. "The Ruby Daughter sent me a gift?"

"She goes by Lady of the Bluffs at the moment."

Liath carefully picked up the torque, turning it in her hands, running her thumb over the ornate knobbed end. "This is from Leinster."

"She said she loved it there."

She blinked, veering toward incredulous with the way her top lip curled like Andrew's did. "But you also said she stalked you for five years."

"Water under the bridge." Unable to resist a sly grin, he glanced at Liath, took a sip of his now room temperature tea, and told her pointedly, "I try not to hold grudges."

Warily, Liath inclined her head. "You are much less angry than when you were eighteen. Still acerbic, but milder." She slotted the torque over her wrist.

Andrew drained his cup and glanced out the window at the violet-tinged twilit sky. *It did not look like Micah's eyes.* "It's been a hell of a lot of work."

"Aye, I believe that." She looked at her own teacup and swilled the dredges left in the bottom with a slight frown before returning her dark eyes to Andrew. "Why didn't you bring your boyfriend with you?"

The question made him flinch. It was benign enough on its own, but it forced him to contrive an answer. An answer that seemed flimsy at best, on the surface. To really understand it, and own it, he had to look into that festering, decades-old wound in his heart. "I'm not proud of you and I." His voice broke. "I'm not proud of how I treated you or how I deal with all the hurt. I thought I could hide it from him. But I have a feeling he's always seen right through me."

"I can relate," Liath murmured thickly.

Andrew jolted as if struck. The connection had been right there all along, but he'd never thought about it like that. How easy it was to abandon the people you love because you're blinded by your own extraordinary wounds. When his throat tightened and his lips strained with the urge to cry, he didn't fight it. He quickly set down his teacup and saucer so he could curl up and hide his face in his palms. Liath's warm hand settled lightly on his knee while he stifled the sounds he made, crying but in control, at last able to grieve without going mad. He didn't stop until his eyes grew dry on their own and his body was an abandoned chrysalis.

At some point, Liath had gotten up and prepared more tea for them. She drank from her cup while gazing solemnly outside as darkness fell. The second teacup rested on her knee, steaming gently. With a trembling hand, he picked it up and soothed his sore throat with its floral warmth.

Neither of them rushed to fill the silence, but it was less fraught than when he'd arrive. Eventually, Liath asked the kinds of questions mothers did to catch up with their distant children, and Andrew was happy to share. She remarked on his accent, how he had scrubbed most of the Scouse out in favor of some hybrid of Minnesotan and Londoner. She fed him sharp cheese and crackers and a tin of shortbread cookies while they talked. Several more cups of tea were emptied and then refilled, and the fire died down and then climbed onto the fresh logs Liath fed to it.

"Bundle up." Liath stood up from the couch several hours later. "It gets cold in here overnight. Phone's on the table there next to you. Turn off that lamp when you're ready. I sleep like the dead, so talk as late as you want. Do you need some blankets or pillows?"

"I've got stuff," he assured her. In the trailer of the snowmobile, he'd separated what he only needed outside and what he would need while he wasn't traveling, and the larger bag with the latter he'd brought in with him. It happened to include the same sleeping bag he'd used in Montana, making it swollen with memories. At the moment, that hurt more than anything.

"Sure." Liath stood near a sturdy ladder which led to an open loft overhead where a faint light shone from a bulb in the ceiling. She slid her flannel off her shoulders and was left in an old tee that said GRANDMA'S SALOON.

He pulled out everything else he needed for the night and then looked back up to see her watching him with her dark, searching eyes. Uncomfortably, he stood with his bundle of belongings under his arm. "I'm not expecting to intrude here for long. If you were...paranoid, like I would be."

Liath hesitated. She held onto the rungs of the ladder. "You're not intruding, child. You never have." Awkwardly, she smiled at him across the room. "Stay as long as you like."

"Wait," he said suddenly as her foot curled around the lowest rung. "When I was coming in, the cabin appeared out of nowhere, like a cloak lifted. How does it do that?"

"Oh." Her eyes glinted with mischief. "The wolf decides."

Andrew stared at her, slack-jawed.

Offering no elaboration, she nodded determinedly and began a slow and careful climb up the ladder. He watched her ascend in silence until she disappeared into the loft, shaking his head before he switched off the stained-glass lamp next to the couch, sitting silently in the moonlight, listening to his mother rustling and the floor creaking under her feet. She clicked on some kind of sound machine that filled the cabin with the whooshing of ocean waves. He hugged his arms around his stomach, nauseous with the strangeness and the comfort of hearing her move around.

Next to the table lamp was the red corded phone, which he picked up off the receiver to tap in Micah's number.

It rang a few times, which was unusual for him. When it stopped ringing, the phone crackled and shouted with the sound of a raucous crowd, clinking dinnerware, and music. Andrew winced, pulling the phone away from his ear for a moment.

"Micah?" he asked loudly into the receiver. "Hey. Hello?"

"Oh! Oh. Wrong end. Okay, I got it. I got it! Don't touch, we're all good." Andrew recognized the sound of Micah clearing his throat. "Hey there, this is Micah Stillwater, and I am *not* drunk."

"Micah? It's Andrew."

"Oh my god. Babe! Babe?" The noise of the crowd intensified. "Guys!" Micah's voice was faint and faraway. "It's Andrew. He's alive! The area code confused me."

"Micah—" His throat constricted, making Micah's name sound strained in his mouth. Andrew tried to summon him back with the urgency in his voice and sheer desperation.

The phone clunked with feedback. "Hey, Andy, it's Sam. Micah's like, six shots deep."

"Sam? I'm so confused. Are you guys out drinking together? Micah hardly ever drinks."

"Yeah, well, he's really upset! What are you thinking? You dodo. Micah is a fricking *golden retriever*."

Andrew shut his eyes. He slumped onto his back on the couch with the receiver clutched so tightly in his fist that his knuckles ached. "Can you let me talk to him, please?"

"No, Chami says it's her turn."

Andrew groaned.

"Hey, asshole!" Chamomile yelled distantly.

"Come on, give me the thing. Hello? It's Ingrid. Don't worry, Andrew. I followed Micah all day. You might remember from when I was stalking you that I am quite skilled at that."

"Yes, you are," muttered Andrew. "Please, can I talk to Micah again?"

"Only if you swear to be kind." Ingrid sounded like an ornery mother. "I don't know if I can charm someone through a mobile communication device, but I am more than ready to try."

"I swear." The vow came through gritted teeth.

For a moment, there was only silence.

Andrew wondered if his mother was listening. It would be funny if she felt sorry for him.

"Hi." Micah breathed into the phone, sounding more like himself. "Sorry. I'm in the bathroom now."

"Micah," sighed Andrew, tearing up.

In the bathroom, Micah's eyes stung as he stared at his blurry reflection in the dirty mirror over the sink. He swallowed several times, set the phone down, and splashed cold water on his face. He used his shirt to dry himself off and then picked up his phone. "You made it."

"Are you all right?"

Micah's voice wobbled like a leaf hanging onto a tree branch in autumn. "No, not really, man! Diana's caveman boyfriend showed up at the tea shop and tried to fucking punch me."

Andrew covered his mouth. "Oh, my god. I'm so sorry. Are you hurt?"

"Actually, no. I went a little nuts. Almost hurt *him.* Got a little Ingrid-y."

Andrew paused. "Maybe that's okay. He sounds like he deserved it. You didn't."

"I'm well wearing. A...aware. I'm well aware." Micah growled. "God damn it, you're killing my buzz!"

"Buzz? Sam said you've taken six shots."

"Just tequila—that's nothing. I could down it by the bottle in business school. I'm no lightweight."

"Please be careful, Micah."

"I'll do as I please." There was an unfamiliar, acerbic sneer in Micah's voice, and it settled in Andrew's stomach like bad curry. "That's what you wanted, right? Gotta set me free. Gotta make sure I can fuck whoever I want, or whatever. I told you I don't do that anymore, but what do I know? Clearly you know better. You always do."

"Micah..." Andrew winced, tears squeezing from his burning eyes. "I'm so sorry I left you down there. I don't know what I was thinking."

There was a long silence on Micah's end of the phone. Andrew thought the connection had been lost, but then, softly and sounding deeply sober, Micah murmured, "Neither do I."

On the edge of a nightmare, Andrew heard the haunting howl of a wolf.

He shivered in his sleep, the deep kind that makes your muscles vibrate, as if the temperature suddenly dropped.

Andrew groaned, blinking and trying to move to pull his sleeping bag up to his chin. But his body remained paralyzed. He sucked in a breath through his nose. Sleep paralysis had only hit him twice before in his life, both times terrifying. Steeling himself, he peeled open his eyes.

A round pair of golden eyes blinked at him; humid, sour breath puffed over his nose and mouth. He bit back a scream, jolting—not paralyzed, then—and the weight on his chest lifted with a whoosh and a thud. Heavy claws scratched away across the floor. Andrew shot upright, searching the dark for a glimpse of the creature. The front door thumped closed with a blast of frozen air in his face. He pulled himself up on the back of the couch to search outside, but there was nothing to see besides the dark slope of the hill and the distant slash of trees.

Andrew's heart hammered in his chest and goosebumps rose on his skin. He pulled his flannel sleeves down over his wrists and flipped the hood up on the sweatshirt he wore on top. Unsettled, loneliness fell heavily on his shoulders.

Maybe he just needed to go home in the morning.

For a while, he stared out the window at the stars big as snowflakes, rolling the blood ward between his fingers while he tried not to cry.

When it became obvious to him that he wasn't going back to sleep, Andrew stood and padded silently across the room. He wanted to inspect the little alchemy station his mum had set up on her counter. He'd never seen something that looked so much like an actual potion bottle. Andrew picked it up and peered inside, but it was currently empty, with not so much as a speck of dust on it.

Beside it was a little chest of tiny square drawers. Andrew peeked inside a few of them. They were filled with herbs and oddities. One drawer had several bird beaks, and Andrew recoiled and made a face.

"Are you interested in naturopathic medicine?"

Andrew jumped, his head snapping up. With her loose hair messy from sleep, Liath peered over the loft at him while she shrugged into a plaid fleece robe.

"Sorry." It had been quite a while since Andrew felt *sheepish* like this. "I wasn't trying to snoop."

Liath climbed down the ladder, stoked the low fire and threw on another log, and then joined him at the kitchen island. "You don't snoop. You observe. When you were a boy you'd do the same thing. In the middle of the night you'd be rummaging through my things to see what you could find. You liked the shells and the pinecones." She gazed past him as if a memory played behind her eyes. "Your dad hated it. You always gave him a fright."

Andrew made a dismissive noise. "Dad hated most things about me."

Liath flipped on the single bulb over the kitchen and then touched the small of his back. "He loved you."

Andrew didn't give in to the petulant instinct to deny it.

She added, "He was very depressed."

"So that's where I get it from."

"Most men that are depressed turn to anger. I'm not saying laying hands on us was ever right. And he *was* a narrow-minded bigot. But it's a broken system, aye?"

"Sure, Mum."

She washed her hands under a quick burst of water from the sink, which wafted a tangy iron smell over toward Andrew. As she wiped them on a dish rag hanging off the ancient fridge in the corner of the kitchen, she scrutinized him over her shoulder. "How about for you?"

Andrew remained in uncertain silence.

"You're depressed?"

"Oh. Yes. I mean, significantly above baseline. As my therapist would say."

"And?" With a frown, Liath hugged her robe around herself. "Has it made you angry?"

Andrew looked up at the rafters, swallowing a sudden lump in his throat. He'd gotten angry at Micah. He'd felt frightened and betrayed, and instead of moving closer, he'd...come here. With a steadying breath, he shook his head slightly. "I'm slow to anger. But I'm quick to run away."

Liath cringed. "You hold up a mirror to me with that sentiment." She gently moved him out of her way so she could reach the drawers. "Now. I'll make you a draught to help you sleep. Valerian root, passionflower, ginkgo biloba. Ground ginger for taste. Most of all passionflower, less so of valerian, and only a trace of ginkgo biloba. Not a recipe, but an instinct." She pinched dried leaves from three drawers and cast them into a crystal mortar. "Grind these." She passed it to him and held out an ebony pestle. He obeyed as she moved around the counter, lit her stove, and placed a kettle on the flames.

"As Druids, each time we encounter a problem, we must work with nature to determine how to make it better. We're asking for what we need, rather than telling it what to do," said Liath.

"It was actually difficult to parse apart what separates the Druids from other pagan spiritual practices." Andrew thought of his notebooks and tomes he used to carry around before he met Micah. "I tried to get most of my information on the Folk from Celtic sources, but it was hard."

She nodded. "That's because we only know of the most effective Druid practitioners because of their bountiful lives or their pacts and cooperation with the Folk. But we don't make the books, or meet as covens, because as I'm sure you know, when you gather too many people in a room, power and greed are more likely to triumph."

He grimaced. "Indeed."

She took a chunk of ginger root down from a hanging basket and started to grate it into a small clear ramekin. As she grated, she hummed and explained, "Sometimes I speak while I work, but there is no script in advance. No incantation already written is ready quite as well as what you decide in the moment to ask for." She glanced up. "And always ask. You are never manipulating nature. You are asking to touch its wealth of life as you shape your will to its offerings."

Even when Micah worked his magic against the Red-wood Queen, he'd whispered a plea to the trees, and they'd chosen to hear him. Even when Ingrid used the Scrying glass, she was shaping her will into some ancient magic that was already there. Maybe all of it was already there, all the magic any of them could ever need, lying dormant until the need spoke to them.

"What's your greatest feat as a Druid?" asked Andrew.

Liath watched him with her dark eyes. Her tongue flicked out to wet her lips. "I asked for it to grow dark and stormy so we could escape from your father."

Andrew blinked.

He didn't think about it as much anymore, twenty-some years removed. But when she mentioned it, the event began playing back in his memories like a reel of distorted film.

Twelve-year-old Andrew was dressed in his school uniform with his backpack slung on one shoulder. His freckles were more prominent then, and he had long bangs that made it easier to veil his eyes.

A few weeks earlier, he'd come out to his mum. He had a massive crush on his best mate, Ryan, and he simply *had* to talk to his mum about it. It felt better now, anyway, not keeping it to himself.

The weather that day was nice and mild for spring, with big cotton ball clouds showing plenty of blue beyond. He let himself in through the unlocked front door, but everything was quiet inside the small, single-story duplex. There was already the sharp tang of beer in the air, so his dad must not have gotten called in to work. Another day with no money always made Edward testy.

Andrew dropped his backpack on the couch by the front door and called, "Mum?"

When she didn't answer, he proceeded toward the back of the house where there were patio doors off the kitchen. The sliding door was open, and he caught his dad's voice on the breeze.

Not quite wound up yet, Edward Vidasche insisted, "You know something about your kid and you've been sitting on it for weeks. What is it, Liath? Don't fucking lie to me."

Peeking around the door frame, Andrew pressed himself against the fridge. His dad was right near the door standing over the folding chair where Liath sat with a cigarette between her fingers. When he was in a tank top, you could see all of Edward's Armed Forces tattoos on his right shoulder.

"If there's something you want to know about Andrew, you should ask him about it," replied Liath calmly, tapping the ash off her cigarette. "I'm not keeping secrets, but if he's not comfortable talking to you, that's up to him."

"What's he hiding?" Edward demanded. He stepped closer and leaned over Liath, and Andrew's heart started to pound. His mum's knee started bouncing. That meant, for both of them, that Edward was winding up.

"Ed, he's just a boy." Liath sounded weary. "He's not doing anything to hurt you."

"There's only one thing that would make you all dodgy like this." Suspicion slurred Edward's words.

Sweat rising on the back of his neck, Andrew fidgeted with the lapel of his school blazer.

"That boy's gay, isn't he?"

"Ed," sighed Liath.

"My son's a fag?" Edward asked again. "How long have you known?"

"I'm not engaging in this conversation." Liath's voice trembled despite how brave she tried to sound.

Clang. The paint bucket they used for cigarette butts went flying. It clattered across the back lawn and hit the clapboard siding hard enough to rattle the glass doors.

Soggy paper rolls stuck to the glass and scattered over the small brick landing.

"Ed, you're drunk. Please just go to bed or something."

"It's your fault!" insisted Andrew's dad. "You coddled him and made him soft!"

"Nobody *made* him gay," Liath reminded him. She always tried to reason with Edward longer than she should. She always tried to keep peace. Andrew, on the other hand, was sweeping the kitchen with a scrutinizing gaze, looking for something to fight with.

"I won't have a faggot living under my roof!" Edward snarled.

Andrew cringed.

Liath said evenly, "Then you should find a different roof."

The aluminum chair scraped; Liath gasped. Her cigarette fell by her feet. Andrew leaned forward.

Edward had her by the throat. With wild blue eyes and sunken, reddened cheeks, he screamed in Liath's face, "You trying to kick me out of my own house, Liath?"

Liath's fingers curled around the arms of her chair. Andrew couldn't see her face from his hiding spot.

Edward choked, "Don't you love me?"

Silent, Liath shuffled her feet, picking up her hand from the chair to push at Edward's wrist in a vain attempt to get him off her neck.

"You really wanna keep protecting that little pansy?" Edward demanded. Andrew could see his knuckles blanch around Liath's throat.

"Always," she rasped.

Edward shoved her by the throat, toppling the chair with her in it. Her head knocked into the bricks. Stunned, she remained on her side, trying to get her elbow under her. As he looked down at Liath with tear-stained cheeks, Edward drew back his boot.

Andrew reached into the space between the fridge and the wall and grabbed a broom. He leapt out the patio doors and jammed the handle of the broom into Edward's gut with both hands.

Edward stumbled away from Liath, gagging and spitting onto the grass. He swung his shaggy head up and glared venom at Andrew.

Andrew held the broom out in front of him and yelled, "Don't touch her!"

"Is it true?" Edward demanded.

"Who cares?" cried Andrew. "So what if I'm gay? I'm still your kid, aren't I?"

Liath ordered, "Andrew, go inside."

"No son of mine can be a fag." Edward raised his hand with lightning speed and backhanded Andrew upside his head. Slight compared to his father's slim but muscular build, Andrew took the strike hard enough to make him stumble. He dug the broom into the grass to keep himself on his feet and then lunged, driving his shoulder into Edward's chest. Liath got up, yanking Andrew toward the patio doors to get him away from his father.

Edward screamed, "Don't do this to me, Andrew!"

"I'm not doing anything," Andrew exclaimed, his head ringing. "You're the one freaking out!"

Liath clutched Edward's forearms—she usually did that, and it occasionally calmed him down. But Edward's streaming eyes were on Andrew and he shoved Liath away. He grabbed his son's collar with both hands and slammed him into the side of the house.

Edward sobbed, "How could you? You're not my son anymore!" Spittle sprayed onto Andrew's cheeks.

Wincing, gagging on Edward's sour breath, Andrew yelled, "I don't care! You suck anyway!"

Edward hit him again; stars swam in Andrew's vision. The stars, and the smell of his dad, and the fact that this was all because of a stupid crush on a boy...Andrew went hot with anger. He threw an elbow, kicked a shin, grabbed a tuft of sideburn, and when Edward let go of his jacket, Andrew jumped on him and furiously pounded his small but bony fists into Edward's face.

Edward fell, and Andrew went down with him, clawing with one hand and punching with the other. Andrew was too small and quick for his drunken father to grab him. He relished drawing blood with his fingernails and pulling out chunks of blond hair.

Liath hooked her arms through Andrew's armpits and hauled him off Edward, who rolled off his back immediately.

"We're leaving." Liath's dark gaze smoldered like embers. "You're never going to touch us again."

"No," cried Edward, scrambling upright, reaching toward them. Blood oozed from scratches on his face and a crack in his lip. He took a step toward them, but stopped when Liath flinched. "You can't go. Please don't go."

"I fucking hate you," Andrew screamed as Liath held him back.

Liath lifted her eyes to the heavens and pleaded, "Rain and dark, I beg for your aid."

Unsure what his mum's characteristically oblique language would do for them, Andrew picked up the broom and flailed it at Edward. Liath pulled on Andrew's blazer, so Andrew pitched the broom at him. It cracked Edward across the chin. Then, it cracked open the heavens. The skies rumbled and split asunder, spilling forth sheets of rain. Heavy, black clouds crowded overhead, sweeping away the daylight, crushing the little backyard with darkness. The downpour soaked them all at once, and Edward slipped, and slipped again on the suddenly muddy grass. He fell, grunting, gasping in confusion, squinting blindly.

Liath ushered Andrew over the doorstop, their shoes squeaking on linoleum. In the yard, Edward crouched on his hands and knees, wiping his face but smearing mud across his eyes, choking on rivulets of rain and squinting in the darkness.

With a vice grip on Andrew's wrist, Liath grabbed her bag from the counter, hauling Andrew toward the front door and picking up his backpack on the way. Splashing into the flooding street under a midnight sky at midday, they escaped Edward Vidasche forever.

At thirty-four, in a cabin on the North Shore, Andrew looked gravely at Liath and told her, "We couldn't have gotten away otherwise."

She looked away, her eyes puffy as she swallowed thickly. "Aye. I am glad that until that moment, I kept in balance with nature. It was willing to hear me. I've spent the last eleven years trying to balance again." She paused, wiping her nose with the back of her hand. "In your teens, I know that I abandoned you and chose to serve myself first. I ruined both of us."

Andrew looked down. He didn't bother denying it when they both knew it was true. An awkward silence hung between them. He didn't want to say anything to hurt her, but it was difficult not voicing his agreement. He often imagined a life for himself where Liath hadn't fallen to addiction.

"I can tell," added Liath, mercifully changing the subject, "that you're very much in balance. I doubt Folk would be ready to call you friend any other way."

He shrugged. "I guess. I try. Yeah."

Liath poured a small amount of water into the tincture and stirred it with a glass straw. "Do you think you feel magic? Around your boyfriend, for example. Or the Ruby Daughter."

He thought of Micah's perfumed emotions. Of the tingling when Ingrid used the scrying glass. Of all the faint feelings that got stronger when he stopped and felt the earth under the soles of bare feet, or spent time staring at the stars. Or Ingrid's ice wall, tingling with power like when feeling returned to a numb limb.

"I thought everyone could," said Andrew honestly.

Liath *tsked*. "Child, don't take that sense for granted. Like calls to like. Magic calls to magic." Pride flashed across her features. "You feel it because you have it."

Chapter Seven
The Fall

In The Squire, Micah hung up on Andrew and dropped his phone in his pocket with fingers that trembled. He went back into the bar, the cacophony of voices absorbing him like an oil spill. He could barely breathe, cinder blocks of emotion on his sternum, cheeks burning.

Micah made it back to their table, which was, unfortunately, the same one where he'd first sat across from Andrew. Ingrid and Chamomile had their arms linked, temples touching as they whispered to each other.

Reaching out, he ruffled Chamomile's hair. She flinched and gave a yell of protest.

"Where'd the kid go?" he asked.

Ingrid swatted his hand off Chamomile's head and then pointed with two fingers toward the bar near them. Sam leaned over the bar talking to a familiar bespectacled bartender; he looked uneasy, and the bartender's eyes were on Ingrid and Chamomile. Micah sauntered over to Sam and hooked his arm around his shoulders, making him jump.

"Whoa!" laughed Sam. "You're quieter than usual. You good? You guys talk?"

"I wouldn't say that improved things," said Micah. He nodded to the bartender. "Another round, please."

"Sam's going home," the bartender said harshly. Her eyeshadow was faded and sweating into the creases of her eyelids, which were hooded as she glared up at Micah through the flashing lenses of her glasses. Micah was trying to remember her name, but he kept coming up empty.

"Um." Micah blinked, defensive, glancing at Sam, whose freckled cheeks were bright pink. "All right. That's fine, buddy. You could've just said."

"I got freaked when you left," Sam said with what Micah was sure he intended as an easygoing laugh. He sounded more strangled, uneasy, like he was afraid of retaliation.

"Aw, why? I thought you liked Chami."

"Well, yeah..." Sam glanced over at the pair of faeries, who were having an animated and hushed conversation with each other. "But Ingrid is so scary. She did so much to scare Andrew. I don't know if I can ever totally forgive her."

Micah paused. "Andrew has."

Sam looked up through glasses that flashed opaque. "I think he's a better person than me. More evolved."

Micah snorted, saying nothing. Andrew couldn't be *that* much more evolved. He was too cowardly to even admit to Micah he wanted a break. But...would he have done that if he hadn't been pushed? On the phone, he certainly didn't sound like he wanted distance.

Confusion lanced painfully through Micah's stomach.

"And anyway," Sam added, "I'm pretty tired. But I paid your tab and I'll call you tomorrow, okay?"

Micah bit his tongue on an acerbic comment—likely *you're such a baby, huh?*—and said instead as he pinched Sam's cheeks, "Of course, little guy."

Sam slowly moved away from his fingers with a tilt of his head. He said carefully, "You're different when you drink."

Micah let Sam go and watched him leave with his hands on his hips. At their table, Chamomile tittered behind her hand before she resumed braiding a lock of her hair into Ingrid's curls.

Looking back at the bartender, Micah asked, "How much did he pay?"

"Sixty," said the bartender disapprovingly.

Micah pulled up the money transfer app on his phone and sent seventy to Sam with a frowning emoji attached.

"Where's Andrew?" asked the bartender, her arms crossed.

"Oh," exclaimed Micah. "That's right. You were here the night we met." Andrew said he'd known her as a kid. "You don't like me."

"I don't trust you," she corrected. "That's all." She filled a pint glass with beer, passed it across the bar at the opposite end, and then returned to him. "Andrew?"

Frowning, Micah hesitated, not sure what could be gained or lost from telling her anything. But the alcohol loosened his lips, and he found himself answering, "His mom's living up on the North Shore. He went up there."

The bartender blinked, her lined lips parting. "Liath is alive? And he went to see her?"

Micah shrugged. "Guess so."

"Interesting." She bent to retrieve a bottle of Patrón, filled a shot glass, and pushed it toward him.

"Why 'interesting?'" Micah demanded. She was definitely feeding him alcohol to make him talk more, but if he was talking about Andrew, maybe that was for the best. He took the shot and tipped it back, making a face as it slid into his belly. "I figured they used to be close."

The bartender snorted. A server slid behind the bar and called for her—her name was Kate, apparently—but she waved her off. "Andrew and Liath? I wouldn't say so. That boy's got a mouth on him when he's angry, and she made him mad. A lot. She was no peach, either. It was like watching two bleeding people rub salt in each other's open wounds."

He frowned. Even this summer, Andrew's irritability had felt muffled and restrained. It was difficult to imagine him spewing hatred. He was always so careful with his words. But...maybe Liath was the reason he was like that now.

Kate raised a salt and pepper eyebrow. "You didn't know?"

Defensive, Micah crossed his arms and bit out, "He never talked about her! Made a point not to, actually."

Her attention slipped away from him as she looked over his shoulder, her jaw going slack. Micah followed her gaze. The table behind him was empty; Ingrid and Chamomile were nowhere to be seen. Micah sucked his teeth. "Bitches."

"It's for the best," said Kate. "They don't belong in here."

Sharply, he turned back to face her and said in a harsh whisper, "Excuse me? What is that, some kind of magical racism?"

Kate shrugged. "You try to fit in. They don't, and they draw attention." She gestured behind him, first at the empty table and then more broadly around it. She was right. Though The Squire was lively enough for late on a Thursday night, there was a ring of unoccupied tables around theirs. As if their *otherness* could be sensed, and Ingrid and Chamomile had scared everyone off.

Micah sighed. When he turned back to the bar, there was another shot in front of him, but Kate had moved away. He watched her prepare a handful of drinks as he inhaled the shot's bitter agave aroma.

Now he was alone, shaken up again with thoughts of Andrew, and...oh, yes. The violent desire to make that Tom person afraid. That was a fun new character development. When he was in the Redwoods, any angry impulse he'd ever had was miniscule and brief. When he was sixteen and found out Sivarthis had only been intimate with him so he could report back to his mates and laugh at Micah's expense, for example. But to be angry at a faerie in the Queen's Guard who was a foot taller than Micah with muscles Micah didn't even think should exist, that would be like engraving his own tombstone.

Not so here. Micah was stronger than Tom. Bigger. And more dangerous. To have that urge to strike terror into a stranger made him feel like a stranger to himself and every emotion he thought he possessed. But right now, that kind of feral energy was a friend to him. He was angry at Andrew, alone in a bar, and absolutely lost.

He shook his head, picked up the shot, and slammed it back.

Time to self-destruct.

"Jeeze, Micah," said Julian, rubbing his eyes, "it's three in the morning. You're completely hammered."

Micah looked up with a spoon in his mouth, swallowing an excessively large bite of ice cream. He doubled over. "Augh! Brain freeze."

Leaning against the doorway into the kitchen, Julian closed his robe around himself and shook his head. "I know you're upset that Andrew left," he said, "but there's no need to be sloppy."

"Sloppy?" said Micah, staggering up to Julian, slinging an arm around his neck.

"Ugh." Julian plugged his nose. "Tequila."

"Sometimes I think you call me names to hurt my feelings on purpose," Micah said. He blew on the concave side of the spoon and carefully balanced it on his nose. It stayed there for a moment and then clanged onto the kitchen tiles.

"I'm being honest," argued Julian. He bent down and picked up the spoon, dropping it into the sink. "You should go to bed."

"You're only honest when you're insulting me!" Micah sang. He blindly felt his way down to the living room with his hands on the wall, flipping on the lights and dazzling Julian's eyes as he trailed along after his son.

"Were you drinking by yourself? You know that's a bad idea for anyone, Micah."

"Oh, no." Micah flopped onto the couch. "I was drinking with my sister."

Julian let out a long sigh. "So is that what you're going to do while Andrew's away? Play pretend with the Folk?"

"Pretend?" Micah sat up. His head spun. He gagged, dropping his forehead onto the heel of his hand. "Woof." When he managed to look back up, Julian had gotten a glass of water from the kitchen, holding it out to him. Taking the glass, Micah said with a sidelong glance at his father, "I'm half from their world, Dad. What makes you so sure I'm not playing pretend when I'm here with you?"

Julian froze, gazing down with his amber eyes round with surprise. Micah sipped his water and glared at the patio doors.

"I forgot how nasty you get when you drink," observed Julian.

Shrugging, Micah said indifferently, "Sorry I have to be drunk to be as mean as you are."

Eyes flashing, Julian snatched the glass of water from Micah's hand and splashed it in his face. Flinching back, Micah yelled, angrily swiping his sleeve across his face.

Spitting water, he spluttered, "What the hell, Dad!"

"If you're playing pretend, then so am I. Do you think I want any of your magical nonsense in my life?" snapped Julian.

"Sorry I'm such a nuisance," Micah said with a sneer behind the water dribbling down his cheeks.

Julian shook his head. "You're missing the point. You always do. Even when you were a kid. Things don't always revolve around you, Micah. Sober up." Bringing the glass with him, Julian shut off the lights in the living room and went upstairs, leaving Micah dripping wet on the couch in the dark.

Slumping into a corner of the couch, Micah covered his face with a pillow and screamed and swore into it.

Julian was right. He needed to sober up. Patting his face dry with the pillow, Micah climbed to his feet, swaying as he made his way to the patio doors. He fumbled with the lock for several minutes until he got it open. Cold air slammed into him, stealing his breath, crystallizing the water droplets left on his face and bangs. He stepped onto the balcony and shut the door behind him, leaning against the glass as a shudder tore through him. Instinctively, he hugged himself.

At least the plants out here were safe from him, already dead for the winter.

Sliding down the patio door, Micah held onto his knees and watched his breath plume out, imagining it was his life leaving his chest, because what was the point anyway?

Maybe he really was playing pretend down here with Julian. Maybe that's even why he was so invested in his relationship with Andrew. Maybe it was all an act. But it wasn't like he knew how to be Fae either. So if he was pretending to be human, and he wasn't really a faerie, then what exactly was he?

"Mr. Stillwater."

Jumping, Julian woke with a gasp and sat up sharply. "Who...who's there?" His heart pounding, he groped for the switch on his bedside lamp and clicked it on. "Wha...Chamomile?"

The small white-haired woman blinked at him. Her long hair was loose under a hat she had pulled politely over her angular ears. She was bundled up in a fluffy pink jacket. She already had Cinnamon purring on her shoulder, marking her cheek with his damp pink nose.

"What're you doing here? It's been years."

Chamomile's large blue eyes gleamed with an inhuman shine. Her expression was neutral, blank, unsettling compared to how lively or mischievous she'd usually looked when visiting the brownstone in the past. "Micah isn't in his bed. I thought he came back here."

"I left him downstairs," grumbled Julian. "Now, I'm going back to sleep. Please leave." He rolled over in bed and pulled his blankets up to his chin. "And do me a favor and get him out of here tonight, too. He's being an asshole."

"Yeah, I know." Chamomile's voice dropped with annoyance. She padded toward his door.

"Chami?"

"Yes, Mr. Stillwater?"

Pushing up to his elbow, Julian felt the lines deepen in his forehead. "Is Micah better off up there with you?"

Chamomile frowned. She was silent for so long that Julian wasn't sure he was going to get an answer. Shrugging, she finally said, "That's for him to say, sir."

Julian sighed. "Always evasive, aren't you?"

She set Cinnamon back on the bed. "Good night, Mr. Stillwater." Without a backward glance, she clicked his door closed behind her and left the room.

She moved silently through the dark house. Goblin eyes were particularly well-suited for the dark, showing her each sharp edge of the steps in grayscale as Chamomile went down the pitch-black stairwell. At the foot of it, though, the living room was empty. Chamomile felt a twinge of irritation. Either she was going to have to keep hunting for that idiot, or she was going to leave him to his own natural consequences. For most people, humans especially, she could do that easily enough. But it was always harder for her where Micah was concerned.

Then she noticed the unnatural shape leaning against the patio doors as she stepped around the couch. Chamomile hauled open the heavy glass door and let Micah fall onto his back against her feet. But his weight was off, his body stiff with cold. As he sprawled across her boots, his eyes remained closed. She could feel his soul still stirring in his chest like a hibernating mouse, but...that was not as alive as Chamomile would like him. Crouching, Chamomile pressed two fingers below Micah's jaw and put her cheek up against his nostril. It took longer than she liked to feel his pulse thump under her fingers and his breath warm her cheek.

She climbed over him onto the balcony, pulling the door closed. Then she braced herself against the bricks of the brownstone, grabbed Micah's wrists, and hefted him into a sitting position.

Micah mumbled, "Let me die."

Chamomile almost dropped him. She blinked, unsettled. Shaking herself, she hooked her arms around Micah's chest from behind him and then back-pedaled into the shadows.

Expecting the pillowy embrace of his large bed, Micah rolled over with a sigh.

The hammock underneath him twisted and ruthlessly dumped him out.

Eyes snapping open, the ground flew toward him as he screamed and flailed in the open air.

He panicked, imagined a broken arm at least if he hit the limestone under him, and tried to scrabble for a branch or something to stop him.

The branches groaned and creaked and came to him, like a dozen bony arms extending arthritic fingers.

It wasn't great; they clawed at his stomach and stabbed into his armpits, but they stopped him from falling straight into bedrock. He gasped and hugged the biggest branch, legs flailing and making the branch wobble.

A faerie with pink dragonfly wings flitted up like a jittery television picture. She blinked, eyes shining black like a rabbit and asked, "Can I help you?"

"Oh my god. Ow. Ow, yes. Please. Please!"

She buzzed around behind him, grabbed him by the middle of his sweatshirt, and lifted his weight off the branch. He let go, and she acted like a parachute as she eased him toward the ground and set his feet on a limestone ledge.

"Th-thank you." Micah's knees wobbled, so he dropped onto his ass on a snowy log. He looked up at the gently swinging hammock overhead. It was about fifteen feet up.

She smiled sweetly with full, violet lips. Her skin had a faint icy blue tint to it. She had pearlescent pink curlicues of hair tucked partly under a fuzzy beanie. He'd seen her once or twice over the years; her appearance was striking and memorable. "I'm Spirulina. You can call me Lina. Now you owe me!"

"Great. Do you happen to know how I got here?" he asked her, pulling up his hood and shoving his hair back off his forehead.

Lina blinked. "You will have to ask Chamomile."

"Of course." Micah leaned his head back and glared at the trees. "Er, thank you. Lina."

Someone with a white afro poked out of a large wicker basket hole and stared at him.

Lina shrugged, tucked herself into a drapey wool shawl, and skipped off through the grove of trees.

Micah dropped his head between his hands. His temples throbbed and his stomach gurgled, and his mouth tasted sour. "Ugh, this doesn't make any sense." Fractured images from his night told him mostly that he had made it back to the brownstone. He remembered a spoon clanging on his kitchen floor. And...Julian, splashing water in his face?

That couldn't be good.

But if he'd passed out in the brownstone, he wasn't sure how he'd ended up in Lilydale.

Chamomile appeared on silent feet and dropped onto the stump next to him. "Good morning." Sliding a basket off the crook of her arm, she held out a mug toward him.

"It is not," groaned Micah, reaching for the coffee that smelled dark and rich.

Chamomile jerked the mug out of reach. "Any thoughts on what you got up to last night?"

"I don't remember," said Micah, apologetic. "I thought I was at home. But I know I pissed my dad off. He threw water on me."

"Normally, I would be delighted," Chamomile observed. She set the second mug of coffee on her knee and then picked up his hand, spreading his fingers out over her small palm. "But I found you passed out on your balcony not long before dawn. And the water from him made your frostbite worse."

He peered at his chapped knuckles and saw small crusty blisters rimming his nail beds. Micah cringed. "Oh. I screwed up real bad last night." He reached for the mug on her knee, and she didn't attack him. Its glaze was a gradient starting at sage and shifting to turquoise, with indigo freckles throughout. Micah raised an eyebrow at

Chamomile.

"Ingrid made it."

"Aw, Red." He grinned.

Chamomile's eyes stayed on Micah's fingers. "It took you a few hours by the fire to thaw out."

"How did I end up in a hammock?" He clutched the mug between both hands, letting its heat seep into his palms, trying to imagine Chamomile hefting his unconscious body around by herself.

"I was hoping you'd fall out like that," she admitted.

"So you hauled me off my balcony, took me here, and then went so far as to *move* me all the way up to a hammock after that, just to prank me. By yourself."

"I don't understand your confusion," said Chamomile.

He snorted, saying nothing, and they settled into silence.

Chamomile plucked an enormous muffin out of the basket with her and took a bite. Crumbs spilled down her chest. She was in a clingy white shift with a deep V, and Micah's eyes slid automatically down over the mounds of her breasts where the crumbs fell. His face heated up as he looked away guiltily.

"Did you want to die?" she asked, muffin stuffed in her cheek. She swallowed and washed it down with a large swig of coffee.

Micah blew on the mug and then took a sip. "No more than usual."

Chamomile choked. Micah gave her a firm pat on her

back, making her spill coffee on her bare legs. He snickered when she punched his shoulder.

More ruefully, he said, "I find it hard to believe that you as an immortal being don't occasionally want it all to end."

Chamomile thoughtfully twirled a strand of her hair. "I suppose it's futile, as I know my life won't end. I just find a way forward when I begin to wander." She glanced at him and said in a voice like tree branches creaking in a storm, "Rather than wandering into circumstances that could kill me, like you did."

"I wasn't planning to pass out on the balcony." He glanced quickly at her. She was still staring at him, so he added, "I was trying to sober up. Unwisely or otherwise."

She nodded, mollified. "Good."

He sipped in silence and cast his gaze out over the quiet compound. It must have still been too early for many Folk to be awake. Snow drifted softly across the steps that went past the kiln throne. Chamomile and Ingrid had some of the only permanent structures in the commune. At their backs, Chamomile's adobo-style hut was made of clay, painted with pink, blue, and white swirls and flowers. Ingrid's was a brick cube, straight across from him on the southeastern point of the camp. Other than their huts and the hanging homes, there were twelve or so heavy canvas tents erected and nestled among red-berry bushes, round bronze-bound barrels, and stacks of logs. There were several small bonfires crackling around the compound, and a large one smoldering down near the western cliffs in the bonfire pit in front of the kiln throne.

Several chickadees hopped over the arched back of a large red toadstool, their black and white wings fluttering as they bent feathery round heads to pick at the scales on the toadstool. Chin in hand, he watched them with a bemused smile until the breeze turned and they soared away.

"Lilydale is really nice," said Micah.

"He realizes, twenty-two years after he arrived in Minnesota," Chamomile said with a sniff.

"Hey, I was busy when I got here. I had to take the GED and get into college. I pretended like I had been homeschooled growing up. Which I guess I kind of was. The Fae education system is...interesting."

Chamomile blinked, looking curious despite herself. When they'd been dating, Micah tried to minimize and ignore his human life. She knew about Julian, and that had been about it.

"What did you study?" she asked.

Micah shrugged and told her, "Dad and I did some research when we got here on what could make me the most money, so I got a business degree. It was *so* boring."

"That is an odd human choice," she said. "The idea that you must do something not for enjoyment but for some sense of stability."

"Modern living makes a farce of independence by making

you unavoidably dependent on everyone else's systems, all the while telling you to find your own way," agreed Micah.

She snorted.

Half of the coffee in Micah's cup was already gone. He peered inside mournfully, watching the reflection of the sky fracture on the dark mirrored surface when he gave the cup a little shake.

Holding her mug with both hands, Chamomile said, "I'm honestly surprised you never had any issues with Fae abilities showing up for you when you spent all that time with humans in school."

"Are you? I was very emotionally repressed." Micah grinned. "If I had nothing to feel, then I had no abilities to show. My classmates had more than enough to say about my eyes, so I knew I couldn't trust any of them." He wagged a finger at her. "Kept me guarded. Andrew did *not* keep me guarded. I am very much *not* guarded with him."

"Perhaps you should consider un-cleaving your abilities from strong emotion," observed Chamomile. "Seems dangerous."

"Anyway," said Micah, standing abruptly, "I have to work today. Bye."

Chamomile watched him rise. Under the navy tone of the dawning sky, her eyes looked ocean-blue. "You have pretty significant frostbite. You shouldn't work."

Micah hesitated. He knew Diana was supposed to work. And he might be too hungover to deal with her professionally. And being at Lilydale could be...helpful.

He sank back onto the log.

Blisters all over his fingers were probably a health hazard, anyway.

"C'mon." Chamomile's eyes danced.

"Oh, all right." Micah sighed. "Then I want to go back to sleep for like, four more hours."

As if it were obvious, Chamomile said, "Me, too. I only woke up because you were squawking so loudly out here."

"Same, here!" someone called from overhead.

"Gotta work on your hammock skills," another voice added.

Glowering at the Folk in the branches overhead, Micah waved and called, "Sorry, everyone!" Then to Chamomile he said more urgently, "Don't make me sleep in a hammock."

"I won't. Come on." Chamomile stood up clutching her coffee. As she went back toward her hut, Micah stared at her swinging hips through her waterfall of silver hair. And there was no one around to make him feel guilty about it.

Micah let out an unsteady breath. He was never *not* attracted to Chamomile. He wasn't a believer that being monogamous made everyone besides your partner unattractive. And supposedly, Andrew *wanted* him to fool around with other people. Why the fuck Andrew wanted him to be unfaithful so badly was still beyond him. But the sting of Andrew's request for a break, and the sting of his abrupt departure, had settled onto Micah's skin much like the frostbite.

Chamomile had been much kinder than Andrew after she'd ended their relationship. She would leave donuts or random new plants on his doorstep. She didn't allow him to avoid her for very long, and refused to let their friendship wither after their romance ended. Eventually, he gave up and got over the lost romance, moving on in their friendship. Chamomile might have worn him down in that sense, but Micah would never be able to look at Andrew again if this was over.

Regardless of forever, their relationship was...paused. He gazed at the white painted door to Chamomile's hut and rubbed his chin.

Some feeling, or some feeling he had been missing, beckoned him toward that hut. It felt like his mouth was watering at the thought of some sweet morsel he hadn't missed until now. Like he'd stopped eating those plastic-wrapped gas station cakes years ago, only to realize with sudden alacrity it was the only thing he was hungry for.

Micah drummed his fingers on his chin, letting out a breath. With those cakes, they never ended up as good as the thought of them. With Chamomile's hut, some whisper in his head told him it wasn't going to be worth it, either. But his resentment was too loud; it pushed down the whisper and stuffed it away.

"Just going in to take a nap," he murmured halfheartedly.

He slowly stood up and cast a long look over the river basin, running his tongue over his top lip. Then drained his coffee cup, and climbed onto the cobbled pathway to Chamomile's door.

Chapter Eight
The Lake

Greeting the daylight with sweat on his back and cold biting his cheeks, Andrew was outside chopping firewood with a narrow-headed ax. It was a peculiar kind of strain, one Andrew hadn't experienced since he'd taught himself sword-fighting in his twenties. The wood smelled sweet, each log splitting with a satisfying *crack*.

He was positioning another log of maple on a wide stump when Liath came outside bundled in a heavy hunter's jacket, her hair tucked up into a wool cap.

"That should do it," she told him, nodding in appreciation at the stack of split logs in the crate next to the cabin. She blew into her folded hands and rubbed them together.

"I had a question," said Andrew, wedging the ax into the stump.

"Go on then." She looked skeptical.

"Can you teach me magic?"

Liath blinked. "You want to learn magic?"

"Ingrid told me the wards and runes I used in my apartment—which I copied from you—are fairly effective. I want to know more. It's likely I'll be around Folk for the rest of my life."

Her eyes lit up. "Is that so? Andrew, are you going to spend forever with this man? This...faerie?"

He touched his necklace. If Micah was able to forgive him for running away to the North Shore, then he was never going to let him go. "I'm going to try to make sure of it. So. Will you teach me magic?"

Gaze lingering on his necklace for a moment, Liath looked away toward Superior, worrying her lip with her canine. "What do you think magic is?"

"Depends." He followed her gaze to the distant water. "Folk are innately magical; it comes from within, and they're born from it. Humans mostly aren't. So, we have to honor the magic around us and understand how we can fit around and within it. Nature, obviously, holds most of the magic. Even the Folk call on it."

She looked slightly impressed. "Andrew. You've walked a good path."

Neutrally, he nodded in agreement. "Thanks. I have another question. Well, an observation, I suppose."

"Curious as ever."

"Something was in the cabin last night. It woke me up."

Liath's face creased with annoyance. She crossed her arms and shook her head. "Fionna must have broken in again."

Raising his eyebrows, Andrew said, "Fionna has suspiciously wolf-like eyes."

"Sorry if she frightened you. She's a curious pup."

"Mother." He couldn't bite the eagerness from his tone. It was hard for anything to surprise Andrew since he first stepped into the world of the Folk, but this excited him. He leaned down to make sure she had to meet his eyes. "Is that the wolf you said decides? You know a *wolf?*"

Liath smirked. "In a manner of speaking."

"Wolves are so cool. My boyfriend's got a kinship to cats, and that's awesome, but...*wolves*, mum!" He grabbed her shoulders. "Let me meet her!"

She laughed. "It's not up to me. She's very strong-willed. She'll meet you when she's ready."

"Ah!" he whined. "Put in a good word for me, at least! I won't be up here that long."

With a shake of her head, she said, "Calm and patience, child."

"Mother!"

Lips twitching, Liath rolled her eyes and pushed his chest. "I'm going to get my gloves."

As he listened to her footsteps crunching away over the snow, Andrew puffed out an opaque breath and turned in a circle. "Hello, Fionna!" he called to the bone-white hills. A gust of wind picked up a spurt of snow and carried it away from Superior. Or maybe the blustery shape was the shaggy back of a wolf. Or perhaps she was both, neither wolf nor snow, but something in-between. "I'm Andrew! I hope we can be friends."

Micah would have loved this.

Not much later, Liath drove them down a nearly invisible road in a rusty red truck with a plough attached to the front bumper. Their progress was slow, the plough cutting fastidiously through snow so deep it almost brushed the door handles. The heat inside the cab wasn't very strong, but Andrew and Liath were both bundled in snow suits, scarves, face masks, and lined gloves under mittens. The temperature wasn't extremely low, but the wind chill would chap skin raw in ninety seconds. It got colder, too, as you neared the lake. The depths of the waters trapped the cold like an old king's tomb, so even when the summer heat was sweltering, Superior still had teeth.

"So, your boyfriend. Tell me about him," said Liath, eyes on the road.

Andrew stared at his lap. "He's only my boyfriend if he doesn't hate me for how I handled myself this week."

Liath raised an eyebrow. "You're worried that after two years, he'll give up on you just because you've had a bad week?"

Andrew opened and closed his mouth. "I told him I wanted a break and he should see other people."

"Ouch." Liath grimaced.

"Don't say that!" Andrew cried. "I...I...didn't want him to, but I...everyone adores him, and I've just been so distant, and..."

Liath sighed, "Child."

"I wasn't going to ask for the break," he added.

"All right, well, he answered your call last night, didn't he? That seems like a good start. Just be patient. And let me see him. I'm dying to know what the Nightshade Boy looks like."

"You've heard of him?" Andrew blinked.

"I heard about him and the Ruby Daughter when they came to Lilydale, aye. That was when we came to Minnesota, too, you know. I wanted to find out what the magic scene was like right away for my benefit and our safety, and it wasn't hard, since everyone was *very* excited to have such noteworthy Folk in Minnesota. I wonder if you two have just been orbiting around each other since then, waiting to collide."

Clearing his throat, he reached into his snowsuit and pulled his phone out of his jeans pocket. It was still out of service when he checked it, which, with a look around at the deserted winter wilderness, wasn't surprising. But it felt more strange not carrying it with him. He pulled up his camera roll and only had to scroll past two photos to find one he'd taken of Micah the week prior, beaming on his bed holding his big ginger tomcat Cinnamon, whom he'd wrapped in Andrew's tartan scarf as if swaddling a baby.

"A cat person," said Liath admiringly. "Very handsome, child."

"He's got a Master's in business from the U of M. He runs a tea shop. But like, that Asian novelty tea. Boba. With tapioca pearls. I mean, the tea blends are still good, and now he keeps my favorites in stock."

Liath screwed up her face. "Wait, why would a prince from the Redwoods need to get degrees?"

"Micah's tried to avoid Fae dealings since his father was pretty messed up by everything in the Redwoods."

"How so?"

"The Redwood Queen had him imprisoned for twenty-two years. She force-fed him Fae-spelled foods to keep him compliant and make him...breed with her."

Mouth dropping open, Liath exclaimed, "Twenty-two years on Fae-spelled foods! How do ye live after that?"

"I would say in large part, he hasn't," Andrew said. "He doesn't even know who he was before the Redwoods. He tried to kill himself a number of times when they first got here. And he's never truly escaped the Fae-spelled foods." He shook his head, thinking of the golden thread looped around Julian's neck while he gazed adoringly at the Queen. "The Redwood Queen stole him back when Micah and I met. He still thinks that was a dream."

Liath shook her head without speaking as the truck rumbled on through the snow. When she finally spoke, her voice had the boiling notes of a kettle about to scream. "It's a miserable life. It's the kind of behavior that makes me resent the Folk. In the tales, it's easy enough to read of wicked acts and feel nothing. But hearing that she did that to a real person, who has to live with the consequences..." She let out a harsh sigh. "I taught you we must be balanced, but what keeps the Folk in check?"

Andrew thought for a moment. "Sometimes nothing, I suppose. But I think Micah checked the Queen's wickedness. Just like with the rain clouds when we left Edward, Micah was able to call on nature to put an end to the Redwood Queen."

"But maybe that was because of his human side."

His brow wrinkled as he looked at her sidelong. "Maybe. But Ingrid and Chamomile aren't wicked either. Wicked things don't love the way they both love him." He hesitated and then said mildly, "And it's not their fault you made the choices you did."

She flinched. "Aye." Sniffing, she said, "Forgive me. It seems I'm a wee bit bitter about the Folk."

"Evidently." They fell silent. Andrew squirmed in the quiet, his own bitterness hanging in the air between them like sulfur. Finally, he said, "That was callous of me. I'm bitter, too."

Liath didn't reply right away, the truck slowing as it mounted a snow-heavy hill, the plough grinding against its fixtures. "We aren't screaming at each other, so we're doing better than we used to."

Inside his gloves, Andrew curled his fingers closed.

"So, is he doing something about it? Your boyfriend."

"About what?"

"The Fae-spelled foods." Liath glanced at him, expression hardening. "You said you went to Lilydale looking for me," she said, ticking off reasons with her fingers. "You knew that's where those cursed baggies of food came from, and you said his father is ruined because of the Folk. That has all of the setup for a campaign that ends the epidemic."

Sighing impatiently, Andrew told her, "Mum, they're only 'Fae-spelled' because it's food the Folk produced for themselves. In the Redwoods, they manufactured it to be a temptation. But the Folk in Lilydale...they're kind of provincial. You're telling me you want four-foot-tall mute brownies to fight and aggress any drug-addled, violent human who shows up demanding an apple?"

"You're very sympathetic to them," Liath noted stiffly.

Andrew bit his tongue and took several breaths. When they reached the highway between the state park and the lake, they sat at the crossroad for a few minutes while cars blew past them with wild spirals of snowflakes spraying out from under their tires. The truck's wheels spun until Liath revved its old growling engine and it made it off the snow.

Andrew finally said, "You're right. When Ingrid was stalking me, I thought every faerie was reprehensible. But now, I will admit that I feel I understand them better than I understand you. I thought you stood for something greater than yourself."

"Ah, so you mean I should have known better," Liath

intoned.

"Obviously," snapped Andrew. "No need to sound so sorry for yourself, mother."

She sighed sharply, drumming her hands against the wheel. The truck slowed; her blinker clicked on toward the right where there was a small but plowed road wending down toward the lakeside.

"Yes, you're right," she said, placating, "I should have known better. I knew it wouldn't be good. I just didn't know...I didn't know it would feel *so* good."

Andrew winced. "Mother."

Hardly hearing him, she said rapidly, "I'm ashamed to say that despite sobriety, despite not having tasted anything Fae-spelled for...how old are you now? Thirty-two?"

"Thirty-four."

"Fifteen years I've been without so much as a crumb of those bespelled foods, and my tastebuds still tingle at the thought. My blood still seems to pump more slowly than it did before, like the magic turned it to molasses."

When her voice fell silent, the truck seemed to shrink around them, its metal skeleton pressing down, making Andrew's muscles tense.

He wetted his lips and said softly, "Terrifying."

Liath gripped a crank on the door and cracked her window, blasting the cockpit of the truck with icy cold. Andrew let her do it without protesting; he could see the rapid rise and fall of her chest.

Things were different now. They were both free of her addiction.

At least he thought so.

"I didn't mean to dredge that up for you," he said. "I'm sorry."

She shook her head slightly. "Do better than me, Andrew," she said. "That's all I ask."

"Actually," Andrew said, realization shafting through him like sunlight through a chink in the blinds, "I think I do better *because* of what you and I went through. It made me cautious, and jaded, sure. But it also made me...open. If I had treated the Folk like they were all wicked, how could I ever have given Micah a chance? And do you know *why* I didn't treat the Folk like they were all wicked?"

Liath didn't say anything, rubbing her mouth as her expression began to return to neutral. She sniffed, letting out her breath in a cloud like she was letting go of the toxins spilled between them.

He continued, "Because you raised me to consider the world on a spectrum, with nuances, not dichotomies. It was only natural to extend this to the Folk once I learned about them. I knew I could be the bad, and they could be the good. I knew who I wanted to be. You and I went through hell together when we left Liverpool, but the lessons you taught me weren't wasted."

The tension left her shoulders; her hands slid down toward the bottom of the wheel as she glanced at him with pride in her eyes. "Aye. You know who you are."

He nodded. "Aye."

"When you face down the unknown without doubting who you are, Andrew Phalen, you will always be more formidable than your obstacles."

Bashful, like he was thirteen showing off a good report card, Andrew stared at his gloves as his cheeks warmed despite the frozen air.

Liath added, "Maybe that's why you fell to despair at the moment. Maybe you've lost yourself a bit."

He took several measured breaths. "I cut out a fundamental piece of who I am when I left you without looking back," he said. "You were a waypoint for me. You were the cairn in the fog that kept me going the right way."

Tears formed on her lashes like little crystals of ice.

"Even after I left you," he added, touching her arm. "That's why I went looking for you after university. My beacon was burned out. I was just feeling around in the dark. So, finding you up here...I'm hoping that I can make a little bit more sense to myself now. And that it can make me a better partner."

Liath nodded after a moment, using the corner of her face mask to wipe her eyes. "I understand it. I've never quite felt like myself since I left Leinster." She thought for a moment. "Forty years ago. God, has it been that long? Feels like yesterday."

"Like you don't have any roots," said Andrew.

"Ah, you know I like tree metaphors," said Liath with a soft laugh that made his toes tingle. He scooted across the truck bench and put his head on her shoulder.

They got out of the truck into frigid wind gusting off the bergs of ice that floated on the lake. He'd last come here as a teen in the summer; this was different. This was transporting. Like he was leagues and leagues away from the Cities, from any trace of warmth or green. It was out of time, not a glimpse of the civilized world in sight yet void of the Folk as well. It was a titan made of waves and ice, impenetrable and dauntless.

Rooted in place, Andrew gazed out at Superior with his chest so tight he could barely take a breath. He tried not to cry, but the tears were already determined to fall.

"She's powerful," agreed Liath.

Andrew nodded, speechless.

She slid her arm around his waist, gripping him tightly through their layers of gear. After a few minutes with only the wind and the waves speaking, she said, "Gichigumi was actually the result of volcanic activity. That's why the basalt is so dark. Imagine, all the heat then. But it's never warm now."

Andrew wiped his cheeks dry as the tears cooled and stung his skin.

She continued, "As Druids, we, like the Folk, and like the indigenous peoples of this land, commune with the natural powers of the earth. I didn't choose somewhere close to Gichigumi by accident when we left the Isles. I've had my fill of coastal cities, but Gichigumi? I'm glad I chose her. Life up here revolves around her, and she protects the land."

Fresh tears tracked down Andrew's face, and he didn't clear them away this time.

"If you can handle the cold..."

"I can."

"...Then follow me."

They picked their way out over the dimpled rocks rising above the nearly-black waters. Winter boots had the wrong kind of grip for sticking to coarse, rounded basalt. But Liath used her hands, and so Andrew did too.

It was because of this that he noticed a large stone between his thumbs that was rich red against the black basalt, banded with ivory and milky green. He gasped and knelt, using both hands to scoop up the agate and lift it for Liath to see when she sharply turned to look at him.

"Oh!" she exclaimed. "The lake gave you a gift."

Andrew turned the agate over in his palm. There was an eye-like geode on the backside, the quartz teeth glittering like dragon scales. He realized that's what the weight of the stone felt like: draconic slumber, storing the heat from the core of the earth. He sat back on his knees to slip the agate inside his suit and into the pocket of his flannel, so he could feel it against his ribs after he zipped himself back up.

Crouched on the pinnacle of the basalt, the lake wind

whipping silver strands of hair into her eyes, she gazed down at him and laughed. "You earth-blessed man."

To keep his eyes dry, he simply gave a dismissive shrug and tried to ignore the swell of his heart.

She led them further out onto the water to a boulder large enough for three or four people to perch upon, and then sat with her calves crossed and her back to the south. He carefully crouched and sat so their spines touched, exchanging some of the warmth of their core, and taking the eastern wind only on one side of their faces. She told him to use his scarf as a shield from the wind, so he obeyed. A deep shudder vibrated his muscles, but not a single thought troubled his mind.

Black waves lapped below them, persistent despite the
cellophane sheets of ice and chunky little bergs that

sloshed around on the water's surface. To the west, cliffs stained red with iron rose high above them, like they were bleeding. The deep green conifers bit into the gray sky as a soft snow started to fall on them. He blinked as he stared at the border between cliff and trees, feeling but not seeing a pair of golden eyes watching him.

Feeling silly, he lifted a gloved hand and waved a little.

"Andrew, there's something about you..."

Andrew lowered his hand back to his lap, but didn't look away from the cliffs. "Go on."

She paused for some time.

"Mum?"

Her ribs expanded and pressed against his shoulder blades. "Never mind. Let me know when you'd like to be out of the wind."

He wanted to pry. But in all his life, it never did him any good. When Liath held a secret in her hands, it would die unspoken if she chose it to be so. He asked instead, "Do I just have to trust him? Forever?"

"Trust him to do what, child?"

"That I'm his choice. That...that a faerie prince wants *me*." He visualized what it must feel like to ride the wild waves in a little boat that rocked with every push and pull of the tide. Only Micah was the water, and he was the boat.

"Andrew, that doesn't sound like his problem. That sounds like you don't believe you're worth it."

Hugging his knees, Andrew wiped his nose on his scarf.

"How could I be?"

Liath paused. "*You* need to answer that. I know your worth. It sounds like Micah knows your worth. And if the Ruby Daughter gave you the favor of her Scrying, then so does she." She turned carefully on the rock and pulled him into her side. "You're the missing piece, Andrew. Find your answer inside."

Before they made their way back to the path carved by the truck's plow, Liath stopped them at the foot of the rusty cliffs they could see from the water. The cliffs cast deep bruised shadows over them, the white sheet of the sky barely visible beneath the wall of rock.

"Look at that," breathed Andrew. "Many down in the cities wouldn't believe we have cliffs like this in Minnesota."

"Come here." Liath gestured as she sank her foot into a snowdrift up to her knee, proceeding carefully, bracing herself against the glittering and barren cliff face. "I found this spot during my sixth winter up here. I don't like coming around here in the summer. Give me a boost, yeah?" She pointed at a lip of rock over her head. Andrew knew better than to argue with her, instead interlacing his fingers with great difficulty through his mittens so she could step into his hand-hold, which she quickly bounced out of and caught both her hands on the lip of rock. Liath scrambled up onto the ledge with fluency that belied her age. When she steadied herself and brushed the ledge free of the heavy clotted snow, Andrew had to dodge the avalanche. Liath reached her hand down and helped Andrew scale the ledge after her with his boots scraping and his stomach dropping a bit as he gracelessly mounted the ledge next to his mother. He wondered how easily Micah could have climbed these cliffs straight up, two hundred feet, no scrambling or struggling like him, just easy inhuman grace.

The ledge gave them plenty of room to climb to their feet and stay away from the sharp dropoff. Liath nudged him as she turned to face the cliff again, running her hands reverently against the gabbro. "The Anshinabe that lived along the shores of Gichigumi were animists. Do you know the term?"

Andrew shook his head.

"They subscribe to the belief that every aspect of the world—the rocks, the animals, the trees, the sky—all have spiritual power. The storms are alive, the rock tells a story."

"That's not too different from what you've taught me as a Druid," Andrew said.

Liath pulled off her gloves and mittens so her slender fingers were bare as she traced the striations in the cliff face. "Aye. Isn't it telling? Animism is one of the most ancient beliefs of man, that we are only lightning bugs flashing for but a moment, miniscule against the life teeming in the world around us." She withdrew her hands from the cliff and held them out to Andrew so he could see that they had taken on the glittering gray quality of the cliff, iron staining her nails rust-red. The effect was dramatic, extraordinary. Magic. Andrew caught his breath. Liath tugged off his gloves so the icy air bit into his knuckles and his fingertips but allowed her to press his palms flat against the cold, immovable rock.

"You have become a drifting leaf as you have lost who you are," Liath said softly, auburn hair brushing her cheeks. "What you need to be is like the rock. Ancient, unmoving, sure of your place overlooking the churning waters and changing of the seasons."

Andrew's hands sank into stone. A little bit physically, but mostly his energy did, like the stone pulled his heart from his chest and told it to *calm*, like it ground down the wounds and the bruises to unblemished bone. His complexion shifted from tones of peach and white into gray and black and deep brown, like he was no longer simply himself but something greater.

"When you feel yourself become untethered..." Suddenly Liath was holding the agate he'd found in her fingers, though he hadn't felt her remove it from his jacket. She took one of his hands off the cliff and set the agate in his palm. "...Then use this as your anchor. Let it ground you again. This agate was shaken loose from the earth when there was fire and earthquakes and calving glaciers and yet, look. It is beautiful and whole on its own." She helped him cup the agate against the cliff and then leaned her cheek on the rock, eyes closed, letting out a long breath. After a moment, Andrew did the same, forehead on the gabbro, the agate sharp against his palm and sturdy against the sheet of stone, feeling his thoughts rub away as if their form was stolen away by the relentless beating of the waves.

It took him a moment of feeling silly as he leaned himself on this ancient earth before he realized this was...this was exactly, precisely what his soul needed. To turn back toward the timeless magic his mum taught him, to quite literally ground himself, to pin his feet back to the earth. This was what he needed to return to Micah, whole and centered, capable once more of loving Micah as much as he deserved.

Chapter Nine
The Fruit

Micah's only sensation was *soft*. The light was soft, the blankets were soft, and his breathing was soft. He easily shut away the guilt around missing work at To a Tea, and felt sure enough he'd be able to deal with one unexpected absence when he went in tomorrow.

Chamomile's canopy was the best part about her dreadful little hoarder's closet of a hut. Most of the inside smelled like an antique shop: tarnished brass, heavy moth-eaten linen, a hundred doilies. But over her canopy she had strings of undying roses wafting their heady fragrance onto the bed, which was stacked with furs and silks and feather pillows.

With his arm crooked and cradling his head, he listened to Chamomile breathe slowly and heavily, her back to him, twitching slightly like a dreaming cat.

Micah reached out with tentative fingers and gently combed through her long hair. There was no trace of blond in the pale light; it was all silver. It spilled like liquid over his hand and transfixed his gaze. He sighed, wistful.

"That tickles," mumbled Chamomile.

"Sorry." He pulled his hand back, awkwardly scratching his collarbone over his shirt.

"Keep doing it."

Micah smiled. He separated three strands with clumsy fingers and then began a lumpy braid. Chamomile stirred slightly, but only to tuck her blankets under her chin. Faintly through her walls, a lyre strummed sleepily.

"Hey, Chami..." He teased the braid apart, running the length of her hair through his hands. It seemed never-ending, much longer than he remembered.

Chamomile rolled over to face him, her hair draping over her shoulder, still threaded through his fingers.

He asked after a moment, "Do you think I'm formidable?"

Chamomile quirked her eyebrow, barely a glimmering smear on her forehead. "Formidable," she repeated.

"Yeah." Her reaction already told him her answer, so he braced himself.

Searching his face, her own expression veiled, she smoothed her hair back from her cheek so her pierced and pointed ear protruded skyward. "You felled the Redwood Queen."

Micah knew that trick. She always answered a question he hadn't asked when she knew he wasn't going to like what she said. He frowned. "Yeah, I know. But that wasn't in question."

Chamomile sighed through her button nose. "No, I don't think you're formidable, Micah."

Micah gave a little growl of disappointment and rubbed his face on her fuzzy pillow.

"I think you can be." She laid her warm hand on his shoulder. "Right now, you're still part of the tree. But you're not the strong trunk, so much as the soft but sweet fruit."

Snorting, Micah looked back over at her. She had a guilty frown puckered on her lips.

Micah pushed himself onto his elbow and propped his cheek against his fist. "It's an annoying, but surprisingly apt metaphor."

"That's my specialty." Her expression relaxed. "I expected you to be upset."

"Nah. If I were formidable, I wouldn't have almost frozen myself to death." He imagined Chamomile, hardly over four feet tall, lugging his six foot frame into Lilydale herself. He knew she was stronger than a human her size would be, but that was...interesting. He'd be draped over her shoulder, while she gripped his wrists and smelled liquor on his breath.

It brought back other memories, of dalliances they had together in this very bed beneath a canopy of the same roses. Maybe it was the smell of the blossoms, or the way they lent a soft pink outline to everything, but it was almost impossible for Micah to stay rooted in the moment. He felt like a careless kid again dating the first pretty girl he met in Lilydale, when he'd allowed himself to act like he wasn't just a human. That was what this all really was, wasn't it? He wasn't human. Human rules, human morality shouldn't matter to him.

His eyes drifted back to Chamomile, who leaned her cheek on her knuckles. She looked like safety, and magic, and letting go of the fears that had ruled Micah for so long.

"You don't handle your liquor as well as you wish you did." Chamomile smirked up at him.

"How did you revive me?" He leaned closer. "Kiss of life?"

Several expressions moved over Chamomile's features like seasons rapidly changing. The apples of her cheeks reddened.

Bolstered, Micah ran his hand along the velvety skin of her neck, coming to rest on her jaw with his thumb dimpling lightly on her cheek. Her long white lashes fluttered closed as he leaned close enough to smell coffee and rose hips on her breath. Micah kissed the pillow of her lower lip as he closed his eyes, finding her docile and open as he pressed their mouths together.

It was brief, but sweet like honey, and soft as a flower petal. Micah lost himself for a moment. He leaned his forearm over her shoulder on her bedding and felt her grasp the collar of his shirt with one hand. Against the rising warmth of their kiss, he pulled himself back.

Chamomile opened stunned blue eyes, blinking several times, her lips making a circle of surprise. "Micah." Her accusatory tone shook him back down into his body, into real life.

He sat back, ankles crossed, knees bent. The spell was broken, and all that remained was guilt, and Andrew's expression of betrayal and disbelief in Micah's thoughts.

"Don't." Micah covered his face, tried to breathe, but he was choked by the floral fragrance of her, the sweetness she left on his tongue. He tried to breathe, tried to pull himself away, tried to remember that she was *wrong* and would solve nothing.

"Micah?" Chamomile's voice went shrill with disbelief. "What was that?"

Still hidden in his hands, he groaned, "Damn it. Instant regret."

"Micah!" she said again. "Andrew is gonna try to fight me!" She scoffed, "That's gonna be such a pain." She sat up and wrapped her silk robe tightly around herself.

Micah rubbed his cheeks. "I-I'm sorry. I'm so—so over-whelmed. And you're so cute when you blush. Like a little cherub."

Chamomile gave his thigh a savage pinch.

Micah yelped, "Ouch!" He swatted her hand away as she came in for another pinch. "What are you doing?"

"Snapping you out of it." The goblin clenched her little knobby fists with a quick shake of her head. "We supported you last night. We made Andrew feel bad. Don't be stupid now."

Micah rubbed the sore spot. "Andrew told me to screw around while he's gone. At least you're not a random person."

"I will not be part of creating that kind of tangle!" Chamomile's soprano voice was urgent like bells chiming. She gave her hair an agitated toss, twisting it around her hand. "Monogamous people can't just turn off their desire to keep their partner to themselves. I can assure you that Andrew doesn't actually want you kissing other people."

"Maybe I don't care what he wants," Micah growled.

Chamomile found his nipple through his shirt and gave it a savage twist, ignoring his squawks of protest and the curses he flung at her. "Quit being a child!" She shifted her weight, climbing to her knees, looming over him with moisture lining the lower lashes of her large eyes. She was desperate, frustrated, disappointed. "I simply do not believe you've so suddenly given up on him. Don't you remember all you've done for him in just two years? You are ready to give that man the world. He's been gone not even two days. Why are you so ready to cast him aside?"

Micah lay with his eyes clamped shut and caught his breath, tears squeezing out through his lashes. "Okay. You got me." His bravado melted as he glanced at Chamomile and received the weight of her disappointment like she'd dropped a boulder on his chest, which was slowly crushing the breath out of his ribs. His expression crumpled. "Andrew discarded me, Chami," he whispered. "He just left. This...this was spite. But also comfort. And...I don't know. I'm lonely. I'm..." With a great sigh, Micah cast his arm over his face and ground his teeth together. "I'm sorry."

Arms crossed, Chamomile glared through the paned window next to them, her matcha skin tone still flushed rosy pink. She fought to push her hair back over her shoulders before starting to braid it instead. She sighed, her head flicking as if casting off her perturbation. Her cerulean eyes darted toward him and then away. "You're a very good lover, Micah. That was never the problem with our relationship."

Micah wiped his eyes dry. He glared at her like a disgruntled cat, only one eye open.

"I knew I could never be as committed to you as you were to me," Chamomile told him frankly. "I have three or four lovers most of the time. I give small parts of myself. Earnestly enough, but only parts, all the same." Her eyes warmed; she smiled, shaking her head. "You give everything."

Micah's throat constricted. He looked away.

"Be hurt," said Chamomile gently, reaching out and touching his face with her small fingers. "But you don't need to pretend like you're not just waiting for him to come home."

CHAPTER TEN
THE FAOLADH

ANDREW AND LIATH WERE outside for most of the day, returning only to the cabin on the hill for meals and to thaw their red fingers and toes. When he had finished cleaning their dishes from a modest dinner of cold turkey, vegetables, and fresh bread, he left his mum rummaging through her herbs and dialed Micah's number on the red phone. It rang a few times again, making his heart hammer.

"Andrew?"

Andrew smiled at the sound of Micah's bright meadow voice. "Hey. Is this a good time?"

"I don't have the best reception. I'm in Lilydale."

"Actually?"

"Yeah. No reason not to be. Like you said, I haven't d..." His voice faded. But Andrew had heard the bitterness. "...about being Fae."

"Right." Andrew grimaced.

"Just gonna get drunk..." Faded. "Since you...and I might..." Static, half-formed words. "I wish you..." Silence.

"Micah?"

"Hello? I ca..."

"Hey, I can't hear you. I'll let you go. Have a good time, but be safe." Andrew paused. "I'm sorry, and I love you."

"Hello? You..." Faded. "...Like I...just...home." Static. "I love you." Micah paused. "You know I do." The line fell silent and then turned to the urgent beeping that told him there was no more connection.

Andrew frowned and put the phone on the cradle. Micah was drunk again. It was almost certainly because of Andrew that he was drinking at all. He'd consumed alcohol maybe twice since Andrew met him, and then it had been champagne on Christmas or one beer at a brewery. Knowing his own selfish cowardice affected Micah this way sparked the impulse to leave *now* and go fix things. But he didn't know how he could fix things if he was still mending himself.

"Andrew," said Liath after a moment, her back to him, "if you're ready to polish that agate, I've got everything set up." She pulled a stool out from under the kitchen bar, which looked more like a science lab now with several sanding tools, a tub of water, and protective gear.

He stood up, hugging his elbows, trying to focus on Liath rather than worrying about how he ruined his boyfriend. "This must not be the first agate you've polished."

"Oh, no. I love hunting for agates." As she sat on a second stool, she nodded to a shelf on the wall with a small army of the iron-rich stones looming over them. "Sometimes I sell them to tourists at the park station in the summers, but only when the time feels right."

Andrew sat on the stool she indicated and rolled the rough agate between his fingers, grinding his teeth in silence. He felt Liath watching him—she always did that, always scrutinized him till he caved and told her everything. But he was older now, and felt fiercely protective of Micah. Just because Micah was angry at him didn't mean he wouldn't fight anyone who said a bad word about him.

Since he was refusing to look at her, Liath set a hand on his shoulder. "You know that you can love someone and give yourself to them whether or not you deem yourself perfect. That's vulnerability."

Andrew blinked. "Are you telepathic?"

"No. Your expressions just have not changed at all since you were a lad," said Liath, nudging his chin. "You grind your teeth when you feel guilty. But there's pining in your forehead. This long little crease over your eyebrows showed up when you were eleven."

"*Mum*," muttered Andrew, because she was *exactly* right.

Smiling with satisfaction, Liath added, "And we have established your self-worth is nonexistent."

With a disgruntled hum, Andrew leaned their shoulders together.

Liath prepared the workspace in silence for a bit. Then

she said, "Believe it or not, I also don't think you were in the wrong to come and find me by yourself."

Andrew shook his head, dubious. "Even Sam was mad at me on the phone last night."

"About what, do you think?" she asked. "Is it how you went about it?"

"Oh, yes. I was very insistent that I wasn't good enough for Micah. Before this depression episode, I at least trusted myself to be loving, and attentive, and, I don't know...I could make him laugh. But I became some kind of shell of a man, made up of my deficits. My addict parents and half-empty teacups left everywhere, and a lazy work ethic." Realization made his heart drop. He had never said this aloud, but it seemed like the time and his mum seemed like the person to tell. "I don't even really like my business, mum. Sam's much better at it than me. All I wanna do is read history books."

"Are you so old and set in your ways that you can't make a change?" She raised an eyebrow.

Andrew frowned. "No, I suppose not."

"And is Micah so supernatural he has no flaws as well?"

"Oh, no." He offered her a humorless laugh. "He always pees on the toilet seat. And he bickers with his dad all the time. And he *always* leaves his dirty clothes all over."

"Sounds like he's allowed to be imperfect, but you aren't."

Andrew glared at her. Liath's chestnut-colored eyes

danced merrily as she propped her chin on her fist.

His eyes drifting up to the shelf of agates, Andrew said thoughtfully, "The cliff, though. That...that was restorative. I can feel myself climbing out of the dark."

She nodded. "I spent many a winter days on that ledge. Meditating for hours. Wishing not just once or twice that I would freeze to death out there."

He flinched, but understood—it was perhaps a more poetic dream of death than when he'd wanted to crash through a guard rail on his way up here.

She stroked his hair and said softly, "It gets better. Keep climbing."

Andrew leaned into her long hand, his throat tightening as he managed a silent nod.

Liath studied his face for several long moments before finally sighing and turning toward the workstation. The air between them shifted, focused. Andrew straightened, attentive. She demonstrated how to use the sanding tools, stressed the importance of keeping the agate wet as you sanded, and explained when to know to switch to a finer grit. Then she handed him the goggles and a dust mask.

Fixing his goggles as Liath turned on the motor for the dremel sander they were using, Andrew said, "So, this wolf. Is she just a wolf?"

"I'm sure you know she's not." The ends of her fire-and-ice hair brushed his cheek as she stood and hovered over him.

He just barely touched the metal to the agate, testing the effects, the water chilling his fingertips as he began to polish off the coarse buildup over the stone's banding. "You told me stories of Nan and the wolves when I was little. Can you tell me another?"

Liath nodded, speaking into his ear as if she were cradling him as a child. "Your nan Natalie lived on a sheep farm three generations old in the hills in Leinster, which is a lengthy drive in from the city center."

"Ah. Hence 'culchie.'"

"Aye. She didn't want me to live in the fast-paced city, either. Why do you think I got out of there as fast as I did?" Liath shook her head. "If only I hadn't. Imagine, Andrew. No Liverpool for either of us. Just Irish hills."

Andrew contemplated the thought as he watched the iron-rich dust settle on his fingers as he wore it off the agate. It had a certain wild and magical appeal, it was true. But no Liverpool would have meant they'd never needed to immigrate to Minnesota. Which would have meant that he'd never met Micah. He slowly shook his head. "It's been a lot of pain, true, but I can no longer wish my life went differently than it did."

"Look at you, accepting the hand fate has dealt you," said Liath, her lips quirking.

With a dismissive snort, Andrew nudged her arm and said, "You let me get you side-tracked."

"Ah, right." She gazed at the blood ward dangling at Andrew's throat, silent for a moment. "Anyway. Natalie grew up during an age where magic was everywhere, and the *faoladh*, the Folk, and the humans lived in open relation with one another. It wasn't necessarily peaceful, but it was collaborative. In the countryside, this relationship lasted much longer than in large cities like Dublin or London, where the Industrial Revolution turned to iron and pushed out the Folk. But for her, living in the Irish hills on what could remain a fairly primitive farm, she had just as many mates who were Fae or *faoladh* as she knew ordinary girls. When I was a girl, the *faoladh* were scarce—moving farther away from civilization, or else falling in numbers to poachers or disease."

"Wouldn't the *faoladh* protect themselves from poaching?" he asked. "Couldn't they reason with humans?"

"Ah. Time to switch to the next grit." She turned off the dremel and held out the next metal tip. Andrew lowered the agate into the water bowl, dried his fingers on his shirt, and pulled out the dremel tip to replace it with the one indicated. When he was back to polishing, Liath answered, "At times, like with the Ryans, yes. Humans and *faoladh* can reason with one another. But sometimes, the *faoladh* were sought *because* they were extraordinary, to be exploited, imprisoned, or controlled, as rare things often are. Not bound by the phases of the moon, they are able to put on their wolfskins at will. They neither prefer to be bipedal or to be beasts, as they felt kinship to both forms, neither wholly beast nor wholly man."

That was a sentiment Micah expressed on many occasions, thought Andrew. A foot in each world, and a stranger to both.

Liath had something burbling in her potion bottle, which played like a bass track behind her storytelling while the sanding held the rhythm. When she spoke of her family and her childhood, her brogue got heavier, making Andrew strain to understand her through it. "When your nan was in her courtship with granddad Phalen, they were walking home to her farm at twilight when they saw an odd woman leaning over a bush, chattering seemingly to herself, prodding the bush with a long broomstick. Your granddad was intuitive and brash—" Here, she paused, an eyebrow raising, eyes roaming over Andrew.

"I wouldn't know anything about that," remarked Andrew, intensely staring at his work.

Her eyes danced. " —And must have sensed something was amiss. He tossed a stone at her feet and drew her attention, and when he did, a wolf shot from beneath the bush and bit off three of her fingers."

"Cripes," said Andrew with a laugh.

"Raving, the woman mounted her broomstick and flew away. Ah. Pause. See how you went a bit too hard here? And keep the stone wetter. Leave that edge be now, it's done. Let's switch grits."

"Wait, are witches real?"

Once he was sanding again, she said without answering his question, "The *faoladh* cast off his wolfskin and was but a boy, wiping blood from his lips and crying, clasping Phalen's hands with gratitude. The boy followed them back to the farm and, feeling for the boy who was seemingly alone, Natalie fed him a warm dinner of sheep's milk and bread, telling him he could stay the night if only he left the sheep alone.

"For three days, the *faoladh* boy wore his wolfskin and stared at the southern hills all day, howling mournfully all through the night. Natalie kept feeding him, though her parents bid her not to. On the fourth morning, a man and woman came to the farm. The *faoladh* threw off his wolfskin and embraced the man and woman, who spoke to him with yips and growls as the wolves do. They all left together without so much as sniffing the air near the sheep pastures. On the fifth day, the *faoladh* family had left an offering on the doorstep of the farmstead—an enormous buck and an impressive doe, and five hares strung on a line, as well as a bloody broomstick with a snapped handle.

"After this encounter, Phalen and Natalie were regarded as having a touch of magic themselves, and the farmstead flourished under them. Your nan swears she saw the *faoladh* boy every year when she went with the family to the Litha market in Dublin, and every year he sent her family home with pelts, lard, and jerky of the finest quality." Liath stuck her foot behind her and patted the deerskin rug.

"This was hers, a gift from the *faoladh* boy she saved."

Satisfied with the smooth yet unrefined shape of his agate, Andrew stopped sanding, placing it carefully in the water bowl. "Is there a family of *faoladh* here with the wolf I saw?"

Liath looked out the windows, sadly shaking her head. "Not to my knowledge. Who knows? I tried to ask around, when she first appeared—it was maybe five years back? Time slides oddly up here. Anyway, nothing came of it, and the DNR denied any movement near here from the local packs, so whatever pack she was with must have been small and avoided detection."

"Is she grown?"

"As a wolf, yes, now she is. She was an awkward gangly thing when I met her, barely capable of hunting. But last I saw, she doesn't look older than...seven or eight as a girl."

"What's your relationship with her?"

Liath shrugged, shaking her head slowly. "It's been a challenge, knowing what to do or not to do with her. I don't want her to treat me as family. I'd rather her be like the *faoladh* boy my ma met, crying for his family until they returned for him. But the longer it goes, the more she breaks my heart, being all alone up here."

Andrew nodded, leaning his cheek on his fist, his eyelids growing heavy. She sensed this at once, patting his leg, standing up from the couch. "The day draws on." She lifted the bottle from the flame using a pair of tongs and tipped it into a transparent teacup. "I brewed you a tea that's helped my mood lift during spells like yours over the years. Drink, and then feel free to rest. I know things are a bit dull up here, without a television or your fancy smartphones, but—"

Andrew shook his head vigorously enough that Liath trailed off. Accepting the cup, he said, "I enjoy the change of pace."

"I have collected some books," offered Liath. She went to her nature altar and stooped down, pulling out a number of thin volumes and returning to him. "Druid folktales, as well as Minnesota natural histories, and books by Anshinabe locals. This one is on the formation of Gichigumi. This is about Laurentia, the old North American continent. The notebooks on the bottom are notes I took after talking to Anshinabe locals about the land."

Taking the stack, Andrew said eagerly, "Ah, this will easily occupy me for the rest of the day. Thank you." He set the books on his knees and flipped through the Minnesota history book, pausing on diagrams and old maps from the time that the state was settled.

When Liath remained silent and motionless, Andrew glanced up at her. Her dark eyes were glassy with tears. She swiped them away and said with a tremulous smile, "I'm just so proud of you." Awkward, she hurried back to the bunsen burner and left him to his books and his flaming cheeks.

Chapter Eleven
The Folk

When he left Chamomile's hut, Micah looked down at his socks and boots next to her door, then experimentally flexed his toes on the ground. Really, it wasn't that cold to walk on. Like floorboards in the winter, but not like walking barefoot outside. He thought Ingrid would be happy if he finally went barefoot in Lilydale like everyone else did.

Pulling out his phone, he frowned while he read his texts with Julian.

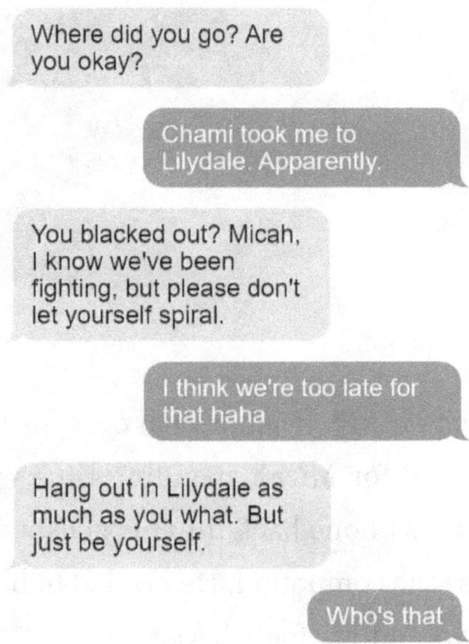

Micah cringed at his own maudlin messages. That was one thing Julian always accepted about him, though. How dramatic he could be. Micah imagined what their life would have been like without magic—he'd have been a theater kid, probably, and Julian would have been in the front row for all his shows.

He typed another message.

Satisfied and strangely emotional over his father's new-found acceptance for Micah spending time with the Folk, Micah slipped his phone back into his pocket and then cast his gaze across the compound. He needed to be busy so he'd stop thinking about his foolish kiss.

Behind the kiln throne, next to the undying garden, something resembling a kitchen was under a thatched clay roof held up on support beams carved with swirls, flowers, leaves, and woodland creatures. A trio of short, green-skinned faeries were busy over a large black cauldron which wafted something savory in Micah's direction.

He sank his hands into his jogger pockets and ducked into the kitchen area to peer into the cauldron. One of the faeries, a small male, jumped when he looked up at him. He was wearing a Pokémon tee.

"Oh! Hello," said a female next to him, her bark-brown hair in a sock bun on top of her head. "You must be...the Prince?"

"Micah is fine," he laughed.

The short-haired female next to her tittered, and the male shook his head in horror.

The one who spoke to him touched her chest and said, "I'm Brynn, and this is Gwynn and Spinn. We're the goblin triplets."

"I love your names! What are you making?"

"Potato-leek stew," answered the female at the end, Gwynn.

"And fresh bread," squawked Spinn, with a slight lisp.

"Can I help at all?" asked Micah.

The three goblins exchanged looks of confusion with their pale green eyes.

"You want to help us?" asked Gwynn. "But you're royalty."

Micah shrugged. "I'm just Micah."

Spinn started to say something, but Gwynn reached over and pinched him.

Brynn piped up, "If you insist, you can cut up some more carrots over on that counter. It's a bit short for you, milord, because we're the regular cooks in the compound."

"That's okay. I can make it work." He stepped past them, his mouth watering at the smell from the cauldron, and then washed his hands with the water at the pump-sink in the corner of the kitchen shelter. He had to kneel to really effectively cut carrots, the trio whispering about him while he worked with a grin on his face.

After a bit, Micah's back was slick with sweat from the

heat of the cauldron, and he'd cut more carrots than he'd ever seen in his life. Now he was mincing fresh garlic cloves, the oil coating his fingertips and the smell strong enough to make his eyes sting.

Back in the Redwoods, the kitchens were carved into a fallen redwood tree and occupied by stony-faced goblins who took no breaks and rarely slept. Their only pleasure had been inventing more ways to hook humans on their desserts. Before feasts—which were frequent—the goblins were whipped in front of everyone and threatened with death if the food did not turn out perfectly.

Here, in Lilydale, the triplets were humming in harmony and flicking each other with nibs of carrots and circles of sliced potato. Spinn, seemingly the runt of the trio, complained the most loudly at his treatment.

Chamomile appeared at the pillar closest to Micah, making him jump and narrowly avoid nicking his thumb. She scowled at his work, crossed her arms, and then looked toward the cauldron. "I hope you're making him work hard, kids," Chamomile said to the goblins.

"We wouldn't dare, Miss Chami," said the goblin with the short hair, Gwynn. It was interesting seeing them by Chamomile, whose skin was still green-tinged but much lighter than theirs.

Chamomile was his height when she walked up to where he knelt next to the counter. "You skulked off," she told him.

"Yup."

She glanced back at the trio. "I need to take him with me," she told them. "Sorry." She grabbed Micah by the back of his sweatshirt and hauled him away from the kitchen.

"Hey!" He fell onto his ass, dropping the knife on the counter on his way down. "I was helping. Let go! Chami, I can *walk*."

She let him climb to his feet but then hooked her finger through the strings of his joggers and dragged him up to the picket fence around the undying garden. She clicked the latch on its tiny gate and let them in. In the winter, they turned it into a hothouse, with a bespelled glass dome above it to keep in the humidity that helped the plants thrive.

The gnome from the night market was inside. She blinked up at Chamomile where she sat on her knees with a basket of strawberries next to her, and three of the red fruits in her hands.

"Hi, Syabira," said Micah. "Better get out of here. I think I'm about to be lectured."

Syabira smiled slightly at them with her shining peach lips. Her ears were small and furred like a deer's, and with her short coiled curls uncovered, you could see the two small ivory horns on her forehead.

Micah flopped into the dirt with his back to the picket fence and crossed his arms, glaring at Chamomile.

"You're going to kill the greenery if you don't fix your

attitude," Chamomile said matter-of-factly. She pointed at the strawberry leaves by his hip, which shivered and bent away from him.

"Oh, so you brought me in here on purpose?"

"Yes," said Chamomile. "Ingrid told me that you killed a plant at work yesterday, so you need to figure that out. I'm not suggesting, I'm telling you that you're going to. If you're going to spend time in Lilydale, you're going to learn to honor it, rather than accidentally killing things because your emotions are out of control. Before, it was the Redwood Queen. But what if it's a loved one? Or an innocent person?"

Micah said nothing, unable to argue.

"If you kill my plants," said Syabira softly, leaning down to speak into Micah's ear, "I would consider cutting off one of your toes."

Micah eyed Syabira, who looked quite serious. "Yes, ma'am."

"May it not come to that." Syabira smiled gently, brushing off a strawberry, dropping it into her basket, and then wandering down to the opposite end of the garden. The leaves stirred against her bare legs as she walked with one foot in front of the other down a narrow soil aisle marked with small round stepping stones.

Chamomile dropped into the dirt, facing him with her legs and arms crossed and irritation creasing her usually delicate features.

"I wasn't supposed to," Micah explained.

"What?"

"In the Redwoods. Connecting with plants for the sake of plants was laughable."

"Why?" asked Syabira from a distance, outrage flashing in her doe eyes.

"The Folk who worked with plants were meant to make thorns or traps or statues of the Queen," Micah said. "That's why I was so excited about you when I came here." He nodded to Syabira. "You wouldn't get away with peddling flowers or running nurseries there."

Syabira cut a glare at nobody in particular before her expression grew tender as she turned her attention to a yellow hibiscus blossom larger than her hand.

"Well," said Chamomile with an indignant huff, "it's different here. Lilydale thrives because we care for it, and it for us, whether someone is directly involved in the gardening or not. And you have an affinity to plants, whether you like it or not."

"I...I do like it," said Micah softly. "I've always liked them. They make more sense than people."

"Aye to that," said Syabira.

Micah looked down at the plants growing merrily on all sides of them. The rich smell tricked his brain into believing it was midsummer. He held a serrated perilla leaf delicately in his hand, allowing the coarse texture to soothe the feeling of his blistered fingertips. As he let his gaze un-focus on the leaf, his pelvis relaxed into the soil, which was cool against his bare ankles. He felt more like himself among the leaves and the dirt, formless and thoughtless, just another living organism thriving in the hothouse. He brushed the leaf with the pads of his fingers—and they suddenly tingled as if going near a lit burner on a stove. Micah sucked in a breath and snatched his hand back. He looked down, turning his hand over. The frostbite blisters were gone.

His mouth dropped open as he rubbed the skin near his cuticles where the blisters had gathered, but it was smooth and undamaged. "Bro."

In the opposite corner of the greenhouse, Syabira straightened, her liquidy eyes going round. She took a small step closer to Micah, curiosity evident on her face before she caught herself and withdrew, but not before she allowed herself a happy little grin.

Chamomile looked unsurprised. Sharp teeth showing, she grinned and shoved his leg with her foot. "Healed yourself, did you?" she said. "Didn't even break a sweat."

"I knew perilla leaves were said to have healing properties, but...how can I just access them like that?" asked Micah.

"When you cast other worries from your head, you might find you can access quite a bit more plant magic than you think," Chamomile said. She glanced at Syabira. "Right, Bee?"

The gnome straightened and paused with a carrot still blanketed in soil dangling from her hand. "All the other things you concern yourself with likely hold you back," agreed Syabira.

Micah gave the gnome a long look before finally muttering, "Easy for you to say, gardening all day and selling flowers all weekend."

Nonplussed, Syabira remarked, "I make a choice to focus all my energy on flora. You could too."

"I don't remember asking for you to join in on the lecturing," Micah said, petulance sneaking into his voice like coffee that brewed too bitter. He heard himself, and embarrassment heated his neck to boiling. How old was he? The gnome glared fearlessly at him until he sighed and said, "Sorry. That was rude."

"Indeed," said Syabira with a sniff, returning her attention to cleaning the carrots.

Micah stared at his knees. He'd never mouthed off to Syabira like that. She'd shown him nothing but patience over the years. He was going to have to make it up to her. Find her a new trowel or something.

Chamomile cleared her throat loudly. "Now that you're done being an asshole, you get to talk to me." He shut his eyes. "You've tried many times over the years to avoid serious conversations with me, but it won't do this time around. We need to talk about that kiss. Your guilt spoiled the enjoyment of it, which is what you get for trying to act like you're not a serial monogamous."

Syabira's gaze snapped back over to them and then just as quickly away. Her black eyebrows rose and her lips pursed; she quickly dug her hand into the soil and resumed pulling up vegetables to make it look like she hadn't heard.

Fortunately too absorbed by his misery to notice, Micah sighed, hugging his arms around his stomach. Setting the perilla leaf on his knee, he said flatly, "I told Andrew repeatedly how committed I was to him. I told him repeatedly how I didn't want anyone else. Look how quickly I turned on that."

She nodded silently. After a few minutes, she plucked a leaf from a mint plant next to her and set it on her tongue. She chewed for a moment and then said, "We don't scorn wounded animals for acting out. I don't scorn you for seeking comfort."

Micah bowed his head and raked his fingers through his hair.

"Besides," Chamomile added, poking his chest, "I know I'm very comforting." When he looked up to glare at her, she winked at him.

"Don't get me wrong," Micah admitted, straightening again and tracing the petals on a strawberry blossom, "you have a soft and curvy appeal."

"I don't need your validation, but thank you." Chamomile dropped her chin onto her fist, raising her brows. "But...?"

"But I want Andrew." He curled his fingers into fists. His bones ached with yearning. "So, so badly."

She patted his hand. "I know."

"Do you think I blew it?"

"I hope not," she said, pulling her waterfall of silver-white hair over her shoulder and twisting it into a rope. "I struggle to imagine someone as rational as Andrew antagonizing you for doing something he told you to do. Even if he's upset that you actually did it."

Regardless, it was going to be messy when Andrew made it home, thought Micah. Many things to talk about. Many wounds to stitch up, perhaps for both of them.

Chamomile looked up over Micah's shoulder as the female goblins carried the cauldron out between them, with Spinn holding a platter with the bread on it behind them. "Ah. Food. I'm ravenous." She lunged with an open mouth at Micah's arm, and he yelled and shoved her away, chasing after her out of the garden while Syabira shook her head at them.

"I thought there were more Folk than this," said Micah as they sat around an enormous fire that was keeping his toes delightfully toasty.

The fire was ringed in with giant toadstools, stumps

turned to seats, and painted boulders laid with cushions. There was a large fallen log sanded flat on top which was being used as a table. It held several carafes of mulled wine and honey mead, pots of tea, and even a crystal-clear pitcher of water that came from a well dug near the frozen stream. But there were only a dozen or so Folk eating, and they left a healthy amount of space between themselves and Micah, Ingrid, and Chamomile.

"Some are reluctant to interact with you," Ingrid told him frankly, her long legs crossed as she sat on a particularly tall stump that seemed to be cut for her substantial height.

"Oh." Micah frowned. Across the fire from him, blue-skinned Lina exchanged an awkward look with a red-haired male sitting under a flannel blanket with her.

Glancing at Ingrid, Micah said more lightly, "I guess Folk might not be crazy about your half-human brother lurking around."

"It's not that," Chamomile said at once.

Adjacent to them near the steps up to the kiln throne, Syabira sat on a large spotted toadstool with her legs crossed on top. She took a sip from a teacup and then told Micah, "We have known you existed for twenty years, but you have made yourself scarce."

Guilt dragged at Micah's stomach.

"Some of us feel that as a wound," Lina explained. She glanced at Nox with the goat pupils, and the goblin triplets, and the chalky-skinned sprite Wex, and then chimed, "Not me, of course."

"No, no. Nobody's obligated to receive me warmly," Micah insisted with a wave of his hand. He awkwardly took a long drink of honey mead, which loosened up his twisted insides. "I have a lot to prove here yet."

"Do you intend to?" Wex's eyes flashed with a challenge. She hiccupped when Lina punched her arm.

Micah nodded. "Yeah. I do." He looked at Ingrid and Chamomile, who were staring at him with particular intensity and matching faint smiles. He dropped his voice to a hushed whisper and said, "Maybe I should bring gifts."

"Yes," said Chamomile immediately.

"You two want to go up to Target with me?" He grinned. Ingrid groaned, "Do I have to?"

"Yes," said Micah and Chamomile at the same time.

As the night grew darker in Lilydale, the fires were lit and reflected off the ice walls like a thousand sunsets. Ingrid sat on the kiln throne primarily because it afforded her an excellent vantage point to watch the Folk revel around the enormous fire at her feet. The golden flames licked at the sky and made the city lights beyond invisible against them.

Micah and Chamomile were engaged in some quick,

complex dance to a frantic song Fethir played on a piccolo. Ingrid suspected they were improvising the moves, but she envied how easily they mirrored each other's rhythm. She envied how they drew the eyes of the Folk. She envied how rapidly Micah had captured the affections of Lilydale with nothing more ostentatious than small gifts and his time.

She was convinced he didn't realize he'd done it yet; in the Redwoods, he was always authentically himself, and it had always gone unnoticed. In the Redwoods, Micah was always in the shadow of the trees and the tall, vicious, brilliant Fae nobility who circled the Redwood Queen like wolves waiting to snap up her leftover kill.

Here, though, Micah stood out among the small, common Folk. They all smelled his noble blood and observed his potential as easily as Chamomile had when they'd first arrived in Minnesota. Around Ingrid, he looked clumsy and small. But not around here. Around here, he became naturally prominent, like a cairn seen through the fog.

Ingrid took a slow sip from a goblet of mulled wine, unconsciously tapping her foot as the jig reached its crescendo. Micah's height was perfect relative to Chamomile's to whisk her around the heat of the fire, wobbling light gleaming on his hair turned to sage in the saturated darkness. He'd pulled off his shirt and was slick with a sheen of sweat. The bobcat skull and antlers tattooed across his chest seemed sacred in this setting, serving as a reminder to the Folk exactly how capable he was.

Ingrid was nauseous with pride as everything fell into place, made sense, justified each stepping stone they'd struggled their way onto through the river of Micah's life. Everything that felt wrong with him, that felt unfair and undue, it was finally, wholly, completely overshadowed by his full potential.

She touched her cheek, startled when her fingers came back damp with tears.

Chapter Twelve
The Ambush

AFTER A DAY AND a night of revelry in Lilydale, moving back into his human role felt cumbersome, frustrating, and unrewarding for Micah. In his office, he stood in front of the row of plants while he held the manager's phone to his ear. With his other hand, he caressed the unhappy leaves on the plant he'd killed earlier in the week. He'd given it a few drops of water to dampen the soil and kept apologizing to it in his head.

"I really don't think that's necessary." Micah willed the phone in his hand to "An occasional no-show doesn't warrant a house call, does it?"

"You and Diana *both* no-showed yesterday," remarked Christina.

Heat crept up Micah's neck. "Yeah. I won't make a habit out of it."

"And this is Diana's second."

Micah rolled his eyes slightly. He didn't know how to tell her how pleased he actually was that Diana had stopped coming to work. Let her disappear.

The aglaonema trembled under his touch. He scowled and took a breath, trying to get rid of his bitterness, but the plant kept shriveling.

Micah slumped heavily into his desk chair. Diana was really ruining his mood.

Christina continued, "I sent a text to your baristas yesterday. Most of them agreed things between you and Diana were pretty uncomfortable the day before. Anna told me something weird happened outside the shop when you left, but couldn't say what it was." Christina paused. "Micah, you have a practically perfect record since you took over the Randolph store. This isn't the end of the world, but it's very out of character for you to allow personal business to get in the way of your work."

"I'm only human," he muttered.

"Say again?"

"Never mind."

"I only ask you to do this since you also told me several months ago you had some concerns for Diana's wellbeing at home. If you say her boyfriend started an altercation with you, aren't you worried about her? I assumed you would be."

"Right." He silenced a sigh. Curse his obvious tendency toward altruism. "I'll go out and check on her." He set the phone back down on the cradle, pressing his thumb and forefinger hard enough into his eyes that phosphenes appeared in his vision.

He pulled out his cell phone to get the number Andrew had been calling from. Though he didn't expect much to come of the effort, he punched the number into the landline on his desk. It rang for about a minute before he hung up.

Micah stood up again, sighing at the aglaonema. "Sorry, buddy. It seems you're a victim of my lack of control. We'll keep working, okay?"

Shrugging back on his jacket, Micah shuffled out of his office. With a mumbled greeting to the baristas, he dropped a bag of peppermint tea into a cup of hot water, flipped his aviator sunglasses onto the bridge of his nose, and left the shop. The baristas watched him leave with whispers of gossip.

"He looks hungover," pink-haired Faith whispered to Colton.

"Peppermint tea is good for a hangover," said Colton.

Anna put a hand on her hip. "Aren't you seventeen?"

"I have an older sister."

Leaning over the counter with a frown of concern, Faith said as she watched Micah disappear down the street, "I've been here two years and I've never seen him that cranky."

"Is he going to Diana's house?" Anna asked them.

Colton shrugged. "If he is, I pity her."

With a swoon, Faith set her hand on her cheek and said, "Real talk, though. Pissed off Micah is *hella* sexy."

Micah couldn't hear them, but his ears tickled with the

certainty they were talking about him as he marched west from the shop. He'd grabbed Diana's address from the employee roster and punched it into his phone GPS. It wasn't a very long walk, but it made him regret that he was hungover for the second time since Andrew had left on his trip. Andrew really needed to hurry up and finish whatever soul-searching he was doing up there.

Micah growled out something akin to a sigh as he scanned the houses coming up on his left. The neighborhood around Diana was cramped and littered, all short and steep front yards and broken down, dented cars parked along the street. Diana's house was small, but tidy compared to its neighbors.

"I do not want to do this," he muttered. "Do. Not. Want. To do this." He kicked the sidewalk with the toe of his boot a few times, glad Andrew had talked him into his own pair of Docs their first winter together. If for some reason their relationship fell apart, Micah suspected he was going to have to completely disappear from his current life. There were traces of Andrew everywhere now.

Grinding his teeth so hard his jaw hurt, Micah climbed the carefully salted stairs up to Diana's front door. There was a metal star in the center of a frosted glass window, so he couldn't see anything inside past the small three-season porch. Micah pressed the bronzed doorbell button and winced at the off-key tune that played. He flipped his sunglasses up onto his head, using them to pin his hair back from his forehead.

The door cracked open a moment later.

Diana peered through the crack and her eyes bugged wide. "Micah? What...shit, was I supposed to work today?"

"Yeah right," he intoned. "You really didn't know?"

Diana's expression shifted several times, from embarrassment into something more calculating. "You shouldn't have come here," she whispered.

"I was told to come here," he said with some bitterness.

"I'm fine," she said. "Bye."

"You don't sound—"

The door slammed.

Micah scowled briefly. Then he realized that was the end of it. She was alive, wasn't she? And, if he was lucky, she would no-call, no-show one more time and be automatically fired from To a Tea. He shrugged and turned on his heel to march back down the steps and proceed with his underwhelming day. He sipped the hot tea, but it only made him think of Andrew.

The door behind him creaked.

"Hey, pretty boy, why are you leaving so fast?"

"Kill me," he muttered, rolling his neck back, flipping on his sunglasses, and glaring into the white sky. He slowly turned around.

Tom stood on his front landing without a shirt on, speckled with small cheap-looking tattoos, arms crossed over his chest.

Curling his lip, Micah asked him, "Do you wanna fight, or something? Duke it out over 'your girl.'" He put the term in air quotes. "'Cause I've got a lot of pent-up aggression. And you know, I'd have a lot fewer problems if your girlfriend hadn't kissed me."

He smiled slowly. "You don't know anything about her, do you?"

"Honestly?" Micah shrugged. "Can't say that I do."

"Diana runs with a bad crowd. You should've kept your hands off her."

"I *literally* didn't touch her!" Micah exclaimed. Then more loudly he called, "Hey, Diana, you should come back out! I'd like to settle this for good."

Tom's eyes glinted. The look on his face twisted Micah's stomach into a knot. For a man who had tried to deck him just this week, Tom looked much less bothered by him than before. He wished his words could crawl back into his mouth, but then Diana reappeared, arms across her chest, wearing a short black skater dress and knee-high socks. Tom sniffed before retreating into the house, pinching Diana's ass as he walked past her.

Her meek discomfort from the last time at the shop was gone. She gazed indifferently down at Micah, her breath pluming in a cloud in front of her lips.

Two wolves battled in Micah's chest for a moment. Was he going to be a manager, or the bitter and lonely man whose boyfriend ditched him because of this girl? *Split the difference,* he thought resolutely. "Why did you tell your boyfriend I kissed you? If you were trying to piss him off, you should have kept me out of it."

"It had nothing to do with him," said Diana calmly.

"Well then what the fuck?" So much for splitting the difference.

Raising her brow, she remarked, "I've never heard you swear."

"Diana," he growled, wishing she wasn't looming over him , "kissing me like that was a dick move. Even if my boyfriend hadn't caught us—and yes, that did royally screw me over, by the way—I didn't ask for it or encourage it. Wouldn't you say it was sexual assault?"

She drummed her black fingernails on her elbow for a moment. "I'm sorry. I had to confirm something."

"Confirm what?"

"That you're a faerie."

Micah's blood went cold. "The hell are you talking about?"

She smiled thinly. "Do you know what my Master's is in?"

"...No?"

"Folklore," she said. She moved partway into her door and stepped into a pair of scuffed up boots. Then she thumped down the steps and stood in front of him, inspecting his expression with her chin tilted back and no warmth in her features.

Micah stifled a snicker. "Good luck in the job market, I

guess."

She curled her lip slightly. "I've seen a dozen woodcuts of the look on your face when you grabbed Tom. You were...feral."

"You sound like a crazy person," Micah said, hands up, heart noisily pounding in his ears. "All I was looking for was some accountability. I'm going to go." He started to turn his back on her.

"I can't let you leave," she said calmly. "I'd like to. I think you're lovely. But it's kind of like a sorority, and I'm the newest pledge."

Ominous nonsense, that. It made Micah's chest clench. A boot scuffed on his left, and a jacket rustled to his right. Slowly, dreadfully, he let his gaze slide off Diana and looked around. Two women flanked him, warmly dressed in layers of black, one with long blue hair, the other with a dark green pixie cut. The blue-haired woman smiled pleasantly, but the pixie-cut glowered at him like she thought he pulled off her hairstyle better than her.

"Have you heard the thing about unicorn blood granting immortality?" asked Diana.

Feeling nauseous but refusing to look as frightened as he felt, Micah asked brightly, "Dude, are you guys witches? Let me guess. Your name is Raven." He pointed to the woman with the pixie cut, and then to the blue-haired woman, "And your name is Midnight."

"No," said the blue-haired woman, "I'm Raven." She

grinned.

Ignoring their aside, Diana said, "Faerie blood...we're thinking it might kinda be the same. Or if it's not quite the same, it might make us feel *very* good."

"Well, I'm not a faerie, so." He shrugged.

The two women exchanged a look.

Diana's eyes widened. She glanced at the two women, shifting her weight. "You are not a human," she insisted, voice cracking. "I thought you were gonna puke when I used that idiom. And sometimes your eyes do this weird color-changing thing. And also, there's no way you dye your hair so often that you can *never* see your roots."

Micah tilted his head and said dubiously, "All...right then."

"And anyway, kissing you confirmed it," said Diana.

"How's that exactly?"

"High emotions are said to smell different in the Folk," said Diana, back in control. "Something like a pheromone. Had to get your heart rate to spike. And as soon as I knew you weren't just into men, I gave it a shot. You smelled like...lilacs and spring grass."

Laughing bitterly, Micah scraped his hair back with his hands, screwing up his beanie. "Holy shit! Honestly, what a relief."

Diana stared blankly at him.

"This makes so much more sense! I didn't lead you on or anything. You're just insane."

The woman with the green pixie cut sneered at Micah. She spat, "Misogynist."

"I think we should take him inside," remarked Diana. "It's a bit obvious, blood all over the snow."

"Don't worry about that," said the blue-haired woman. "I'll clean up after him."

"I don't like where this is going," Micah muttered. If Andrew were around, he'd already have his sword out. Hell, if Andrew were around, he'd probably already be fighting.

"Diana," Micah said to her with eyebrows raised to make sure he didn't glare at her, "I know this isn't your speed. I believe you think it is, but I refuse to accept the fact that I've totally misread you ever since you started working with me." He scanned her barren yard. About all it had in his favor was a small pair of silver birch trees guarding the front door. Glancing back at Diana and—and comparing her to that girl Cirrus, actually, with the chokers and fishnets and amethyst moon, Micah said honestly, "And I did not expect you to be a witch. But listen. I still think you're cool, and if you tell these lovely ladies to stop trying to intimidate me, I'll forget all this ever happened, okay?"

The two women pulled out athames—sharp, shining ritual blades that hooked at the tips to improve the ability to *rip*.

"Cool." Micah's voice was a thin little gasp.

"I'm going to enjoy this," said the green-haired witch.

Like falling through ice that would soon freeze him to

death, Micah sank into a cold sense of acceptance. These women were going to try to kill him.

The green-haired witch snatched his collar and then thrust the blade at his neck with savage confidence. With a yell, Micah jerked back, popping the lid off his tea and splashing the scalding contents in her face. The witch screamed, pawing at her quickly reddening face with her gloves.

He somersaulted forward, slamming into Diana's knee with his shoulder. She buckled and went down, and he let his remaining momentum carry him up to the slender trunk of the leftmost birch tree.

The blue-haired witch hefted Diana back to her feet as Diana swiped the snow off her dress. Diana pulled her own blade out of a pocket on her hip and unsheathed it. Her arm trembled visibly.

On his feet and matted with snow, Micah tuned them out for a brief moment, backed against the birch tree. He snapped off a branch the length of his forearm and gazed fondly down at it.

Trees in winter were just sleeping, right?

Micah twirled it between his fingers, inhaled deeply, and breathed out, "*Wake up.*"

And it did.

The branch exploded just as the three women rushed him like a trio of ringwraiths. He spun the stick, now thick as his wrist and jagged with newborn offshoots. It disarmed the green-haired witch almost at once, her athame spinning away as Micah thrust the end into her stomach and jabbed. She went down heavily, grunting, spitting out a clot of blood into the snow.

Stepping back, Diana gawped at him as if she hadn't quite believed her own theory until this moment. Micah closed in on her and raised the staff as if to strike her. She cowered back, covering her face, forgetting she was holding a knife.

Micah lowered the staff and deadpanned to her, "You're *so* fired."

Her jaw dropped, and horror flooded her eyes. Her lips started to form his name. But—

Pain erupted in his shoulder and wrenched a guttural cry from his chest. He dropped heavily to his knees. Bending forward, Micah groaned while his vision tunneled beneath the lightning bolts of searing pain laced across his back. Diana's feet shuffled away from him. Instinctively taking her cue, Micah leaned onto his elbow and kicked his leg out behind him. He connected with one of the witches and felt them trip heavily over his calf.

Panting, Micah rolled onto his back and glared up at the green-haired witch as she righted herself and smiled down at him with cruel delight, his blood freckling her cheeks. Micah used the birchwood staff to struggle back to his feet, breaking into a sickly cold sweat, the strength in his muscles sapped by his wound.

The blue-haired witch reached to withdraw the blade, but he spun the staff like a propellor and it bit down into her arm with a loud and sickening *crack*. She screamed; her forearm snapped like a twig. Staggering back, tears springing into her eyes, she turned and fled down the street.

The other witch gave a feral yell, flinging herself at him with fingers curled into claws.

Micah jumped back, but his knees buckled.

As he started to fall, the air smelled of mulberries, and Ingrid thrust herself free of the streak of shadows between himself and the witch. Ingrid caught him by the waist, while he steadied himself with the birchwood staff. Then she wound back an arm and landed an exacting punch in the witch's face.

The green-haired witch dropped like a stone, blood gushing from her nose. She scrambled back on her ass, eyes widening, tongue lapping up her blood as it streamed over her lips.

Ingrid followed her into the snowy yard with bare white feet and vengeance in her arrow-straight back. Her tall, slender form coruscated bloody red light that reflected off the snow like tail lights in the dark. A breeze Micah didn't feel toyed with Ingrid's loose curls.

She gazed down at the witch and said calmly, "You must not know whose blood you shed."

The witch drew a cold iron dagger with hemlock berries

wrapped around the pommel and lashed out at Ingrid. Ingrid kicked her leg back, the blade missing her. The green-haired witch wound her legs around Ingrid's other ankle and tried to stab again.

"Hey!" Micah leapt on top of the witch, his knee smashing into her groin and the birchwood staff falling against her throat like a lethal proclamation. The witch gagged, spittle flying from her lips.

"Don't fucking touch my sister," Micah snarled, bearing his weight down on the birchwood staff so corded muscles jumped in his forearms despite how his fingers tingled on his left hand.

The witch's eyes bugged. Her hands scrabbled at his wrist as the staff crushed her windpipe, so her gasping lungs no longer made a sound, no longer gathered air. She grabbed his pinky and bent it back to disarm him, but Ingrid's alabaster hands appeared on either side of Micah's, like interwoven threads on a vicious tapestry. Together they held her down as they watched the life drain from her face. Growing impatient, Ingrid gave the staff a savage downward thrust, the witch's throat emitting a wet and final crunch.

The green-haired witch spasmed and lay still. Her glassy eyes turned dull, staring heavenward. The smell of urine rose off her body.

Micah swallowed sour bile as he clambered off the dead witch and fell onto his uninjured elbow. He clutched the birchwood staff to his chest, trying to drag his eyes off the witch, but her death worked on him like a paralyzing curse. Ingrid moved over the body, her fingers under nostrils as if checking for breath while her eyes quickly roved over Micah's face, his back, as if trying to see through his chest to assess his injury.

A tiny sob captured both their attention. Micah looked over the snow to the walkway where Diana stood frozen. Horror wiped her expression blank; she seemed unaware of the tears leaking down her cheeks, as if she were too numb to notice. When she saw Micah looking at her, she dropped her athame. It clattered onto the salted pavement under her feet as she put her hands in the air, palms forward in surrender.

Ingrid turned toward Diana with the sharp grace of a predator, making the woman yelp. The scarlet-eyed faerie looked fearsome, terrifying, otherworldly. She was unbothered by her bare feet on the frozen ground, unbothered by the wind in just a wool dress that seemed to have turned blood-red after she killed the witch. She wore sprigs of winter berries behind her tall, pointed ears, but the red of the berries looked gruesome, like splatters of blood.

"Oh. Oh, no. M...madame, spare me," said Diana, eyes round and wide and dripping tears.

Ingrid walked on silent bare feet up to Diana, gazing disdainfully down at her before reaching out and grasping her chin in her hand. Her rings glinted like spirit lights bobbing on her bone-white fingers with sharp black nails dimpling Diana's cheeks.

"Madame, please," Diana begged, tears bright in her eyes and wet on her face.

"Ingrid," cautioned Micah, "don't kill her."

Ingrid cast her crimson gaze sidelong at Micah where he knelt on the ground. Her calm cruelty faltered. She blinked, irises like glinting garnets. Then she narrowed her eyes and looked back at Diana. She said evenly, "You will say your friend broke her neck from a slip on the ice. You will denounce this practice of black magic. And you can expect that if we meet again in similar circumstances, I will be merciless."

Diana trembled under Ingrid's grip. Her eyes became unfocused for a moment as the command settled into her bones. "Caty broke her neck," agreed Diana. "I don't do dark magic anymore."

Micah used the staff to try to get back to his feet. But he was too weak, too shaky, too numb to move his limbs. Blood leaked freely around the knife in his shoulder; he could feel the warmth spreading down his back, disturbingly hot in the winter air. Micah tried one more time to stand, but he slipped and hit his left elbow. He cried out as the impact ricocheted down to his palm and up to his spine, so intense that his vision spun momentarily into blackness.

"Ingrid," he moaned.

Ingrid yielded and turned away after giving Diana a sharp shove that knocked her down onto her ass in the snow.

The Ruby Daughter squatted in front of Micah. She inspected him in silence with her expression carefully blank—it told him more than he wanted to know about the state he was in. Then she held onto his hips and put him on his feet as if he were a child. He clutched the birchwood branch in one hand and leaned into Ingrid as he shuffled alongside her, barely able to breathe without the pain overwhelming him.

Diana watched in silence, shaking in the snow where Ingrid left her.

When they got down onto the sidewalk, Ingrid grasped Micah by the waist and then stepped them into the shadows. But he didn't see where they went. A comforting blanket of unconsciousness threw itself over him. He passed out.

Moments later, Ingrid lowered Micah onto his belly on her nest in her hut. She told the candles to burn hotter. As she pushed up the sleeves of her dress and knelt beside her brother, she touched the blackened iron handle of the athame protruding from his flesh, which was sliced into his trapezius muscle on the edge of his scapula.

Startling Ingrid with her sudden appearance, Chamomile arrived in her shelter and hurried over to the bed in the corner. When she leaned over Ingrid, Chamomile sucked in a sharp gasp. Gracelessly, she clattered through Ingrid's belongings by the door on a black shelf that held medicinal herbs. Chamomile returned with an armful of jars and stepped over Micah's prone body to kneel above his head. She poured steaming water from a pitcher into a large dish and dropped a terry cloth inside. Ingrid watched her, waiting, holding a linen kerchief in her palm, hovering over the handle.

Chamomile lifted her bright, serious gaze. Then she nodded.

Ingrid grasped the handle of the athame and yanked, tossing it toward her door with a hiss. Chamomile moved in at once with a compress and pressed it down with both hands as blood stained the cotton pad red immediately.

"What happened?" Chamomile demanded, a tremble in her voice. She held down the pad as she prepared another and then quickly switched them out.

"Witches," Ingrid told her. She picked up the bloodied pads and set them on the table over her shoulder.

Chamomile spat a complicated string of foreign words. "They were going to bleed him."

"He was handling them well, but the one I killed was old. I could feel it."

Chamomile grimaced and confirmed, "You killed a witch?"

"She would have killed him. I did what was necessary." She moved to help Chamomile as the smaller faerie struggled to free Micah's right arm from his jacket. Ingrid peeled it across his back and down his other arm while Chamomile reached inside and pressed another wad of cotton to his shoulder while they disrobed him. The sweatshirt was worse, more tedious than his jacket by far. Ingrid ended up holding the heavy dead weight of his torso against her chest while Chamomile pulled his arms free, working with one hand while still pressing on his wound. When the sweatshirt was just around his neck, they laid him gently back down on the pillows while Ingrid pulled it over his head.

Chamomile went to work silently. With the wet cloth she

wiped away the blood coating his left side. She wrung it out into a bronze bowl. Blood pooled at the bottom; the sight made Ingrid light-headed. Then she wiped down his back once more while Ingrid maintained pressure. Finally, she gently moved Ingrid and her compress, quickly wiped the stab wound and then packed it with a small bunch of leaves. The leaves stymied the free flow of blood immediately.

It was then that Ingrid realized she'd been holding her breath.

Chamomile used a mortar and pestle to grind more stems into a creamy paste before coating the wound with it. Ingrid helped manipulate Micah's heavy form so Chamomile could wrap medical dressing under his armpit and across his chest so it wouldn't budge.

She taped down a large piece of gauze and then sat back on her heels. When she looked up at Ingrid, her eyes were shining. Swiping the back of her hand across her nose, Chamomile looked back down at him and ran her fingers through his pale green hair shining under the candlelight. "Should we tell Andrew?"

Ingrid sighed through her nose. "We can let Micah decide when he wakes up."

Chapter Thirteen
The Child

Night fell, and Liath was snoring upstairs before Andrew tried to call Micah from the red landline next to the lamp. It went to voicemail. His stomach twisted with guilt. It certainly was not so late Micah would be asleep, and it was hard to imagine him missing all Andrew's calls without noticing. Even if he was still in Lilydale, Andrew would have expected him to at least try to answer.

Perhaps, Andrew thought with a surge of fear, Micah was done waiting for him to come home. He thought back to their conversation in Micah's room where...where he'd *told* him to sleep with other people, like an idiot. Like a coward. If Micah had listened and sought out a new sexual partner, it would take all of Andrew's self-control to not resent him for it. And yet this was what he claimed he wanted. For Micah to be free. If that turned out to be best for him, Andrew...simply had to accept it. The thought brought a rush of bile to his throat, sharp and coarse and sour. Cowardly fool. He was going to die alone now.

He hugged his arms across himself, trying to bring down his heart rate. His hair was wet from a shower under water that tasted like iron, and braided on top the way Chamomile had taught him, so he'd tied the hood of his sweatshirt tight to keep the cold off. His cheeks were sticky with a frostbite poultice Liath had at the ready.

Even before the worry about Micah seeped back in, he didn't feel tired at all. The day had been too novel, too wild for him, leaving him with an emotional high and his brain spiraling. The work and insight it took to tap into his own natural connection to the wilderness was exhausting, but...he could *feel* it. Nature spoke back to him, made him slip between the cracks of the sky and the bark of a tree and the grains of snow. It felt like he'd turned on another frequency of existence like donning a pair of 3D glasses at a movie, hitherto denied to him just because he didn't know how to look.

Holding the polished agate over his head so the translucent parts turned to fire in the moonlight, Andrew tried dialing Micah's number one more time, but it still went to voicemail. Then he picked up his phone and rummaged through the settings to see if he could do anything to boost his service signal. But the X in the corner tray remained, and he shook his head and powered it down.

He slid onto his back and stared at the vaulted rafters, counting whorls absently in the weak light from the moon that shone inside. His eyes traced the white moonbeam back to the window and tried to find the stars, but the moonlight cast shadows on the interior of the cabin, which flashed on the windowpanes and obscured the view. It made him almost pine for the stars.

With a sudden burst of resolve, he unzipped himself from his sleeping bag and padded to the front door. He pulled on his wool gaiter under his sweatshirt hood and his jacket hood, and then wrapped his head up in a scarf before he pulled the orange snowsuit on over all of it.

After breaking two packets of instant heat and jamming the crinkling plastic bags in the toes of his boots, still damp inside, he stuffed the boots onto his feet. Then he broke two more packets that he held in his palms and sank his hands into his multiple gloves and mittens.

When he stepped outside, he was reminded that this was the North Shore in the middle of the night. The cold bit through his gear in an instant. But he settled in with the discomfort. He crunched through existing footprints until he was away from the cabin on the other side of the hill from his idle snowmobile. He plopped down cross-legged into the snow, and then tilted back his head and gazed at the stars. There was some light pollution eastward and southward from the surrounding towns, so the stars still didn't quite compare to that night in Montana. But winter starlight was especially bright, like the veil between the earth and heavens was thin and pierced by a million needles of brilliant light.

He let his mind wander, allowed his thoughts to roll over him with a menagerie of feelings that came and went. Worry in his stomach, anticipation tight in his groin, anger in his forehead and his jaw, sorrow heavy on his shoulders. They were all back, after he'd been numb to them for months. It hurt more to feel, but he was alive again.

A soft sigh drifted into his ears. Andrew dropped his head immediately, heart fluttering with excitement. A dozen paces away, that familiar cloud of living snow crouched silently and watched him with sunspot eyes. When Andrew remained still, blinking slowly, the form took a cautious step toward him. It fell under a beam of moonlight, which spilled like milk over its shaggy coat. Andrew smiled slightly as a pair of golden lupine eyes blinked back at him. It stalked toward him slowly, one large clawed paw at a time.

He *might* get eaten. That was a choice, he supposed.

The wolf approached him with its nose quivering. Its face was round and tufted. One furred, gray-tipped ear swiveled to the side.

"Hello, Fionna," Andrew said softly.

The wolf's other ear swiveled in recognition when he said her name. Keeping her keen eyes on him, she lowered her head and sniffed his hand on his knee, a paw crunching in the snow near his foot. The moonlight turned her heavy winter coat to tones of silver and charcoal, with pale white around her eyes and under her chin. She stretched out her neck and sniffed at the exposed skin around his eyes with warm and damp breath ghosting over his cheeks.

A cloud clamped over the moon, washing darkness over him and the snow. He blinked until his eyes adjusted to behold a girl in the wolf's place. Her eyes were unchanged, precious metal gleaming behind long, dark lashes in the middle of an oval face with full squishy cheeks. Her lips were dry and cracked but quirked slightly with a curious grin. A mane of tawny hair fell down to her shoulders and got lost in the fluffy parka that her wolf pelt had become. Her movements were no more tamed now that they were bound within the body of a girl; she was crouched in the snow, head cocked to the side, crawling toward him on all fours.

Slowly, Andrew raised his hand to give her the same kind of little wave he'd done the day before by the lake. She froze, eyes flicking to his hand as she settled back on her knees and raised her little stubby fingers back. The girl would have fit in with primary school children and was built thick around the middle, but her limbs looked knobby and stretched out. As Andrew set his arm back on his knee, the girl crawled closer. She stretched out a finger ending in a sharp dirt-clotted nail and tugged down his mask under his chin, peering thoughtfully at him. Andrew swallowed a gag at her foul canine breath, a grin climbing onto his lips at the absurdity of the encounter.

"Boy Liath," said the girl, her husky voice like a bark.

Considering the sentiment with a slow nod and a shrug, Andrew pressed his hand to his chest and said, "Andrew. Liath is my mother."

"Mo-ther." Fionna's head bobbed. She pressed her hand to her chest in imitation and then peered up at Andrew as she tipped herself over into the snow and rolled on her back with glee.

"You must not be cold," he said with a laugh. In response, she reached for her head and gripped her messy bangs, giving them a ferocious yank and shifting back into her wolf body as if donning a cloak. Andrew shook himself as goosebumps scattered across his skin, scratching his cheek and pulling his mask over his mouth. The wolf's long legs kicked toward the blanket of stars as she shimmied along her back, her long mauve tongue lolling out from between her ivory fangs. When he was about to reach out a tentative hand and touch her furred ribcage, she shot back to her feet and wound her way behind Andrew, dropping her weight against his spine so he jerked forward. It forced himself to his knees, which elicited a joyful yip that could have come from a domesticated puppy. Urged on by her excitement, Andrew stood up as she circled around his legs with her thick, heavy tail swishing. He reached down and patted her back, which was sturdy and warm enough for him to feel through his layers of gloves. She wove around again and butted the crown of her head into his palm. He scratched behind her ear and down into her cheek, barely able to penetrate the fur, although she leaned hard into his hand, whistling like a screaming tea kettle. She reared back and threw off her wolfskin so she could wrap her arms around his neck.

Andrew gasped as he stuck out a foot to keep his balance, grasping the girl's waist. He tried to straighten, but so true was her grip that he simply lifted her off the ground. Swinging her legs around his waist, she clung to his shoulders as she kept whining, sounding barely human. Andrew held onto her as his heart climbed into his throat. How many years had it been since this little girl touched someone? How many times did she run into humans who chased her away or screamed when they saw her as a wolf?

After a few minutes embracing under the moonlight, Fionna slid back onto the snow and blinked up at him. She pointed down the hill and hopped up and down.

"Oh, I can't leave..." he began. But maybe that wasn't true. Maybe it was time to go home. And to tell Micah he'd never wanted a break in the first place. He was just...broken and doubtful.

Fionna threw on her wolfskin and scooped her lower jaws through the snow, munching on it like a sno-cone. Understanding, Andrew crouched, picked up a clump, crushing it into a ball.

"Ready?"

He tossed the snowball into the stars; Fionna threw back her head, mouth open as she leapt into the air and caught the snowball before landing with an elegant thud. He laughed as she pranced in a circle and opened her jaws until he crouched to do it again.

Andrew climbed back into the sleeping bag on the couch not long before daybreak. His hair was slightly frozen, as were his toes. His legs hurt, sore from running through the trees with a wolf pup. He could feel his cheeks were hard and wind-chapped again. Once he rolled onto his side, he was asleep almost at once.

Something was wrong when he woke up. The ocean waves seemed louder than when he'd fallen asleep. But...no, that wasn't quite it. Andrew blinked and rubbed an eye with the heel of his hand. Liath stood across the room over the kitchen island. He started to sit up, jostling the cord around his neck so the cold twist of wire brushed the hollow of his throat. It felt...lighter. Confused, Andrew looked down.

The vial was missing.

Moving carefully so he didn't make a sound in the sleeping bag, Andrew slid his legs over the edge of the couch. His toes hit something odd and he looked down. There was a white sound machine producing ocean waves on the floor at the foot of the couch. A childlike part of Andrew wanted to believe that Liath wanted to let him sleep. She no doubt had seen all the footprints—man and wolf both—tracking over the hills outside her cabin.

But...

History was not friendly to this belief.

He stepped lightly across the deerskin rug until he could see over his mother's shoulder. Liath gripped the uncorked vial of Micah's blood between her thumb and forefinger as she swilled a potion bottle in her other hand. She held the glass over the open flame of the bunsen burner, watching the deep red liquid bubble inside.

Andrew reached over and snatched the vial out of her fingers.

She gasped and spun around. "A-Andrew! I...hoped you'd sleep—"

"The fuck are you doing, Liath?"

She looked down at the potion bottle in her fingers. She opened and closed her mouth and then looked back up at him without speaking.

Teeth gritted, Andrew growled, "I asked. You. A question."

Liath's shoulders hunched; she grew guarded. "I...wanted to experiment."

"What is Micah's blood supposed to do?" he demanded, hot indignation rising in him.

Liath hesitated. "Fae blood is said to have many powerful properties. I want to find out what."

"Were you hoping it would make you high?" sneered Andrew.

Liath flinched. Her earth-brown eyes hardened into coal. "I don't know what you expected from me, Andrew, but I was bound to disappoint."

"You're right." Andrew ripped the bottle out of her other hand and cast it onto the floorboards to shatter at their feet. "Enjoy the rest of your pitiful life, Mother." He gathered his things and threw open the front door, barely stepping into his boots and marching down the steps outside in just his jeans and sweatshirt. Andrew threw his backpack and sleeping bag in the trailer of the snowmobile, climbed onto the seat, and tore into the wilderness.

Once the cabin was out of sight, he released the clutch. "Fuck!" he roared, climbing off the snowmobile, kicking clods of snow. He screamed again at the heavens until his throat felt raw.

Then he dropped onto the snow, burying his face in his forearms, letting heavy shudders wrack his body until he didn't know if it was grief or the cold.

The wolf snuck up on him—he jumped when her wet nose thrust into his ear, loud and hot. Andrew's head shot up.

Fionna's golden eyes beheld him with her canine eyebrows lifted. Her tail wagged slightly, her ears cocked sideways, and then she stuck her neck out and licked his cheek.

She put her head on his arms and forced him to inhale

the musk of her fur. Hesitantly, Andrew pressed the side of his face into her scruff and leaned his arm on her shoulder blades. Of course *now* his eyes were burning. He and the wolf stayed in their strange but comforting embrace until his fingers and cheeks were numb.

"Excuse me," Andrew managed with a sniff. "I have to go home."

Fionna scooted away from him when he spoke, but stayed near as he dressed properly in his winter gear. She whistled again as he climbed onto the snowmobile and put on the helmet.

"I can't stay with Liath anymore," said Andrew. "She isn't healthy for me." He revved the engine into life.

Fionna gave a whine of protest.

"I'm sorry," said Andrew. "There's someone I have to get home to. Hopefully."

The wolf scampered under a hemlock, bringing the two of them full-circle. He gunned the snowmobile past her, but she shot back out from under the tree and ran after him, her legs pumping, her tongue flapping out of her black lips.

At first, the sight of her made his heart drop with dread. What was he supposed to do with a wolf attached to him? If he couldn't get her to go back to Liath, she'd be wildly vulnerable to being spotted by humans, who could panic and likely shoot her. Leaving her to fend for herself didn't seem like an option, and bringing her back to Liath would mean he would have to see her again. Even if he were at his most noble, instead of angry and lovesick, he couldn't bring himself to do that. With another quick glance at Fionna, he cut some of the gas. She did a little leap to thank him.

The edges of buildings emerged after an hour. He slowed down and searched the trees around him for a glimpse of Fionna. Finding her obscured behind a pair of spruce, Andrew called, "Fionna, you have to turn back. I don't want people to see you." He swallowed and added more softly, "Thank you for your friendship. You were the best part of this trip."

Fionna emerged with her head low and her ears back. She padded across the muddied snow toward him and set her chin on his knee. Chest tight, Andrew slowly lifted his hand and scratched her heavy scruff while she released another low, sad whistle. Then he gripped the handlebars again and briefly revved the engine. Fionna picked up her head, pointed her maw toward the heavens, and let out a short howl. The hairs on the back of Andrew's neck stood up. He gritted his teeth with resolve and sped onward.

It was surreal being back in the fluorescent lights of the ski shop. He returned the keys and the trailer as if in a dream, and didn't put up a fight when they said they weren't returning the rest of the week's money. He pulled off his hat and scarf as he made his way with heavy steps back to his Saturn in the parking lot, staring up at the lightly falling snow.

Maybe he shouldn't have stormed out of the cabin. Maybe he was proving to himself he hadn't changed a bit since he was a teenager. That it was so easy to betray him, and for him to turn away. But she'd taken the blood ward off his neck in his sleep, and ruined it...proving she hadn't changed since he was a teenager, either. They were both still so toxic to one another, bringing out their worst sides, falling into old patterns almost immediately.

For a moment, overwhelming disappointment, renewed abandonment, frustration and guilt misted his eyes, but he shook himself and rubbed his face. There would be plenty of time on the drive home to cry. Plenty of time to try to guess whether or not Micah would forgive him. Plenty of time to hope that by the end of the day, he would be in Micah's arms, feeling his heartbeat against his cheek.

Peeling off his snowsuit, Andrew opened the driver's door on the Saturn. He packed everything back into the trunk and slammed it shut with finality.

"Bark!" exclaimed a little girl's voice. Andrew spun around just as the wolf girl threw her skinny arms around his waist and squeezed him with disproportionate strength.

"Fionna, I told you...oh, you probably can't understand me, can you?" He patted her head, trying to pry her arms off him, but she kept her hands clasped and growled softly until he let her go.

Fionna blinked up at him with shining yellow eyes and a

quivering chin. Her hair was pushed back from her forehead and behind her very human looking little ears. In daylight, it looked like she wore a luxurious fur coat and suede pants. But she was barefoot, her feet scarred and callused. Her lips were grayish and chapped, and her cheeks were coarse. As a human, she looked woefully neglected, destitute. How was she supposed to know her human body needed more grooming than she did as a wolf? He wasn't a good judge for how old she would be as a human, but now that he could see her better, she didn't look over ten.

"Alone," she yipped sadly, shaking her head.

"Okay, okay. Let me look at you." He started to crouch, and she let him go but held onto the hem of his coat. He squatted next to her, Fionna all but nestling into his chest.

"I thought Liath took care of you," he said. "Sort of."

"Alone," she whimpered again, and then burrowed against his collar. Even her hair smelled like sweat, like dog, like sap from hemlocks. But then again, she'd probably never had a bath.

"Mum must not have been great company for you, eh?" Andrew said softly. "I think she tried to keep you wild. I get it, but...that's not enough for you, is it, child? You're bound to get yourself in trouble up here, I bet. And anyway, it doesn't feel right, leaving you behind as a little human who looks this rough." Fionna looked like she was posing, rocking on her heels, hands behind her back, blinking her large eyes. Like a child wanting to get adopted. "You wouldn't be able to scare anyone in Lilydale though," he mused. "You wouldn't even be the most feral thing there." Andrew snorted, "*Chamomile.*"

She stepped back from him and pawed his cheek with cold fingers. "An-roo," she said. "Fionna." Then she pointed to his car. "Come...come with." She nudged his hand with her forehead.

He sighed, "Honestly, Micah would love you." While she watched him expectantly with her saucer eyes, Andrew grabbed the handle to the back door and pulled it open. "Come on then, little one."

Fionna bounced in a circle and yipped, and then clambered on all fours onto the bench in the backseat. She folded up her limbs and sat tall and proud with a lopsided grin.

Andrew reached into the backseat and pulled the center seatbelt out and around her. She growled at him, but he gave her a dirty look and proceeded to buckle her in. Fionna leaned against the seatbelt with another little growl, pulling the shoulder harness into her mouth and gnawing on it.

"Stop it," said Andrew, just sharply enough for her to infer his meaning from his tone. "We have a long drive." He put the strap back down onto her shoulder. "You should sleep, or else just relax, okay? I can get you something to eat and drink. But otherwise, I'm eager to get home."

As if she understood all this. But she certainly liked

staring at him while he talked, like she'd never gotten to listen to a human speak for very long.

"Are you sure you don't want to stay here?" he asked.

"An-roo and Fionna," she said with a furrowed brow.

"Okay. Okay." He held up his hands. Then he closed her in the backseat; she leaned forward to watch him in alarm until he got behind the wheel and closed his own door. The car took two tries for the engine to turn over. Fionna jumped, gasping and grabbing the bench.

"You're safe," he said in a soothing tone. It took her a moment, but she slowly relaxed and leaned back, biting her lip with her small human teeth. In the mirror, Andrew watched her pick up the snow scraper from the floor by her feet. She gave it a swashbuckling wave, giggling.

"No," growled Andrew. She put it down almost at once, still biting her lip, a dimple appearing in her cheek. "Oh dear god," he muttered, rubbing his face. "You're an adorable little rascal, aren't you?"

She yipped several times and kicked a bare foot into the back of his chair. Then when he put the car into drive and backed out of his parking spot, Fionna's eyebrows shot up. She grabbed a fistful of the seatbelt as she bared her teeth with displeasure.

"Hey, get used to it. It's safe." He paused and said, "Magic."

Fionna blinked and found his gaze in the rearview mirror where she stared at him for several long seconds. She had shaggy taupe brows that lowered on her forehead as she repeated with a nod, "Magic."

"I hope you understand we're not coming back here for a good long while," Andrew told her as he turned onto the highway. "I'm not coming near that woman ever again. Say 'bye, Liath.'"

Fionna turned in the seat and looked through the back windshield. She touched her dirty fingers to the glass and repeated, "Bye, Liath."

Andrew's heart wrenched, and he swallowed again, more painfully this time. But he focused on the road as he got up to highway speed, and then some, more than willing to speed if it would get him home to Micah any sooner.

Fionna fell asleep with her head against the bench when Andrew was flying down Highway 61. He plugged his phone into the auxiliary cable and then started a call to Micah.

It went to voicemail.

Chapter Fourteen
The Repair

Buzz.

Buzz.

Buzz.

Micah stirred, facedown, the last vibrating ring of his phone in his back jeans pocket rousing him from darkness.

He blinked, blind and empty. Under his bare chest it was soft and plush, and heavy blankets lay atop him up to his neck. He was cozy enough, but in the way of waking from a nightmare. The fire pulsing in his shoulder left nothing to doubt: the fight with the witches had been real.

"You're awake."

Soft candlelight flickered to life. Micah struggled to turn his head, grinding his teeth at the pain from moving his neck. He looked up at Ingrid sitting with knees tucked up to her chest in the corner of the bed by his head. She was stringing clay beads onto a thread.

"H'long was I out?" he mumbled.

"Sixteen hours or so," she answered, sliding a bead down

that clacked quietly into its neighbors. Her gaze flicked back up, dark and worried. "How do you feel?"

"Awful." His eyes stung, and he shut them and started to take a deep breath. It was an immediate mistake, and he shuddered as he released what little air he took in. He managed to grunt, "Can you make it better?"

"Yeah. Chamomile left something here. It's willow bark and...something stronger." She picked something up off the ledge over her head. "But we have to sit you up."

"Fine."

Ingrid slid a hand under his belly, and he got his right forearm under himself with such trouble it was as if he'd never moved a day in his life. She supported most of his weight until he was finally on his knees. His vision rocked like he was a capsizing boat and his mouth filled with saliva. Slapping his hand over his mouth, Micah groaned and hurriedly swallowed down the urge to vomit.

Ingrid gave him a little shot glass and held onto the small of his back while he tipped it down his throat. He made a nasty face and stuck out his tongue, and she traded the empty glass for a mug and helped him wash down the shot with mulled wine. Micah drained the mug and felt it settle warm and heavy in his stomach. "It's bad. Isn't it?" he asked, feeling his pulse hammering in his shoulder.

She nodded. "It was a long blade. It tore some muscle. And you still have a sensitivity to iron, even if it isn't like mine."

Micah closed his eyes, since any other movement would hurt. "I'm grateful you were there."

"I am too." When he looked over at her, her slender brows were low over her narrowed eyes, glinting with a dozen candle flames that turned her irises to garnets.

Micah asked in a whisper that barely used the air in his lungs, "Did you tell my dad what happened?"

"Chamomile did. She thought it best. But she minimized the extent of your injury. Said you would stay here for a bit."

"That's good." The shot seeped into his bones, clearing his head slightly, dulling the pain so he could almost endure it. "Can you help me up?"

He used her shoulder to push himself to his feet while Ingrid steadied him with a hand under his forearm. She put the branch of birchwood in his fist and braced his elbow while he transferred his weight to the shaft of wood, which notched into the brick floor and kept him planted. It was as thick as an arm bone, and almost Micah's height, trembling as if excited to be held. Ingrid's lips curled with a proud smile as she witnessed him reunited with the staff. The humming in her blood recognized man and magic twining around each other, eagerly exploring this new channel to communicate and flourish. Spring-green dust crawled through the veins in Micah's knuckles, racing away from the staff and up his forearm. The staff creaked quietly as a fizzy glow moved from his hand, into the wood, and up to the pale, jagged broken end of the branch. It illuminated the slivers of the wood with jeweled green light. Micah blinked, disbelieving, lifting his gaze from the staff and fixing Ingrid with luminous amethyst eyes which, just briefly, were ringed in evergreen.

"You've never looked more like yourself," she told him.

His chest rose and fell in a quick, sharp gasp, tears lining his lashes. Slowly, the light faded out of the branch except for a soft glow on the end like a plastic star losing its charge on the ceiling.

Chamomile's entrance into the hut had been silent, but based on the look of awe on her soft features, she had seen the entire sequence of Micah and his staff calibrating.

When Micah turned around, Chamomile stood in front of him holding a long scarf. He jumped, hunching his shoulders automatically. Baring his teeth, he groaned and shut his eyes for a moment. Inhaling through his nose, he opened his eyes as he exhaled.

"I need to tie up your arm," she told him, and then climbed onto Ingrid's table so she could reach his shoulder. She carefully bent his arm across his stomach and then used the scarf as a sling which she looped over his neck. "It needs to be mostly immobile, but I regret to inform you that you will need to move it regularly, which will not be enjoyable." Inspecting him with a frown, she let out a sigh, then pecked his cheek with a kiss.

He smiled a little and hugged her small waist.

"The liquid was to fortify you." Chamomile was all business. "This should maintain your wellbeing." She gripped his jaw in her hand and then pried open his mouth.

"Hmph!"

Chamomile set a small leaf-wrapped pebble on his tongue. "Swallow."

He did, and then groaned. "I'm not a dog! I could have…"

"Shut up. I'll be keeping you medicated for a few days to help you heal and make sure you aren't in agony. You're to notify me at once if you feel worse, feverish, or faint. I'll be watching you."

"Who are you, Ingrid?"

The accused scoffed loudly behind him.

"You terrified us," Chamomile told him. "Don't get hurt like this again."

"Yes, ma'am."

"What's this?" She gave his staff a light shake. "You finally have a conduit?"

"I don't know." He gave her a look like she should have known he wouldn't know what it meant. "But it tickles and feels safe."

Chamomile nodded, glancing once more at Ingrid as her expression clouded. Micah felt too tired to ask her about it. He made his way slowly to Ingrid's door like an old man with a cane. He glanced at his untied Docs, but left the hut barefooted instead.

Small, doe-eyed Syabira stood up near Ingrid's door with

a bundle of spruce in her hands wrapped in red ribbon. "You're awake." Expression soft, she spoke like a refreshing breeze. "What a relief."

Micah grimaced. "Does the whole compound know?"

Syabira nodded, her cloud of curls bobbing. "Word spread quickly that you were wounded by a witch. We are all aggravated by that. It's...ominous."

"Tell me about it." He dropped his gaze.

"But we also heard how well you handled yourself," Syabira added. "I remember when you first arrived in Lilydale. You were hardly yet a man, and so reluctant to be among the Folk, and certainly unaware of your natural gifts. Not so now."

"I'm working toward formidable," he remarked dryly.

Syabira smiled kindly. "For being so young, you are well on your way." She curtseyed slightly, and then trudged past him and disappeared behind Ingrid's hut.

After she walked away, Micah snorted and rubbed his neck. "That's right. Youngest forty-two-year-old ever."

Awkwardly leaning his staff into the crook of his elbow so he could use his phone, he flipped through his notifications. They were mostly from Andrew, some from Julian, and one or two from Sam.

He blinked, his sluggish brain trying to make inferences. Andrew had texted him? He tapped on it.

Hey, love. I'm on my way home. I hope you're okay. I hope you can forgive me for all this.

The text had come in almost five hours ago, early in the morning. Micah gasped. The movement sent a lightning bolt of pain through his shoulder and arm all the way to his fingertips. His vision blurred. Groaning, he rubbed his eyes with thumb and forefinger and took several shallow breaths to try to collect himself. Without uncovering his eyes, he tried to gather the idea to himself that...Andrew would be home soon. Micah would have to face him. Looking like *this*. Sitting on...how many days had it been now? Was it really only four? Based on his feelings of anger and betrayal, it felt like it had been years.

And he'd kissed Chamomile. Micah's knees went weak. He wobbled against the staff and half-fell down the steps, making his way like an invalid toward the seats around the fire pit. Sweat rose on the small of his back as he made it to a squishy white toadstool and held his breath while he gingerly sat.

"Here," declared a faerie with twists of white hair and skin gray-brown like maple tree bark. They held out a puffy pastry that Micah took gratefully, and then filled a crystal cup with water and set it within Micah's reach.

"Thanks, Nox." His voice was hushed.

Nox nodded, their rectangular pupils thoughtfully beholding Micah before they sat on a stump next to him. "The witches shouldn't have harmed you, under our circumstances," they said in a voice formless as the snap of bark breaking off a tree trunk.

Micah snorted. "Agreed." He fell silent, greedily emptying the water cup before taking a large bite of the perfect pastry. Getting stabbed worked up an *appetite*.

Or maybe he was just anxious. Okay, terrified. Because Andrew was going to be home soon. And that might mean he was about to tell Micah that the lake had cooled his feelings, that they were over, that Micah might as well have died outside Diana's house.

He pressed his forehead into the heel of his hand, goosebumps rising on his skin as the pastry threatened to come back up.

Scratchy but toasty wool fell over his shoulders. He sat up, blinking. A plaid flannel draped over him as Nox settled back onto their stump.

"Hey, thanks," Micah rasped, winking at Nox.

"There is always a spare cozy blanket in Lilydale," said Nox with a sage nod.

Micah grinned, taking another bite of the pastry while Nox filled up his water. As the faerie settled into silence, goat eyes returning to the fire they stoked with a large stick, Micah tried to let the warmth and the bonfire and the butter on his tongue trick him into believing everything was going to be fine.

The sky was velvety navy blue when Andrew pulled onto the curb opposite Sylvandale Road in the city of Lilydale. He was almost out of gas, his bladder was nearly bursting, and so was his heart. He had rehearsed his conversation with Micah a dozen times, the last handful of which were had aloud, while Fionna slumbered in the backseat with an apple juice clutched in one hand.

For most of the trip, Andrew had avoided thinking about his mother. He'd gotten used to doing that over the years, after all. It wasn't the first heartache from her, and honestly it wasn't even the worst. She'd been meaner when she was coming down from a Fae food high. This time, she had simply betrayed him.

Andrew let himself out onto the road, the quiet of the street enveloping him and the cold nipping his nose. He stretched aggressively, groaning, sore from folding his long legs for hours and hours in the car. He let out a large plume of warm breath into the air, slipped back on his jacket, and zipped it up to his chin. Edging around the boot of the car, Andrew pulled open the passenger door and leaned down in time to see Fionna jolt awake, a bark whooshing out of her little lungs. She jerked against the seatbelt, her apple juice sloshing noisily in her hand. Her darting eyes were fearful, the pupils huge. Then she found Andrew, and a toothy grin spread across her chapped lips. She reached for him and came against the seatbelt, glared down at it, and put it in her mouth to gnaw on it with an agitated whine.

"I'll let you out, kiddo, just, hold on. We're going into the woods, but you have to stay with me, okay? It's not...it isn't as wild as Up North. I don't want you to get lost or run into anyone."

Fionna stopped struggling while he spoke, though he suspected by the furrow in her little forehead that she had no idea what he was saying. She followed his hands as he grasped the buckle for her seatbelt.

"Stay with me." Andrew spoke firmly the way people commanded their dogs. "Okay?"

"Okay." Fionna tried out the word in her mouth like a new flavor of tea. She gave her apple juice a shake and then pitched it at the floor of the Saturn.

Andrew stifled a sigh, unbuckled her, and then immediately grasped her hand. She blinked at her fingers in his, and then clambered out onto the road. Fionna craned her neck back, snuffling audibly like a dog, looking down the residential street across from them with a wide-eyed and curious gaze.

"Mistake," muttered Andrew. "This was a huge mistake." He locked the Saturn with the key in the front door, stuffed the keyring in his jeans pocket, and turned to face the guard rail. Fionna was already tugging on his hand, leaning over to peer down at the steep drop off buried in undisturbed snow that was glowing in the twilight.

Entering the bluffs by Sylvandale was much more treacherous than going from the Brickyard Trail, but it was at least a mile closer to the faerie compound. And he was in a hurry.

"We're going slowly," Andrew told the pup sternly, and hypocritically.

Eyes alight, Fionna stuck her leg over the guard rail, blinked up at him, and nudged his hand with her cheek. Andrew obliged, climbing into the snow and letting himself slide into the trunk of a barren linden tree. Fionna didn't falter, the grace of her wolf form seemingly transferring into her gawky little human body as she bent to sniff the base of the tree, pawing at the dead leaves clinging to the underbrush and squeaking with excitement. She let Andrew brace himself on her hand as they picked their way down nearly vertical outcroppings of limestone, ducking under scraggly branches, weaving around decaying logs.

Her body stiffening sharply, Fionna's snuffling suddenly intensified. She pulled out of Andrew's grip and donned her wolfskin, jaws opening, nose skyward. Andrew, it turned out, was using her to steady himself much more than he realized. He immediately lost his footing, his boot skidding over loosely packed snow and plunging him onto his hip and his shoulder. The snow was so deep he got a face full of it, straight into his mouth and ear and nostrils.

Through his wintry vision, he saw the little wolf bounding through the snow, tail pinwheeling gleefully as she took off after a panicking squirrel. But when Andrew sat up and spat snow with a curse and a growl, Fionna froze. She turned back, ears forward to find him, then swiveling back as she hurried through her tracks and back to him. Whistling, Fionna snaked under his arm and helped him stand with his hand on her sturdy back. Andrew grumbled a complaint, his joints singing, but they relentlessly trudged on until the frozen creek and the cobbled fence was in view distantly beneath them.

Down below, Ingrid raised her head in her hut, inhaling deeply in a manner quite similar to Fionna. She raised an eyebrow and then finished folding her bloodied blankets. The frightening and coppery stench was overwhelming, but she was certain she smelled something else out of place. She set them on the bricks near her door and then let herself outside, sniffing again. Something odd hummed against the northeastern gate into Lilydale, and it was on the air as well. It smelled...wet. She slid through underbrush and snow-touched bushes up to a small gap in the cobblestone fence and an even smaller archway through the ice wall.

Dressed warmly with most of his red hair obscured by a

hat and a hood, Andrew crouched in the arch ahead of her. He was dappled with caked-on patches of snow, his cheeks bright red.

With some relief and some admonishment, Ingrid began, "I see you've made it home—"

Andrew looked up at her, fearful as a fox, eyes wide. One hand was braced on the cobbles, and the other held the scruff of a small, fluffy timber wolf with eager golden eyes.

"—Andrew," finished Ingrid, like a mother whose child had brought home a turtle from the park.

"Uh. Hi. I brought some Oreos. But they're up in the car." He adjusted his boot against the foot of the ice wall.

The wolf's thick tail wagged, just slightly, cautiously, hopeful. She bent muscular legs while her pink tongue lapped her lips in appeasement.

"You brought home a *faoladh*," Ingrid said blankly.

"Um." Andrew felt his face contort. "How exactly do you know about *faoladh*?"

"How could I spend time in Leinster without spending time with the local *faoladh?*" She crouched to be nose to nose with the wolf and scratched her chin. "Let me see you." Her voice took on a gentle quality Andrew had only heard once or twice in two years, and only then when she was speaking to Micah.

Fionna threw off her wolfskin at once. The tawny-haired girl hopped from foot to foot, uneasily avoiding Ingrid's gaze as she reached out and wrapped her hand around two of Andrew's fingers.

"So young." Ingrid clicked her tongue. She glanced up. Andrew gaped at her with wide eyes. "What?" she asked irritably.

"I...she's submissive to you," Andrew said.

"Canines are to me what felines are to Micah." Ingrid shrugged. "All the better when they are magical."

Andrew rolled his eyes almost imperceptibly. "Naturally."

"I would be jealous of me, too." She sniffed.

Now he didn't hide his eye roll. "Great, so, uh, can she stay here for a bit?"

"What were you planning to do if I said no?" asked Ingrid as she straightened and fixed Andrew with a withering glare.

"Uh." He blinked at her. Then finally he shrugged. "Oh, I don't know. I wing things all the time. Does that mean you're saying yes?"

"Of course. She's a good girl. Aren't you?"

At Ingrid's sweet tone, Fionna instantly pulled back on her wolfskin, bouncing around Ingrid's feet before rolling onto her back and showing her fluffy white belly. Ingrid crouched and scratched the *faoladh*'s bristly winter coat.

Andrew edged past the threshold into the compound and let out a happy sigh as he unzipped his jacket and let it drop off his shoulders. "I'm permanently frostbitten."

Ingrid pinched the back of his knee and made it buckle,

surprising a yelp from him as he bent a knee.

"You deserve the frostbite," Ingrid snapped. Standing, she ordered the *faoladh*, "Come along, little one. I'm sure he didn't feed you properly."

Fionna's tail wagged and she licked her lips again, but Andrew shot a hand down to her head with a quick, sharp look at Ingrid that he tried too late to rein in.

"Calm down, dad," remarked Ingrid with a raised eyebrow. "She's simply submissive to me. She is still yours. Consider this like a doctor's appointment."

Reluctantly, Andrew scratched Fionna behind the ear, nodded faintly, and removed his hand. Fionna immediately thrust her snout toward the ground, snuffling loudly and wagging her tail. Ingrid's gaze slowly shifted from Andrew to the *faoladh* as she took a graceful step after the wolf.

Before she could get away, Andrew asked hurriedly, "Is Micah here?"

Ingrid waved her hand over her shoulder at him, and Andrew assumed that was...not a no. With an indignant huff, he sloshed through barely solid ice collected on the steps, following them toward the heart of Lilydale. Pale, fragrant campfire smoke rose from the large fire pit near the western cliffs, drawing Andrew in with the hope that he could use it as a vantage point to find Micah.

A white-haired faerie stoked the fire, looking up with eerie rectangular pupils when Andrew approached. Andrew thought for a moment that the faerie was alone, but their gaze flicked away from Andrew with their brows raised on their charcoal-colored forehead. Andrew followed their line of sight and—

The flames parted like curtains, flashing off hair green like sea glass curtained forward over a bowed head. When the fire-tending faerie looked over, Micah raised his head. And then he saw Andrew.

"Micah." Forgetting his misgivings, the sight of his faerie prince struck like dawn breaking after the longest night.

Warped though he was by the sheen of heat, Micah's expression was wrong—haunted, agonized.

Andrew halted, hands curling into fists as he called unsteadily, "I...can I...can we talk?"

Micah's face crumpled. He managed to nod before dropping his head onto his hand as Andrew rushed across the clearing, fingers of heat from the fire clawing against his legs. Micah was sobbing before Andrew even reached him, the heartbreak and pain in that discordant sound pushing Andrew to his knees in front of Micah's toadstool. Andrew started to reach for his knees, his fingers tingling before they even made contact, but he froze. Micah hadn't spoken, and Andrew had broken his heart this week. He couldn't touch him yet.

Micah sniffed and smeared his hand across his face. The flannel blanket slid down from his tawny shoulders.

Andrew bit back a gasp of horrible disbelief. "Micah?"

Deep purple bruising marred Micah's tattooed chest, partially obscured by several lengths of hospital bandaging wrapped around him. His left arm hung in a makeshift scarf sling. "Wh-what happened?"

As Micah's face crumpled again and fresh tears leaked out of his burgundy eyes, Andrew grazed his fingers over Micah's shoulders. His skin was hot like sunbaked stone, damp with sickly sweat. Andrew hung onto him, murmuring pacifying nonsense and a whisper of, "Breathe."

It took several minutes before Micah could breathe again, his ribs aching and his shoulder burning. The touch of Andrew's hands on his scorching skin was like a cool breeze, like finding his way home, like a balm on his wounds.

"I...I-I got ambushed by Diana and her friends," he rasped. "She didn't *like* me, Andrew. She was setting me up." When he managed to look up at Andrew, his eyes were burgundy with fear, but flickered plum-purple when Andrew took Micah's face in his hands and crushed his lips against the hinge of his jaw, an apology and a plea in the gesture. Micah couldn't help but wind his uninjured arm around Andrew's shoulders, smelling unfamiliar shampoo and something rustic and feral in his hair. He shuddered as Andrew grazed his lips along his neck and onto his collarbone.

Against his chin, Andrew whispered, "I'm so sorry. I'm s...I'm so sorry, love. I should have been there."

Micah nodded. "I wish you had been. I wish you hadn't left me like that. I know you needed to go see your mum, but...god, like that?"

As Andrew pressed the heels of his hands into his eyes, he explained, "I did all of it wrong. I never wanted a break. I just...wanted to be right, and I got so lost in the fog that I didn't believe you'd ever want to shine your light on *me*."

"I know." Micah smiled weakly. "You just got so stubborn, Andrew. Can you try to listen to me next time, please?"

"Yes," agreed Andrew with a little curling smile. "I promise."

Tilting his chin, Micah brushed their lips together. Almost immediately, just as Andrew tasted the strange medicinal quality of his lips, Micah pulled back, his eyes growing wide.

"What?" Andrew asked, alarmed. "Did I hurt you?"

"I-I kissed Chami," Micah blurted. He clamped his hand over his mouth. "I'm so sorry. I don't want that over our heads at all. It was so stupid, but...I was lonely, and angry, and none of that's an excuse, I know, I hate that—"

Before he could keep rambling, Andrew held up his hand, and Micah fell silent almost at once. Micah's confession hit a wall of numbness inside Andrew that wasn't ready to thaw yet. It made sense, and Micah had been with Chamomile before, and it was devastating and yet, was it? Andrew had pressured Micah to do something like that.

"Do you want to be with her?" he managed to ask, which was the most important part of whatever transpired between Micah and the goblin—who would most certainly be dealt with later.

Incredulity flashed across Micah's features. "Of course not!"

Andrew nodded slowly, swallowing around the tightness in his throat. "That's good." He coughed into his sleeve. "I'm...I'm hurt, but you were too. I'm disappointed, but I was prepared for this possibility. I had to be. I told you to do it."

Biting his lip to keep it from trembling, Micah shook his head. "Not *really*, though. I get that now."

"Regardless." Andrew's eyes slid shut. "I'm happy you regret it. I'm happy you don't wish for a life where you could go back to be with someone like Chami."

"I only want a life with you." Micah cupped Andrew's cool, high cheekbone in his palm. Andrew nuzzled into his hand. "But you can be angry at me, okay?" Micah let his hand fall to grip Andrew's fingers. Coffee-dark eyes fluttered open to gaze thoughtfully at their joined hands. "I want you to know I can handle it. I want to handle all of you. Not just the parts you're working so hard to control. I...Kate, at the bar, she said you used to scream at your mom, and..."

Andrew sighed softly. Micah's hand around his felt like a safe harbor. Like he could never become unmoored again.

"Yelling and screaming makes me feel worse." He thought guiltily of all the things he'd said to his mother. Years ago. Just this morning. "It did then, too. I worked through that kind of rage in therapy. I don't want to be like that anymore. And I've barely begun to process my time with my mum, and I come home to find you injured? A kiss with Chami is the least of my worries at the moment." Pulling out the elastic from his shiny hair, he combed through it with his fingers and gazed up the hill at the kiln throne.

Micah was briefly spellbound by Andrew's hair—red enough when not lit with firelight, now looking like it was made of magma. He'd been captivated by Chamomile's hair in her hut, it was true, and she was a faerie…but Andrew looked ethereal too, with the planes of his face carved in the sharp relief of golden firelight and deep blue shadows, with his hair glowing, with his eyes deep pools of darkness. Micah wasn't even conscious he was reaching out until the smooth strands of Andrew's loose hair slipped between the pads of his finger like water.

The gesture tugged a smile from Andrew's lips, which drew Micah in like he was a moth, curling his fingers against the nape of Andrew's neck, pulling him in to kiss him again. This time, they both melted into each other like the heat from the fire turned them to candle wax. Gingerly, Andrew threaded his arms around Micah's waist, well below his bandages even though the risk of injuring him further still pinched at Andrew's thoughts. He opened his lips to welcome Micah's tongue and let out a breath that turned into a moan of relief and desire. The soft sound made Micah grip him tighter and almost pull his hair before he caught himself, letting their kiss end with a sigh. Andrew's eyes kept glowing like embers as he leaned on Micah's knees, lips glistening, the collar of his scoop-neck shirt falling below his clavicle, which almost pulled Micah in again to taste the wilderness on his skin.

Andrew tore his eyes away from Micah's features, distracted by the taste of fresh-cut grass that landed on his tongue out of nowhere. He blinked, peering around Micah's scuffed and stained jeans.

A creamy white branch of birchwood, strong but slender, leaned against the toadstool near Micah's legs. It stayed close to him despite how its height really should have made it tip over, like it wasn't comfortable with the idea of not touching him. Andrew hardly needed to ask what it was; Micah's springlike magic emanated from the length of birchwood like an incense stick.

Andrew glanced up with his brows raised. "You have a magic staff now," he observed.

"Yeah." Micah blushed. "Formed in my time of need, and whatnot. Chamomile called it a conduit." He picked up the staff with his good arm. Micah turned it in his palm, the staff bringing a giddy skip into his heartbeat until he set it in Andrew's hands. To Andrew, it seemed to breathe in time with the shallow rise and fall of Micah's belly.

"Micah," whispered Andrew, rubbing one of the coarse little knobs of darkness in the wood. "This is bloody amazing. I'm so impressed."

Micah shrugged and then immediately bared his teeth in a grimace, flinching and reaching for his wrapped shoulder.

Flinty dark eyes tracked the movement. "What did she do to you?"

"Her witch friends stabbed me with an athame." He blinked, shellshocked. "Iron, too."

Andrew became still as a predator with eyes on his prey. His eyes narrowed, and his lips pressed into a thin line. After a long moment, he set the birchwood staff by their feet and leaned his forearms on Micah's knees. "Can I kill her?" He sounded flippant, but his eyes turned to stone with his question.

Micah's throat tightened, making his voice tremble. "I-I appreciate that, but..." He shook his head slightly and explained, "We worked together once after, um...the blizzard. It was pretty awful. I was really mean. So then she no-showed. The district manager sent me out to do a wellness check on her."

"How'd she know about you?" He glanced up. "Did you tell her? That you're half-Fae?"

As he stroked Andrew's cheek like he would a cat, Micah shook his head. "No, of course not. She had this hypothesis that I...that I would smell different, and from what you've told me, that's correct. So as soon as she kissed me, she confirmed it, and—"

"Oh, no." Andrew groaned.

"What?"

"She wanted to exploit your blood," he ventured.

Micah's brow furrowed. "How the hell would you..." His eyes followed Andrew's hand as it dug in his jeans pocket and withdrew the partly emptied vial of the blood ward. "Huh? What happened to that?"

"Liath decided to experiment with it while I was asleep

this morning."

"Andrew..." sighed Micah, shoulders slumping, his hand coming up to cup Andrew's cheek. "Shit. I'm sorry. That's really disappointing."

"Yes. It would be, if I weren't so accustomed to her disappointing me." He rolled the vial between his fingers and then wedged it back into his pocket. Acknowledging Micah's grimace with a fleeting smile, Andrew said, "So it seems when we were apart, everyone was out for your blood. What even is it expected to do?"

"Fuck if I know." Micah shrugged, and then froze, baring his teeth with a moan of pain. "I need to quit with the shrugging," he groaned, squeezing Andrew's offered fingers. "We can't do this again. Shit goes down when we're apart."

"I promise you," swore Andrew, "next time I'll stay and fight."

Parting his lips to let out a steadying breath, Micah picked up Andrew's hand and spread it over his cheek. "That's all I need to hear." He drew Andrew close with two fingers on his chin, lashes fluttering closed, waiting for Andrew to kiss him. Wrapping an arm around Micah's neck, Andrew obliged, tender and gentle. It sewed up the rift between them leaving only a scar behind.

Micah opened his eyes with a smile. Then he gasped. "What the—wolf!" He hooked his good arm around Andrew's waist and jerked him away from the fire as a shaggy timber wolf slunk toward them with wary golden eyes, its head down and ears erect. Micah's sudden movement settled without mercy into his bones, pain stabbing through his chest. He gnashed his teeth and burrowed into Andrew's collar, fingers digging into his hip. "Fuck," he moaned. "We're gonna die."

"It's all right." Andrew kindly patted Micah's head and rested his hand there. "She came home with me."

Micah peered through one eye as Andrew extended his hand toward the creature, which trotted toward him with a steady and suspicious eye on Micah. It thrust its snout into Andrew's palm, shimmying under his hand so he petted the whole length of its tawny spine. The wolf then touched its wet black nose to Micah's hand where he clasped Andrew's waist, huffing hot air onto his fingers, nosing underneath his palm as if trying to get him off Andrew. But, fearlessly, Andrew shooed the wolf back with a shove to its scruffy throat.

Micah's eyes grew round as saucers, jaw dropping open. "What the hell."

"Ingrid said it was fine." Andrew wore the look of a student getting in trouble and claiming another teacher had given him permission.

Managing to wrench his gaze from the wolf—who still stared intently at him—he turned an awestruck stare toward Andrew. "What."

"Her name is Fionna." Andrew rubbed his thumb inside

the wolf's heavily furred ear. As it blinked at Micah, its pink tongue stuck out between its lips.

"What!" Micah broke out of his shock with a shake of his head. "How do you know? Is it like me with cats?" On cue, the wolf lifted its large front foot off the limestone, swiping its black-padded paw over its head and then...as if throwing off a blanket, the wolf was a girl.

"What!" squawked Micah.

"Fionna!" announced the girl, throwing her arms up, sucking in her lower lip when she smiled in a way that was immediately evocative of the expression she'd just had as a wolf.

"Oh my god." Micah squished his cheeks between his hands. "Look at you! Fionna? It's so nice to meet you!"

"Meet." Her voice was kind of like a bark. Then on knobby knees she shuffled closer to Micah and sniffed the space where Micah's chest pressed into Andrew's waist with the same frantic intensity as she had as a dog. "An-roo?" she asked, scratching her chin, poking at Micah.

He laughed. "I'm Micah."

"I love him," Andrew explained, winding his arm through Micah's and clasping their hands together.

"Love," repeated the girl, nodding knowingly. She sniffed. Fionna's head tilted to the side as her uncanny gaze shifted back to Micah's face. She sniffed again as if she caught a scent, scurrying around him. The heat from her little body pressed into his shoulder as she investigated the gauze. She growled—a high-pitched noise that vibrated in Micah's chest. "Witches!" she gasped, back-pedaling and bumping into a large stump.

"Um." Andrew gripped Micah's hand tighter. "Why does she know that word?"

Micah snorted. "It's us. Of course it's all going to connect."

"Fionna, we're safe here." Andrew stretched out a hand toward her. "No witches. Promise."

She nodded faintly but stayed away, clambering onto the stump, tucking her knees into her chest, drumming her thick little fingers on her shins. "No witches."

Unwinding their hands, Andrew stood up, propping his hands on his hips. "It's getting late."

"Not really." Micah made a face at the sky. "Isn't it, like, five?"

"I got up early." Andrew glanced down with a wry crinkle of his eyes and reminded him, "You got stabbed."

"Ew. Don't say it aloud. It's freaky."

"When did it happen?"

"I don't know. Sometime yesterday afternoon. Ingrid said I was sleeping for sixteen hours or something. I'm not tired at all. Chamomile force-fed me medicine."

Andrew eyed him for a moment, deciding whether or not to say something snide. As the silence stretched longer, he chose not to, looking up at the rest of the compound. "Well, I'm not leaving you, so I'm going to go speak with Ingrid."

"Aw," whined Micah as Andrew strode determinedly up the steps toward her hut, leaving him alone around the fire with the wolf over his shoulder.

Andrew found Ingrid near an open-walled structure behind the kiln throne, speaking to a male faerie with moth wings folding and unfolding between his shoulders. The male glanced past Ingrid as Andrew approached, opened his wings, and launched off the ground. Flapping haphazardly, the male landed on the structure next to them, looked down at Andrew, and hissed.

Saluting the faerie, Andrew turned his eyes toward Ingrid.

Her lips curled in a smirk. "You certainly fear the Folk less than the first time you came here with Micah."

Andrew shrugged. "I'm not afraid of *you* anymore, so why would I be afraid of them? You could eat them for breakfast. Tell me you haven't bitten a faerie here before."

"Hm," was all Ingrid said.

"That's what I thought. Where was Micah sleeping?"

"In my hut," she answered. She ducked into the structure next to them. There seemed to be an enormous black cauldron inside. When she turned back, she extended a sealed bottle of water and a package of cheese crackers toward him.

"Oh. Wow. Thanks."

"Sarcasm?"

"Nope."

"Hm," was all Ingrid said.

"Is there somewhere else Micah and I could sleep tonight? I...I don't want to leave him again, especially not while he's injured."

She nodded in understanding. Striding away from Andrew, she stuck her head into a conical canvas tent close to her shelter. A pair of Folk squawked in alarm but scrambled outside immediately.

Andrew watched them with a swallow of guilt. But the two Folk chattered excitedly, "It's for Micah? We mean...Prince Micah? Wait. What should we call him?"

"Prince Micah," he repeated under his breath. The Folk must have warmed considerably to Micah while Andrew was out of town.

Ingrid murmured something.

"'Micah' is *not* adequate," insisted the shorter faerie, a male with sunset-orange skin and fawn legs, who was dressed in an oversized sweatshirt and slippers. "He is the child of the Redwood Queen, like yourself, milady. He needs a title."

"Sorry, your Ladyship, but he's right," said the blue-hued female beside him. Her hair looked like a tuft of cotton candy. She was draped in a purple scarf which allowed her rainbow-flashing dragonfly wings to sit comfortably between her shoulders. "We could pay it no mind when he wasn't here often, but now..."

"Wasn't there something with nightshade?" asked the

male.

Ingrid glanced imploringly over at Andrew.

Andrew shook his head. Nightshade Boy didn't seem right anymore. That was Micah's child self. His half-formed uncertain identity when he still desperately wanted to be human. That staff, though—it was a signal that Micah was changed. Grown up. Capable. Andrew rubbed his stubbly cheeks thoughtfully.

The two faeries turned glinting liquid eyes on him, waiting expectantly.

It had to be related to plants...and if Ingrid was a Lady, Micah had to be...

"Lord...Heartwood," he blurted.

The female faerie squealed and clapped her hands together. The male gave Andrew a look like he knew Andrew had just pulled that out of his ass.

"Lord Heartwood!" trilled the female. "I'm telling everyone." She spread pink dragonfly wings on her back and buzzed into the air.

Brows raised, Ingrid stared at Andrew.

Feeling a little pleased—at least he hadn't said something embarrassing—he shrugged, breaking the seal on the water and taking a long swig.

Ingrid shook her head at him. Then she stooped into the tent and emptied it of the faerie couple's belongings, most of which looked like musical instruments. She set them in a tidy stack and then peered inside calculatingly.

Andrew came to help her and then asked, "So, what is your conclusion about Fionna?"

"Be more specific." She straightened. There was a gilded chest outside her hut that she opened up on silent oiled hinges. She lifted out stacks of sweet-smelling blankets and set them in Andrew's outstretched arms.

"Well, for one, she seems to have innately taken to you."

"Magic calls to magic." Ingrid waved a hand dismissively.

"Hm. My mum said the same thing."

Ingrid gave him a folded futon mattress which he spread on the cobbled floor of the tent, and together they stacked piles of blankets and pillows and made a cozy cocoon bed like Ingrid had. Slightly hunched, Ingrid hung a large glass jar full of bouncing faerie lights from a hook at the crown of the tent. She put a pitcher of water and a large bowl in the corner, and then several towels beside it. She set a pink bar of soap dense with herbs and flowers on top of the towels.

Ingrid gestured to the setup. "This is what we typically do for grooming, but I'd be open to figuring out a more modernized arrangement for as long as you need to stay."

"Yeah. I suppose it's best if he heals from a magical wound among magical Folk," agreed Andrew.

Ingrid nodded. "Based on Julian's temperament, I don't think it would be good for him to see Micah until he's in better condition. For you, I will send someone up to the grocery for a selection of human-made foods. I don't expect you to nor hope you would consume Fae-made foods unless we know they've stopped affecting you."

Andrew looked skeptical. "What do you mean? That it's not a permanent effect?"

Ingrid hesitated. She crouched next to the cocoon bed and hugged her knees. "It's only a hypothesis at this point, but...Micah is half-human, and is not affected by Fae-spelled foods because he grew up on them. And you and him regularly...er...exchange...fluids."

Andrew blushed.

"I'm wondering if he may help you build up an immunity to Fae-spelled foods."

"Maybe." Andrew looked down. "The addiction thing is all...a bit fresh for me, though, so I'm not ready to chance it." When Ingrid gave him a blank look, he pulled out the half-gone blood ward from his pocket and held it up, explaining, "My mum used to be hooked on Fae-spelled foods from here, you know. So I think when she realized I had Micah's blood on me, she couldn't resist...seeing what she could do with it, I guess."

Ingrid frowned, setting her chin on her curled fingers. "Disappointing, I'm sure."

"Very much so."

"It's true for full Fae blood, you know. It's very power-ful to humans. It usually kills people if they ingest it on purpose," Ingrid told him. "In the moments before death, it's very hallucinogenic. We sometimes did it on purpose to people in the Redwoods."

"Of course," sighed Andrew.

"Not many people get to spill half-Fae blood enough to know what it'll do. For you, his blood ward did make you immune to Fae charm. But I don't know why blood would hold significantly different properties from other fluids, hence my hypothesis."

Andrew fingered the vial for a moment before nodding and setting it down in the tent. "I like the possibility that she just wanted to...cure herself or something," he said. "It's clear the use of Fae-spelled foods was still affecting her."

"I'm sorry your mother succumbed to that kind of temptation." Ingrid couldn't say it if she didn't mean it. "That must have ruined your time together."

"I enjoyed the rest of it, mostly." Andrew gave a dismissive shrug. "That's more than I'm sure you can say for your mother."

She grimaced. "Indeed."

"I'm grateful you were willing to use your skills to give me the chance to see her again, even if it ended like that." Andrew smiled gently. "I appreciate you, Ingrid."

She looked as uncomfortable as he did when someone expressed their gratitude, swirling her finger over the tassels on her sash. "Um...um...I appreciate you too, Andrew."

He grinned.

Fionna shoved her head through the door flap and whistled a whine at them, ears sideways on her head.

For her part, Ingrid looked relieved about the interruption. She shooed the wolf back through the flap, and Andrew heard Fionna gurgle a long whining growl in protest. They followed Fionna outside, under a dark sky with the ice wall reflecting a myriad of lights back at them—the cool white of the stars, the burning firelight, and the milky yellow dots of the city lights.

He glanced between Fionna and Ingrid and asked, "How...civilized can she end up being?"

"With diligent teaching, relatively so," answered Ingrid. She fixed her wool shawl and tucked a curl behind her long, sharp ear. "She isn't going to be a simple pet. But she won't be like a true human."

"Darn. I was hoping the shapeshifting timber wolf I brought home from the wilderness would be really low maintenance. Like a goldfish."

Ingrid glared at him with eyes that flashed crimson.

Andrew snickered. "You're just jealous you can't be sarcastic."

Sniffing, Ingrid didn't dignify him with an answer. She ran Fionna's furred ear between her fingers. Some understanding passed between the two of them, and Fionna planted her butt on the ice outside the tent, hind legs splayed awkwardly and her thick tail whumping against the limestone.

Micah appeared past the curve of the land, wearing the heavy flannel blanket like a cloak with a hood, rumpling his hair over his brow. "What are you two getting up to?"

"We're relocating," said Andrew as Micah used his birch staff to pick his way up to them like a hobbling old wizard.

Micah walked up and leaned against Andrew, burrowing into the blanket. Only a tuft of his hair stuck out like a green sprout. Holding one corner of it in his good arm, he reached around and pinched Andrew's ass. Andrew yelped in surprise and garnered an odd look from Ingrid. Within his blanket, Micah chuckled with satisfaction.

"Lord Heartwood!"

Andrew and Ingrid exchanged a look. He said, "She wasn't kidding about telling everyone."

A small crowd of Folk materialized in the dark, some holding lanterns with flickering flames inside so that the eerie light danced over colorful and excited faces.

"Who?" Micah emerged from his blanket looking bewildered, hair askew. He blinked at the crowd and cast a blank look between Andrew and Ingrid.

"Lord Heartwood, how goes your wound?"

"That's you." Andrew thumbed Micah's chin with affection.

Micah furrowed his brow. "I'm Lord Heartwood?"

"Seems so," agreed Ingrid.

"Since when?"

"Couple of minutes ago," said Andrew.

"According to whom?" Micah's bewildered look persisted.

"Your knight." Ingrid nodded to Andrew.

"Yes, the Auburn Knight bestowed you with a legendary title!" trilled the blue-skinned pixie Spirulina, playing a jaunty scale on a fiddle tucked under her chin where she buzzed over the heads of the ground-dwelling Folk beneath her.

"How did you decide that?" asked Micah, his eyes swirling to lavender as color painted his cheeks and a crooked grin showed his bright white teeth.

"'Cause the heartwood of a tree in the center is the sturdiest. Difficult to break." Andrew added more quietly with heat in his eyes, "And the sweetest wood."

"Good god." Micah shook his head at the heavens.

Andrew snorted and started to laugh, draping his arm around Micah's neck.

A small, pale pixie exclaimed, "I heard you slayed a dozen witches, Lord Heartwood!"

Micah wormed his fingers up over his blanket cape. He scratched his stubbly cheek and slowly shook his tilted head in bemusement. "That tale is growing fast."

"Hey!" Chamomile pushed through the crowd of Folk with her bow and arrow in hand. She cocked an arrow and stepped up to Andrew, Micah and Ingrid, turning to the crowd and aiming at them. "You should all know better." She paused. "Lord Heartwood needs space and rest. He'll visit when he's ready. Go away!"

The Folk of Lilydale dispersed with whispers of gossip

rippling amongst themselves. A piccolo started whistling in the air as fat snowflakes began to drift down upon the bluffs.

Spinning in the snow, Chamomile demanded, "Lord Heartwood? Who decided that?"

Ingrid pointed at Andrew.

"Do me," Chamomile said.

"Boyfriend-Kisser," said Andrew at once.

Micah slapped his forehead.

"*He* kissed *me!*" Chamomile's cheeks turning fuchsia. She looked jumpy, casting an uncertain look up at Andrew, wielding her bow in front of her as if preparing to defend herself.

"He what?" Ingrid's eyes widened.

Chamomile hunched her shoulders, avoiding Ingrid's glare.

Micah and Andrew exchanged a look.

"It's fine," Andrew felt the need to add. He reached out to pat Chamomile's head, and when she let him get close enough to do so, he pivoted and pulled her ear instead.

Chamomile squawked and snatched Andrew's hand, but Micah swung the birchwood staff and broke them up.

"Knock it off," said Micah. "I'm the one who did something wrong. And I got a titty twister for my trouble."

Andrew snorted. "Oh. Good."

Micah scowled.

Ingrid's eyes were on Chamomile, faint irritation making

her lips purse. She said without looking away, "Micah, you need more rest. This tent is yours now."

"Oh. I thought Lina and Leif were staying in there." Micah gestured to the tent as Fionna started furiously scratching herself behind her elbow.

"They were happy to vacate," Ingrid told him. "Good night, you two. I'm happy you're back together."

"For the record—" Chamomile poked Andrew's hip, "I am too."

The two females strode off together toward the trees, and Chamomile began gesturing emphatically.

Micah whispered, "I think those two are fucking."

"Oh, definitely." Andrew nodded. "Remember when they went off together in Montana? How could you *not* want to have sex out there?"

"I know. It was so romantic." Micah smiled dreamily, reminiscing on his first time being intimate with Andrew. His cheeks grew warm. They stood beside each other in silence for a moment, both imagining, both stepping a little bit closer to each other.

Clearing his throat, Micah said, "So you got us our own tent, huh?"

"I'm not leaving you tonight," explained Andrew, "and I couldn't bring myself to sleep in your sister's bed."

"Why's that?" Micah asked with a crooked smirk.

Andrew opened the tent flap. "Don't get any ideas." He hooked a finger through Micah's belt loop and tugged him into the tent.

Beaming, Micah surveyed the small but cozy space as he lowered himself carefully onto the cocoon of blankets. "Is it a bad idea? Maybe. Did I already think about it? Obviously. Do I want to do it anyway? Also, obviously." Micah touched his shoulder gingerly. "And I mean, Fae drugs are doing good work."

Andrew pulled off his flannel shirt and then his sweatshirt so he was only in short sleeves and his jeans. Micah watched him with ridiculous excitement, and when he caught him staring, Andrew opted to pull off his tee as well. The slight chill in the air rose goosebumps on his skin and turned his nipples to pebbles.

He climbed onto the blankets as Micah slid the flannel blanket off his shoulders and watched Andrew with a swirl of silver in his irises. They simply drank in the sight of one another for several beats. Andrew's limbs tingled, and his stomach tightened with arousal. He forced himself to look away, clutching his knees.

"I don't want you to push yourself too much," Andrew told him, voice strained by desire.

Micah threaded their legs together, scooting closer, Andrew's breath stuttering when Micah trailed his fingers along his pale wrist. When Micah caught his lip between his teeth, Andrew's eyes slid down to watch, his red lashes veiling his hungry gaze.

"As if either of us could resist." Micah lifted off

Chamomile's sling as he beckoned Andrew with a crooked finger.

Andrew carefully undressed Micah, happy to separate him from his clothes spoiled by the sharp smell of his spilled blood. Micah moved very little, obliging, his face glowing with a rush of color. His bandaged chest heaved with ragged, eager breaths.

After Andrew slid out of his jeans, Micah guided him onto his lap. He left his injured arm at his side, but used his right to loosen Andrew up, their noses and foreheads almost touching. They kissed softly at first before Andrew's tongue roamed into Micah's mouth to begin a languid dance.

Andrew ran his hands through Micah's smoke-scented hair. He separated their lips and gasped, leaning over Micah's uninjured shoulder when Micah entered him; he trembled, clutching Micah's neck, moaning his name.

The injury, their time apart, the fear of what was to come, it was all forgotten as they shared their ecstasy. Their bodies kept a slow, deep rhythm, slick with mingling sweat, glistening under the magic of the faerie lights overhead. Micah paused every so often when his exhaustion strained against him, but Andrew kissed his jaw whenever he went still and waited, patient, panting and tightening his thighs against Micah's bony hips. Eventually he moved off Micah's lap and onto his stomach, allowing Micah to shift position and bend his shoulder less as he knelt behind

Andrew's pale, slender limbs.

After reaching shuddering satisfaction together, they held each other in silence, trembling with relief. Micah curled himself behind Andrew with his arm draped over him. Lacing their fingers together, Andrew squeezed his eyes closed as he fought the urge to weep in relief. Being back in each other's arms was a reprieve, like they were finally through stumbling in the fog and had made it home.

Chapter Fifteen
The Staff

IT WAS STILL DARK when Micah climbed out of the tent wearing his green jeans and a knit blanket draped over his shoulders. He hadn't managed to get his arm back into a sling on his own with Andrew sleeping, but leaving his left arm limp at his side was tolerable enough.

When he emerged Fionna lifted her shaggy head. She blinked amber eyes at him, and Micah felt a pang of guilt as she made him think of his father. Julian would be horrified if he knew what had happened. But it might also be the case he would start to be happy if he didn't quite know everything.

The wolf inspected him in silence as he inspected her. She looked like an ordinary beast with her tawny paws delicately crossed and her strong shoulders drawn back. But then when he kept watching her, her thick pink tongue poked out the side of her lips and made her look silly and...not quite like an animal. Her tail thumped once against the ground.

Micah held his fingers out toward her. She bowed her head and let him scratch the coarse fur between her ears. As if satisfied, she then laid her head back on her legs and closed her eyes.

Micah sat cross-legged beside her, laying the birchwood staff across his knees. He experimentally closed his left hand into a loose fist. His fingers tingled, and his shoulder cramped. From the little he knew about physiology, the tingling told him there was nerve damage in his shoulder. Scowling, he set his fingers on the staff and curled his good hand around it.

Truthfully, he had no strong feelings at the moment. This week was the longest Micah had been in Lilydale at one time, and it was so...unexpectedly lovely. The Folk in Lilydale were simple and sweet, wanting to experience simple pleasures and play all day.

But the sense of rightness was offset by life below in the human city. A dead witch. The nasty way things were left with Diana. Not to mention his tea shop. The kids were probably going insane with curiosity.

The contrast between the two worlds, and the sweet and the sour, was enough so that it all canceled out.

He was so overwhelmed that it all jumbled into numbness.

Good.

He had a point to prove. With himself, and the strange dual natures fighting within him.

For so long, he couldn't do anything. He just watched things happen. Or they happened to him whether he liked them or not.

Then, after he met Andrew, something began to open in him. He had power in his blood.

But it was locked away where intense emotion was his only key. It was just...no way to continue.

Honestly, Micah thought, staring north toward the glinting skyscrapers downtown...he deserved more.

He deserved to be formidable.

Chewing his lip, Micah looked back down at the birchwood staff he'd snapped off a sapling and claimed for himself. If that small stick could grow, then so could he.

Micah ran the pad of his thumb along the small ridges of the branch. Splinters pierced the whorls of his skin and left behind pinpricks of blood in the wood.

He settled the seat of his pelvis more heavily into the ground, took a shallow breath, and visualized the branch sprouting triumphantly back into life.

Something stirred deep in his belly, tickling its way up his sternum, along the cleft of his lip and to the crown of his head. He watched with distant delight as the branch rippled and cracked like an eggshell, the wood splitting first where he'd left a thin trail of his blood.

Bright green leaves broke through the fissures, twining hungrily into the air, small and wrinkled at first and then uncurling into glossy green coins.

His lips twitched. But it wasn't enough.

Micah shut the door on the stream within himself feeding into the branch.

Immediately, the small leaves withered and floated off the staff and onto the packed snow under him. The wood smoothed back down, the bark unruffling like a preening bird.

His heart lurched with a strange grief. He acknowledged the grief of life waning, and then released the feeling.

Micah used his good arm to stand the staff up in front of him like it was a mirror of his spine as he sat erect in the cold winter air.

He frowned faintly, considering his options. Beside him, Fionna twitched in her sleep.

Micah searched for that piece of raw energy that was tickling inside him. He told it to move, nudging it along his arm, through the palm of his hand, and up the birch to its gnarled end facing skyward.

The point of the staff began to spark with soft green light, emanating in the dark like the light on a radio tower.

Micah's lips parted. He leaned on the staff and pulled himself to his feet. Gingerly, he reached his injured arm forward to touch the light with one finger. It felt like...him.

Planting his feet, he swung down the branch and tapped its glowing tip on the skeleton of a dormant cluster of lilies. The light danced off the tip of the staff and onto the dry, papery leaves, which began to stir as if someone stepped into them. Beginning deep down near the stems, the color of the leaves grew brighter, supple, stretching out as if waking from a long sleep. Long spindles of lily stems curled up and the heavy buds emerged before his eyes. Bright orange petals unfurled, trembling slightly in the cold.

Tears springing into his eyes, Micah started to grin.

Obscured by the leaves of her winterberry bush, Ingrid sat cross-legged outside her hut and watched Micah unnoticed. When he brought the lilies back to life, Ingrid's lips split in a joyous smile as she leaned against her door and hid her tearful face in her hands.

To Be Continued

Join us soon for the final installment of The Heartwood Trilogy, *Promise Me, Lord Heartwood*.

Find your way to www.heartwoodtrilogy.com for all the information on the trilogy and to subscribe to my newsletter for updates.

ACKNOWLEDGEMENTS

THE FANTASTIC MOMENTUM FOLLOWING the release of *Deny Me, The Nightshade Boy* has many people to thank. The local bookshops eager to speak with me and stock my book really made this whole thing real. Cream & Amber which hosted my book launch party, Next Chapter, Subtext Books, Comma, and of course Tropes & Trifles welcomed me with such warmth and excitement for events or lengthy chats.

My online street team headed by Victoria Day has given me a stronger sense of community than I have ever had in my life. My editor Quinton Li who is personally and professionally a champion of my work, Olivier Way, Cat Treadwell, Alycia Davidson, Vera, Sol, Olive, Briar, and everybody who has signed up for ARCs or my newsletter are all the only reason why *Rend Me* managed to still see the light of day.

I want to give a big shout-out to my husband of seven years, Ryan, who will never give up on me even at my brattiest.

About the Author

Z.M. Celestaire (they/she) is a writer, artist, and therapist. Writing and art have been a hobby for some twenty years now since they were a goofy little middle schooler, which is actually when both of the Heartwood Trilogy protagonists were created. Z.M. fell in love with fantasy as soon as they were listening to their dad read C.S. Lewis before bed, and grew up devouring tales of dragons and sassy princesses, city magic and the Folk. Z.M. is fierce advocate for social justice.

Z.M. lives in Saint Paul, Minnesota, with their spouse, human child, and fur children.

Visit Z.M. on social media under the handle @artcoffeecats.

PRAISE FOR DENY ME, THE NIGHTSHADE BOY

"I devoured this book in a day and can't wait for more from the boys and their human (and not-so-human) friends." — RK Ashwick, author of *A Rival Most Vial*

"This book had me going feral, devouring it in a quest to see a happy ending for Andrew and Micah." — Iris Esta Cansado, book blogger

"There's something in this story that is wild and magical that speaks to a life beyond that of human memory. It left me yearning in a way a story hasn't in a long time." — Sebrina Eden, author of upcoming Faultlines series

"The prose is not only rich with beautifully written metaphors, but feels very visual." — CJ Aralore, author of upcoming *Gravity's Fire*